DREAMS AND DESIRES

BOOK ONE

BY

PAUL BLADES

Dark Visions Publications
darkvisionspub@gmail.com

Other books by Paul Blades:

The Maddy Saga:

PART ONE: THE DREAM MAN

CHAPTER ONE

Dr. Kelly Jameson wasn't the kind of person to believe in dreams. Her life was devoted to science. She had gone directly from medical school into research. Few twenty-seven year old women had the opportunity to run her own lab and supervise her own staff, as small as it was. She loved her work, and if it were not for her friend, Adele, she might never have taken any breaks from the sometimes tedious routine. Adele would tease her that she was "wasting that beautiful body away." And so she dragged her to singles' resorts, shamed her into donning a scanty bikini, and practically pimped her out to the pretty, tanned and sexually hyperactive young men she met there. So far, Kelly had resisted their false charms.

Kelly had long, thick, beautiful, auburn hair, the color of burnt orange, that went down to the small of her back. Her features were delicate, almost child like, something that made her job of being taken seriously by middle aged foundation trustees and international health bureaucrats difficult. And prancing around in a two piece set of fabric small enough to fit inside of a jelly jar was not the way for her to develop the persona that would unlock the coffers of the powers who could help bring her visions to reality.

When they returned from a weekend in Cancun a month ago, she had told Adele she was through wasting her time and energy in finding a mate. She would concentrate on her work. Adele's response was to leave a brochure about Mardi Gras on her desk this morning.

Adele was one of her staff, her right arm. She handled all of the considerable and tedious paperwork necessary for the tasks of responding to the foundation's constant demands for information on her work, collating the results of experiment after experiment, managing the payroll, paying the lab's not inconsiderable rent and other expenses and, most important of all, cheering Kelly up.

For the last two years, Kelly had been working off of a grant from a major foundation working to discover a medicinal enzyme which would counteract the presence of heavy metal contaminants in drinking water. It was an intractable problem, especially for third world, pregnant women. If a medicine could help women pass the pollutants through their systems instead of on to their fetuses, birth defects would be substantially lowered. She had protocols for research which could keep fifty technicians working full time for several years. She believed she was on the right track. It was just a matter of the right formula, enough time and enough money.

Unfortunately, each lead had to be meticulously pursued to its bitter conclusion. The last couple of papers she read at symposiums in her field had not been well received. Her case supervisor from the foundation which had funded her to date was not forthcoming on her chances for grant renewal on her last visit. She hoped time was not running out. She just knew she was right!

There was just so much to do and so little time. That was why her recent tendency to drift off into a fugue-like state was so disconcerting. She found herself staring off into space, straining to pierce the fog surrounding the dream man. He was tall, trim, well built. After each dream, when she awoke, she would try to recall his face without success. It was something she just couldn't focus on, though his features seemed strong and determined, forceful. He looked familiar, like he was someone she should know. When she tried to bring his visage into mind, he seemed strange, almost other worldly. He wasn't really smiling, and his expression wasn't exactly friendly, more like inviting. And yet, there was something about the man that struck fear into her, as if he had some power or force about him she should be wary of.

In the dream, he was naked, and his lack of clothing was natural, as if draping his body with even the finest cloth would somehow diminish him, cloak him with the impedimenta of a civilization or culture far beneath his noble carriage. The man would look at her intently, his eyes mesmerizing. Then he would reach out his hand to her. He would be standing amidst some kind of mist or fog. His lips would move. And then she would wake up.

Kelly could not remember exactly when she first started having the dream, but it was months ago, sometime during the summer. At first it seemed strange but inconsequential. Then it kept returning again and again. Now she was having it practically every night.

The dream was disturbing for more than just its content. Lately, she had awoken from it every morning in a feverish, aroused state. Her breasts would be aching with need and her hand would be fondling the lubricated folds of her sex. She would be sweating, her sheets all a tangle as if she had been struggling with some demon. This morning, she had fondled herself to a wrenching, mind blowing orgasm, shuddering with pleasure as the ill defined face of the dream man haunted her.

Kelly's sexual life was not what you would call satisfying. In fact, except for her occasional bouts of self administered bliss, it was non-existent. It was not because she lacked any of the attributes to attract qualified potential lovers. Her face was attractive, with well proportioned features, good, clean lines and voluptuous lips. She was about 5'6" tall, had sweet, curvaceous hips, long, well toned thighs. Her breasts were more than ample to fill her hands when she stood before the full length mirror in her bedroom after her shower, looking over her well trimmed, appealing body, wondering if she was, as Adele was constantly telling her, wasting the best years of her life.

In college and high school, she had dated; she was no sexual amateur. But once she realized that all her hard work in school had developed a sharp, analytical mind that needed to do great things, the pursuit of sexual gratification had seemed puerile. Not that there was anything wrong with sex. She had loved the sensation of a rampant cock in her belly, the feeling of sexual power it gave her to reduce her boyfriends to quivering, blubbering pools of pleasure. And the taste and smell of a man's loins in heat had often been enough to make her orgasm when the stiff wad of flesh began to throb and pulse in her mouth, delivering a stream of salty, bitter, piquant essence.

In fact, it was what she was thinking about this very minute. She was sitting at her desk, her chin in her hand, wistfully looking out her curtainless, industrial style, office window, watching the early December winds push the bare trees to and fro. Her other hand was on her lap resisting the urge to caress the insides of her thighs under her stylish, tan business skirt. This intruding recollection of the titillating sensation of hard, hot flesh brushing across her lips, filling her, had come upon her suddenly. It was connected to the dreams in some way, she knew that. Her breath had become heavy and her breasts seemed to have swollen. There was a tingling feeling on the tips of her nipples, a feeling echoed below in the apex of her thighs.

"Earth to Kelly! Earth to Kelly!" The sound of her friend and work associate's friendly voice startled her. She turned to see her bright face in her doorway. Adele, a Southern belle, was a spunky and vivacious 23 years old and had short, straw blond hair, cut into a shag. She said she liked to keep her hair as only a small issue in her life. She had pretty, sparkling, blue eyes, was tall, at least two inches taller than Kelly, and had a long, languorous torso. Her breasts filled her buttoned lab coat quite well and its calf length hid the thrilling thighs which would otherwise have been revealed by the short, stylish skirt she wore underneath. It was Friday and party time for Adele. She didn't want to waste a single minute of her Friday night going back to her apartment and changing. 5:30 to 8 was happy hour at Gene's Tavern over on Broad Street and she always met some friends there after work at the end of the week.

"Are you lost in space or something, honey?" Adele asked Kelly, in an exaggerated drawl, humored at finding her boss and friend staring out the window.

"No, no," Kelly responded, dragging herself away from her salacious reverie. "Just thinking."

Adele was well aware of her friend's worries. Although they were separated by four years of age, they had developed a close friendship over the 18 months Adele had worked at the lab. She was a godsend, relieving Kelly of many of the distractions that took her away from her principal tasks. They had dinner often, sometimes talking shop, but often regaling each other with tales of episodes of their past licentiousness or, in Adele's case, her present, their wishes that men could be more like women, well in some ways anyway, and deploring the scarcity of acceptable male companionship.

Kelly had not told Adele about the dream. She would have felt silly doing so. She didn't want to endure Adele's pop psychoanalysis of her randy subconscious, particularly since it would be based on a combination of her community college survey course in psychology, the platitudes of Dr. Phil and the horoscope pages of Star Magazine. Kelly was a graduate of Johns Hopkins Medical School. She had a bachelor's degree in applied sciences with a minor in behavioral studies from Princeton. She didn't need Adele to tell her that her dream was sparked by a deep seated need for a mate, that the mysterious male figure represented her vague notions of what she really wanted in a man and her fear of commitment to one. And what would she say about the subject of her lewd reminiscences? She would tell her she needed to get laid!

"You think too much," Adele returned, smiling. "I think your brain is getting burned out."

Kelly laughed. She knew her friend was only kidding. "I didn't know you could think too much," she said.

"Oh, yeah," Adele said, her lithesome body half in and half out of Kelly's small office. Her right hand was on the door frame above her head and her left hip was pushed out saucily. "If you don't watch it, I'll find you here someday with green stuff running out of your ears and your eyeballs hanging out. Why don't you come out with me? We'll have some fun."

"I can't Adele, I've got to finish some paperwork. The Edelson grant application is due next week. If our current funding peters out, I've got to have a back up."

"Grant, schmant," Adele answered in her Southerner's version of a Yiddish accent. "You can work on it tomorrow while you recover from your hangover. Let's go get some mai tai's, some dinner and then go dancing. I guarantee you'll have your heels in the air by the end of the night." Adele swayed her thin, graceful hips playfully. "There's lots of horny men out there, honey. You've got to get yourself one of them."

Kelly frowned. "I don't need a horny man in my life right now, Adele."

"You look like you need something, honey," Adele told her. "You were lost in some kind of cloud. I know you're work is important, but everybody's got to let loose once in a while. You can't do your best work if you're grumpy and miserable. Come on, let it go, get wild!"

Kelly found it hard to maintain her resentment of the younger woman's presumption that she knew what she needed. Adele was a light hearted soufflé compared to her fried liver and beans. It was good to have a friend.

The professionally dressed woman released her frown and gave Adele a warm smile. "Thanks for you concern, Adele. I really appreciate it. But I just can't tonight. Call me over the weekend. Maybe we can have lunch on Sunday or something. That'd be nice."

Adele, seeing her efforts at bringing some excitement to her friend and boss's life were in vain, smiled back. "Okay little miss busy bee. I'll call you tomorrow some time. Or not, depending on how the night works out. I may be wrapped in the arms of a 6' tall, broad shouldered, handsome, independently wealthy, Latin lover. And if I am, I'll be damned if I'll take a break from jumping his bones to call you!"

The women laughed. "Good luck, Adele," Kelly said. "And if you find this guy, see if he has an older brother, okay?"

"Will do, boss," Adele replied.

Soon afterwards, Kelly was alone in the lab. The three young, female, lab assistants had jumped ship immediately at the stroke of 5 o'clock. It was if they had been poised at a starting line, ready to pounce into their weekend at the very moment the minute hand hit the 12. She didn't blame them. They were all lively, pretty girls, less than a year out of high school.

Having a wholly female staff made Kelly's job easier. It wasn't that she felt men were less competent than the girls. Well, maybe they were, taken as a whole. The girls seemed less likely to call in sick, horse around or be distracted from their tasks. She had had several young men working for her at various times and for short periods over the last two years. Some of them were better than others. But it seemed they could not get past working for a young, desirable woman. Either they would melt into a little pool every time she called them into her office, or they would smile and smirk at her while she was giving them instructions. And if she leaned next to them, making any form of bodily contact while she peered over their shoulders to make a visual observation of some reaction or development, they would get flustered and start mumbling or stuttering. And they liked to look at her tits.

Kelly tried to dress conservatively: plain business suits, slacks and modest blouses, all worn under her lab coat when she was not at her desk. But she could not disguise her voluptuousness. She was not as well developed as Adele, but she was no slouch either. More than once, when she had called one of the young men into her office to discuss some protocol with them, some employee issue or anything at all, she would look up from her paperwork to find their gazes drawn to the soft, smooth mounds on her chest. They would blanch with embarrassment when she caught them, but their focus would continually shift up and down, up and down, from her eyes to her tits and back again as they were talking. No, the girls were much better and she hoped and prayed none of the male applicants she rejected ever sought counsel with the Equal Employment Opportunity Commission. Just how would that look to the foundation grant committee?

Kelly's lab was located in half of a red bricked, light manufacturing building situate in a small, mostly residential town in southern Virginia, called Jacksonville. It was one of more than two dozen Jacksonville's around the South, all named after the mercurial Confederate general. Kelly was from New Jersey and her suburban upbringing had not prepared her for the sometimes yahoo ways of the locals. She had never been to a Piggly Wiggly before coming here, nor had she ever eaten shredded, barbequed pork for lunch.

The ubiquitous rebel flags and decals on the revved up, jacked up pickups, many with the seemingly standard 30.06 shotguns mounted in the rear windows, were slightly disconcerting, making her feel like she had moved to some foreign country armed to repel an imminent invasion force. But the rents and wages here were cheap and general living expenses were low. It helped to stretch her grant money. She sometimes wished, however, she had located the lab in one of the other mostly economically depressed towns in the area with unique names like Splintersville or Gate's Corner. There were seven Jacksonville's in Virginia and her mail was constantly being misdelivered.

But then she wouldn't have found Adele. And she might not have found the beautiful little farmhouse she lived in, at least a half mile from the nearest residence, and built adjacent to a fast running, musical brook. Many a night she had finished her waking day by sitting on the long, covered, wooden porch and listening to the sounds of the water dancing off of the stones in the stream, enjoying the vista of bright stars in the clear night and sipping a hot cup of chamomile tea. She did some of her best thinking there.

She had to laugh at Adele's reference to a theoretical, 6' tall, broad shouldered, handsome, independently wealthy, Latin lover. Although they had often joked about their common fantasy, she was as likely to find one as Kelly was to find a pearl in the oyster crackers she liked to have with her soup at lunch. There had been some corporate development in town. But the executives were either married or grown up boys who raced off to one of the other more populous urbanized areas of the state in their sleek sports cars at every opportunity. Adele knew that. She was a local, one who had made the enlightened decision not to marry an indigenous, high school football star right after graduation and have two babies, a hound dog and a divorce by the time she was 22.

No, Adele was probably going to hang out with some of her girl friends tonight, go dancing at the Rainbow Club, a 'B' grade disco at the other end of town, and maybe, just maybe, catch one of the overdressed, over confident, oversexed, executive types on a night he had been unable to make it out of town, or if his wife had. Adele was no home wrecker, but she wasn't so particular she would reject a coital prospect just because he had a pale, circular ring of flesh around his finger where his wedding ring should be.

Kelly worked until just before 8 o'clock. She spent most of her time reading journals she reviewed regularly for developments in her field. No telling where the clue that would advance her research would come from. And if she could not immediately assimilate the importance of all the details, she would ruminate on them later, hoping the synapses of her brain would bring her a revelation her mere conscious mind could not.

The office was separated from the lab area by a partition made of glass from about waist level up. The lights in the work area were dimmed, but she could still see the long lab tables, the burners and reagents stored on them. There were two large, cooking racks on the far wall and a large cooler. Adele's workstation was to the far left, an oversized, green metal desk with battered, five drawer, metal, filing cabinets behind it. Adele's desk was a mess, something that sometimes offended the well ordered Kelly, but her assistant always seemed to know where everything was, and filed and finished all of her reports on time. Kelly liked to be in control and it irked her sometimes that she had to rely on Adele to produce this file or that. She had learned, though, to tame her obsessive tendencies and let go of the urge to impose her own order on Adele's domain.

Kelly loaded her small briefcase with more work and donned her light, fall jacket. It was warmer here in the South than her New Jersey home at this time of year, but it was early December and the air was close to cold at night. She closed the door to her office, and then, after she had conducted an inspection of all of the girls' work stations, locked the lab and left the building.

The other half of the single level, light manufacturing building was occupied by a metal working outfit. They specialized in fabricating small, precise, surgical tools, minute, metal parts for sophisticated machinery and some other secret government projects. She had met Mr. Hardings, the shop owner and manager, when she had moved in. He was a grey haired, slightly roly poly, avuncular man with a large, bushy, salt and pepper mustache. He had helped her select some of the local tradesmen who she needed to set up her lab and had saved her a lot of money. He was also the landlord and often inquired when they met in the parking lot as to how her grants were going. She dreaded the possibility that someday she would have to tell him she couldn't pay the rent. Every time she saw him, her financial pressures came to the forefront of her mind. On the other hand, it was nice to have another operation in the building, especially one that had a 24 hour security guard. It made her feel safer as she walked to her car in the practically empty parking lot to know that somewhere someone was watching over her on a security camera. She had developed a strong sense of self preservation from living so close to crime ridden, urban areas up North and she discounted the comments of her old friends who still lived there that it was so nice to live somewhere where there was no 'crime problem'. Well, they hadn't read the local newspaper and didn't know about the raft of burglaries, shootings and miscellaneous mayhem that occurred in even this bucolic locale.

No one disturbed the attractive, young woman as she walked the forty or so feet to her car. She beeped the locks and opened the door to the driver's side of her 2 year old, leased, silver Sentra. Before she got in, she looked wistfully back at the building. So much of her dreams and hopes were tied up in the neat, 50 year old, red brick structure. "Soon," she thought. "Soon, we'll get it. The big break." She just knew it.

CHAPTER TWO

It took Kelly about twenty minutes to reach her rented farmhouse. There had been some apartments and condos that had been closer to her place of work, but Kelly had chosen the more remote location because of its isolation and beauty. She drove up the long, gravel path to the old, wooden structure. The inside had been renovated with new, modern, efficient appliances, clean, freshly stained and varnished wood panel walls, a large, elegantly tiled bathroom. But the outside looked like it could have served as headquarters for some Confederate brigadier. The roof was a dark, grey slate and the exterior was covered by long, grey and brown, misshapen wooden slats. It may have looked like a ramshackle shack from the outside, but it was warm and comfy on the inside and it was home.

The fields surrounding the house were covered with short, brown grass. The owner had reserved the right to farm the hay from the property and two weeks ago had shaven the last, long, wavy stalks. The empty fields gave the homestead a desolate feeling. There were copses of tall, bare maples around the edge of the property and the looming, purple Shenandoah Mountains, miles away, appeared like huge, silent sentinels.

Kelly trod quickly up the warped wooden steps, across the porch and into the house. She was in her place of sanctuary. She threw off her coat, letting it drape across one of the antique, stuffed chairs she had bought from an auction house over in Taylorsburg and went directly to her bedroom, flicking on the light. She had a large, four poster bed as a centerpiece to the room with heavy, dark dressers on either side. The bedspread was thick and warm in the chilly nights and was embroidered with small pink and lavender flowers. The double windows were surrounded by heavy curtains, light beige with long, dark brown borders. Her oversized, fluffy pillows sat on her bed at the head, beckoning her.

Kelly was tired. It had been a long day and a longer week. But she wanted to decompress from her day before retiring. Besides, even for an old maid like her, it was still a little early.

She quickly cast off the short, shirtwaist jacket that went with her suit, undid the buttons to her blouse and drew her slim arms from the sleeves. As she was unfastening her dainty bra from behind her back, she cast a sideways glance at the uncovered window. Who knew who was lurking out there this late at night? It was moonless, and with the lights on it seemed as if the windows were the barrier between herself and some strange, dark dimension. Her mind filled with a vision of some creepy, rag tag redneck lurking out in her yard, peering in and groping his grimy loins as she undressed. She shivered at the thought, but continued undressing none-theless. She knew in her heart there was no one out there and she would be damned if she would give in to superstition or wild imaginings.

Kelly dressed herself in a baggy, old, orange and grey, Princeton sweatshirt and a pair of sweatpants. She had doffed her two inch heels, practical yet dressy enough to make a good appearance if a sponsor or potential sponsor should drop in. It was why she wore the suit. She would have been much more at ease in a pair of jeans and a t-shirt, but she always wanted to make sure she could make a good impression. She slipped into a pair of comfortable, cloth slippers and headed for the kitchen.

A little more than an hour later, Kelly was sitting curled up on her sofa in the small living room. She had broiled and eaten a small piece of boneless chicken breast and steamed a couple of stalks of broccoli. A wide, stemmed, wine glass sat on the coffee table with the remnants of three inches of the dark maroon merlot she had poured herself. She was on her laptop, surfing lists of recently published scientific articles and ordering a few. The TV was on and the credits for the latest episode of the Sopranos were rolling upwards. The show was one of her few indulgences, many of the scenes being shot not far from where she had grown up with her working class family. Thank God for the Internet, Amazon.com and cable television. Even way out here, the trappings of the modern world could be brought to her home in an instant.

The shapely woman yawned and stretched. Right now, she thought, Adele was probably just getting warmed up. Well, good for her. But Kelly was tired and she wanted to get back to the lab early in the morning to check on some of the experiments brewing in the low temperature oven. She shut down the laptop and clicked off the TV. The dishes she left in the sink for the morning. She turned off the lights in the living room and kitchen and entered her bedroom. She shed her sweats and, clad only in her lacy, bikini cut panties, went to the bathroom to perform her evening rituals.

Watching herself in the bathroom mirror, Kelly took the time to brush her thick, wavy hair, her mind drifting absentmindedly. She saw before her a pretty girl, trim, with fine, round breasts which pointed upwards at the ends. Her skin color was light and luminous. Was she wasting away, she asked herself. She had broken up with David soon after she moved here, the pressures of the long distance relationship too much. It had not been much of a relationship, anyway. He was a pleasant convenience, someone to spend some time with and with whom to satisfy her cravings for sexual release. There had been no one since.

She wondered if Adele would make a connection tonight. She imagined her wrapping her long, lithe legs around the hips of the imaginary Latin lover, moaning with pleasure as he plowed her furrow with his hot, hard cock. As she repeated her mechanical brushstrokes, her mind a thousand miles away from what she was doing, Adele's face in the fantasy became her own. She imagined the feel of the thick, rigid manhood scraping across her bud of pleasure, scouring the inner walls of her wet cleft, the pressure of the man's strong chest against her breasts, his hips pounding into hers. She licked her lips. Her breathing began to become labored. Her free hand unconsciously looped under one of her breasts and massaged it, her thumb and forefinger trapping her stiff nipple and squeezing it until she brought herself a twinge of pain.

Suddenly, Kelly came awake. What was she doing? Her crevasse had moistened and she was showing a blush on her chest just above her breasts. She was startled at her lasciviousness. This was not her at all! Her body gave a little shiver and she put the brush down. She turned out the light and went into the bedroom.

When she entered the room, Kelly turned on the bedside lamp and turned off the overhead. The room was cast in a soft, almost eerie light. She looked down at the bed. Would she dream again tonight, she wondered. Would her lusts be raised again by the image of the strange man beckoning her? She was actually apprehensive about going to sleep. The dreams were so real. Lately, the dreams were lasting longer and longer. She could see his lips forming words; he seemed to be calling her. The smoothness that had characterized his appearance seemed to be giving way to lines and bulges and curves. The fog, or what looked like fog, was thinning. In the early dreams he had been far away, in the distance; now he was coming closer and closer.

Last night, she felt like she could just reach out and touch him. She sensed her dream-self yearning for him, desiring him. But her yearning, her desire, was tinged with a deep foreboding, as if when she finally made contact with him, placed skin to skin, she would cross a Rubicon from which there would be no return. She looked again at the double windows. She felt as if there was someone watching her. But who could it be? She stepped to the windows and drew the curtains closed after checking to make sure the sashes were locked. A hint of unexplainable panic ran through her mind and she went out to the living room, bathed in the glow of the dim light from the bedroom, and checked to make sure the door was secure. It was.

What was wrong with her? She had never felt like this before in this house. It was her island of peace, away from the world. If she could not feel safe and secure here, where could she? She tried to reach into her rational mind. No one was outside, she told herself. No one is inside. Dreams can't hurt you. Okay, so she was randy. She was a vibrant, normal, young woman, after all. Sexual drives were entirely natural, beneficial even, placed in every one to assure the continuation of the human race and allow everyone to experience the pleasures of their own bodies.

And there was nothing wrong with bringing pleasure to your own body. Masturbation was a good way to get release. As long as it did not become an obsession. She usually performed this self service about once every other week. Maybe she would do it tonight. It would help her get to sleep.

But was it becoming an obsession? She had brought herself off this morning, almost unconsciously, while awakening from her dream. And she had spanked the monkey the day before too. And Wednesday. And several times last week. What was happening to her? Was she becoming obsessed? Lately, she had found herself drifting off into sexual reveries several times a day. Were the dreams driving her sexual needs or vice versa?

Kelly quickly slipped under the sheets and drew the warm comforter over her. She reached out and flicked off the light. It took only a few seconds for the silence of the house to enwrap her. Through the windows, she could hear the rippling of the stream outside. The wind had picked up and she could hear the double paned glass shifting slightly as it blew against them.

Her body warmed up quickly under the covers, the coolness of the sheets quickly fading into a comforting reflection of her body's heat. She was on her side, facing the windows, her legs curled up, her arms around herself. She let her mind drift and, soon, she felt her hand easing down her torso over her hips and over her legs. Her skin felt so good, soft and clean. Without thinking, she rolled onto her back and drifted her fingers along the inside of her thighs. She raised and spread her knees so she could caress them down their length.

Why not, she thought. It wouldn't hurt her to get off. Her pussy was already burning with need. It only took her a moment to shuck off her panties, kicking them off of the ends of her feet at the bottom of the bed. She brought her hands to the crux of her thighs, ran them through the carefully trimmed, wiry hair and softly pushed her engorging labial lips together. It felt so good. She drew her fingers along the slit for a while, parting the lips slightly, up and then down again, letting the tingle in her loins develop. She moaned lowly as her fingers sensed the moisture of her arousal. She gasped when they brushed against the hardened nubbin at the apex of her needy sex.

There was no stopping now. Kelly let her right hand continue to draw pleasure from her softening pussy and brought her left hand up to massage her aching breasts. They were hard with the blood of her lust. The heat of her hand sent rivulets of pleasure through her. She imagined the coffee brown skin of her imaginary bedmate covering her, his long, glistening, shoulder length, black hair falling over her body. He was kissing her breasts, running his rough tongue over her teats, sucking on them hard, squeezing her mounds firmly in his large, strong hands while his cock slowly eased its way into her depths. It was her and Adele's fantasy Latin lover, the man who would bring her everything: love, passion, strength, warmth.

Kelly's breath began to get short and her heart began to thump in her chest. Her fingers massaged her clit, pressing on it, running little circles over it, pausing only to dip into her well of sexual heat to draw out her oozing moisture, and then covering it until it was slippery and rolled under her sensitive touch. She could feel the telltale signs of her orgasm building inside her. She was thrusting her hips back at the hand in her loins as her thighs began to shudder. "Ohhhhhhhh!" she moaned. "Ohhhhhhh!" Suddenly, her mind became overwhelmed with the flood of pleasure that rushed to it. Her pussy began to throb and contract. She spread her legs wider, her knees almost touching the mattress on either side of her, drawing her long, graceful legs up. Her hand rubbed harder and faster on her loins. She arched her back as she felt her whole body electrified with ecstasy. "Oh! Oh! Oh! Oh!" she called out into the dark room at each convulsion of her sex. In her mind, her lover was pounding his lust into her, filling her void, forcing apart the sides of her enflamed inner flesh. It seemed to last forever. She wanted it to last forever. And then she moaned again, "Ohhhhhhhhhh!" as she crested her lust and her pussy's spasms finally begin to subside.

When the tremors of her orgasm faded into a bliss that seeped into every pore of her body, Kelly rolled to her belly and fell asleep.

* * * *

They say even the longest, most involved dreams take only a second to flash across our minds. Kelly wasn't sure how long she had been sleeping when the dream began, but she felt sure she had long ago descended deeply into somnolence. She was standing nude in a huge, grassy field. It was bright and sunny with large, fluffy, bright white clouds fleeing across the deep blue sky as if pushed by strong winds. But no breeze caressed her naked form. The air around her was still and heavy.

Across the field, which was strewn with a wonderful array of brightly colored wildflowers, she saw the man approaching. He wasn't walking, more like floating, and his body was enwrapped with a swirling fog.

He was coming closer and closer. He was also nude, and the fog that surrounded him had sprinkled him with its droplets, making his smooth, hairless chest shine and glisten in the sun. He had long, black hair that touched his shoulders and flared back behind him as he approached. Kelly felt her passion begin to rise as he neared her. He was no more than twenty feet away from her when she saw his lips begin to move. His right hand extended from his body, palm up, like he was inviting her to take it. Kelly's mind filled with the urge to flee. But her body wanted to stay, wanted to reach out and accept the strong, compelling hand in her own. His eyes, though, belied his gesture of amity. They were dark and foreboding. As her hand, seemingly of its own will, extended towards him, she felt her own eyes locked into them, felt his gaze piercing her brow, entering into her mind.

Suddenly, the man was upon her. The misty shroud still enveloped him. She was trying to tell her dream-self to back away, to withdraw her hand. Some part of her consciousness struggled to bring herself out from this entrancing night fancy. The dreams had never gone this far before and she knew that some barrier was about to be crossed, that whatever happened now, somehow things would not ever be the same. It was too late. She wanted to stop, to break the mesmerizing gaze of the man's sharp, fierce eyes. But her body would not obey her. She was lost.

The dream Kelly slowly reached her right hand into the swirling mist. When her disobedient fingers made contact with those of the man, she felt a flow of energy pass into her. Her mind reeled with the pleasurable sensations being sent through her body. The man waited, his hand now grasping hers. She saw his lips forming her name, calling out slowly in a deep, inviting voice, "Kelly…Kelly…Kelly…." He seemed to want something. And then she realized he wanted her to pull him to her, that he needed her efforts to cross the misty barrier which separated them. Again, her rational self said, "No! No! No! Don't do it! Don't!" as she felt her arm drawing back, bringing the man towards her.

Kelly gasped as the man's body emerged from the swirling field of mist that surrounded him. He was inches away from her now, his naked body fully visible at long last. His smooth chest was well developed, his stomach taut and firm. Heat radiated from his torso like a plinth. His arms and thighs were thickly muscled, his face clean shaven and strong. She looked down as he moved to press his body next to hers and saw his long, thick manhood was erect. For a moment, a fearsome regret passed though her mind. What had she done? Then the man leaned forward. He placed his large, strong hands on either side of her head and pressed his lips onto hers. Her lips parted and she felt his hot tongue enter her mouth.

A wave of lust passed through the excited, young woman as she felt the tongue explore her mouth, dance against hers, sending hot passion into her very soul. She sucked and played with the hot invader eagerly. Something was passing between them, something more than mere lust. She felt as if her mind was being probed by the strong hands on her head. Something was wrong! This was more than a kiss! The strong, broad shouldered man was exploring her, drawing her essence from her and filling her with his will.

Suddenly, she was no longer standing, but was on her back with the dream man lying beside her. Keeping one hand on the side of her head, his hot tongue in her mouth, he drifted the other down along her neck, across her heaving chest and captured first one breast and then the other, massaging them, caressing them, causing another wave of passion to pass through her.

When the hand dropped to her belly, it brushed over the wiry bush that surrounded her sex and then slid a thick finger down the already wet slit between her nether lips. Kelly moaned. She spread her legs invitingly. Her hands were on the man's body, exploring the firm flesh, receiving an exciting flow of energy wherever they went. Their lips had separated and the man had pulled his head back. His eyes bored into hers. It seemed as if she couldn't look away, not even blink, as the brown pools, cold and hard, drew her in.

The man shifted himself so he was between her outstretched legs. He took hold of his hard shaft and presented it to her fevered, distended nether lips. She felt a moment's panic when the fat, round head pushed aside her outer labia and delved between them. But the sensation of his entering her was overwhelming. The hard rod of flesh eased its way forward, making the interior flesh part seemingly of its own accord, inviting his penetration. Slowly, he pressed deeper into her. She felt herself being filled. She groaned with passion, her hands gripping the large man's shoulders. When he had sunk his manhood fully into her, his pelvis bone meeting hers, he slowly began to withdraw, dragging across the tender flesh of her sheath, running the top of his cock along her hard, electrified pleasure bud.

The sensation of the man's languorous stroke drove Kelly wild. She wrapped her arms around his back, slid her legs down his hard, flexed thighs. Their lips rejoined and the impassioned young woman's body shuddered with delight. He began to rock back and forth within her, increasing his pace almost imperceptibly, until he was gliding in and out of her lush canal at an almost frenzied pace. Kelly rocked her hips back at him, meeting each thrust of his with a powerful push. She could feel her blood getting hotter and hotter. Her whole body tingled with the foreshadowing of her impending climax. And then it hit her. She felt her pussy throb and spasm. Her body shook and her back arched. "Ohhhhhhh!

Ohhhhhhhhh!" she moaned into the stranger's mouth. There were no thoughts in her mind but the appreciation of the waves of ecstasy that flowed through her. When her pulses of pleasure began to ebb, she felt her passion begin to rise again as the man, not missing a stroke, continued his relentless plowing of her burning sex.

It was when her body began to shudder and quake with her second, wrenching orgasm, her mind protesting at the almost painful pleasure, that she felt the man's body stiffen. A low, strained sound emanated from his throat. His thrusts became hard, his hips colliding with hers, presaging his climax.

Suddenly, it was as if a veil had been lifted from her eyes. She was not in a dream! She was in her own bed, not in some flowery field! This was real! How could that be? A strange, unknown man was fucking her! Panicked, she tried to beat at the man's body, her hands balled into little fists. She tried to free her mouth from the man's ardent kiss. She writhed and rocked her body in futile protest. And then he came. She felt the throbbing and jerking of his cock deep within her. The sensation of his fluids jetting into her womb sent her into another mind numbing orgasm. She grabbed his shoulders with her soft, frail hands and pulled his body towards hers. Her legs wrapped around him, drawing his cock deeper into her pulsing crevasse. Each contraction of her pussy's muscles sent a wave of excruciating pleasure throughout her flesh.

Kelly was practically breathless when the man's thrusts slowed languidly to a stop. Her body was slick with perspiration and her blood pounded in her brain. It took her several moments to recover a semblance of equilibrium. The man's head lay next to hers, his forehead on the bed. She could feel and hear his hot breath as he recovered from his expenditure. His chest rose and fell heavily on hers. Her mind filled with misery and fear. Somehow, someone had broken into her home, had stripped off his clothes and interposed himself in her dream. She was shocked that her newly lascivious nature had prevented her from detecting his real life invasion of her bed, that his assault had so easily integrated itself into her subconscious.

But here he was, as real as herself. Kelly whined involuntarily and began to writhe and twist her body. She tried to shout out, to scream a protest into the night, but her voice was silent. For some reason, she could not push out a sound other than an inarticulate, barely audible, "Arrrrrrrgh!" from her throat. The room was shrouded with darkness. She could not see the flesh of the body that had taken possession of her other than as a shadowy form, but she could feel it, his heavy torso lying on top of hers, his strong legs between her thighs, his hips pressing against her hips.

The man seemed to have fallen into some kind of faint. Kelly struggled to push him off, terrified lest he should awaken. She felt weak, drained and he was too heavy. The man had taken her energy from her, she was sure, just as she was sure somehow he had deprived her of her voice. Then, the body above her began to stir. She felt his chest slide across hers, slipping over her sweaty breasts and belly. His torso rose, his lips found purchase on the side of her neck, kissing it, teasing it with his tongue. His hand covered her left breast, kneading the pillowy flesh gently, capturing her nipple between its fingers, stroking it delicately. She realized the man was still hard and still inside her. Her mind revolted against the pleasurable effects of his languid attentions. She struck at him with all the force her tired arms could muster, moaning her protests. But when the thick, hot cock slowly began to renew its movements along the course of her womb's canal, her mind was jolted back into passion.

Kelly cursed herself for her wantonness as the man's prick drove her again to lust. She felt shamed at her inability to control her fevered reactions to his assault, humiliated that he could force her so easily to succumb to his desires. Silently, he stroked in and out of her agitated pussy. If only he would talk, say something, taunt her or mock her powerlessness, then, perhaps she could muster her resources to oppose him. His quiet, determined, almost other worldly insistence on his pleasure and hers, though, subverted her need to resist him. For just a moment, Kelly imagined this was still a part of her dream, that she would awaken, sweaty and spent, alone in her bed. This hope quickly passed. The man's flesh was too real. The sensations of his body against hers were too substantive, too actual in their detail to be anything else.

The man's heat and strength was intoxicating. He again took possession of her lips and thrust his hot tongue inside her. She moaned into his mouth as her crisis began anew. Her body rocked and shuddered as she came, her mind short circuited with pleasure. When she felt him discharge himself into her, the spasms of his cock sent her over the precipice of her passion one more time. Then she passed out.

CHAPTER THREE

The morning found the couple curled against each other, the woman's unconscious body spooned inside the man's wider arc. It was he who awoke first. Slowly, his mind focused into consciousness as his eyes took in the strange, new surroundings.

This was his fifth jump. It was always the same. If the jump was successful, that is. No amount of casting into a largely indecipherable, other universe could prepare one for its reality. It had taken quite a while before the technicians had found an acceptable subject. They had rejected a number of them as either insufficiently passionate or lacking the strong, independent intelligence that would cast a secure enough link across the void. For if the jump was not successful, well, no traveler ever had survived an unsuccessful jump. Their essence was dissipated in the barrier between the two realities.

The man didn't have what we would call a name as much as a reference. Its sound, if approximated in the verbal tones of English would be something like "Rrrrrrjjayammmm", or to get even closer to our language, "Raijamoon." The ideas of self and identity which we find so essential to our psyches did not exist in his home universe. So much was different. There was no real, corporal separation from the Whole. He, and we'll call him 'he' for purposes of convenience, was more like a kind of facet, a rivulet in the stream of race consciousness. Not that he didn't have individuality, a separateness from The Whole. It was just, well, different, as foreign to us as our universe was to him.

It took many time periods of training to develop the mental capacity to be able to adjust to strange, new environments. And to take on the bodily form of an inhabitant, to prepare one's mind for sexual congress with an alien being, no matter how pleasurable it was to the new corpus one occupied, took an exceptionally flexible and fearless nature. But the Whole had the ability to manipulate its resources, concentrate aspects of itself. He and a number of other peaks of the Whole's existence had been infused with the mental resources they would need. He was the best, the place where the Whole had streamed the purest, densest accumulation of courage, adaptability and strength. The fact he had survived five jumps proved that.

But now he was alone, separated from the Whole, on his own. He would need to adjust, gain strength, become familiar with the flesh he now possessed. For many, many weeks of our time, the physical reality of the male humanoid body had grown and developed. It had sprung from a kernel, initiated when the technicians had focused on the human female's psyche. Her need for sexual fulfillment was strong, and her yearnings, pushed by her, in human terms, superior mental strength, had stretched over the thin membrane between dimensions. They had learned long ago how to focus on and intensify those yearnings from many types of beings in many dimensions, and had isolated and focused on her as a single subject out of millions of possible ones. As Kelly's preoccupation with her unsatisfied lusts became stronger and stronger, encouraged by her night time contact with Raijamoon's universe, the physical being he was to inhabit grew from his own substance and of that of the Whole, slowly taking form, until, finally, last night, her passion had been strong enough to pull him through, his body, features, mannerisms all dictated by the visions in her mind.

The acts of sexual congress they had performed together had solidified his existence in this realm as a human male, approximately aged 35, strong, healthy and energized by the far superior intelligence he possessed in his newly found mind. They would need to continue. The young woman was now his connection to this world, a sort of 'familiar'. For although he was here, the connections to his old world would eventually draw him back unless his presence was sustained by her lust for him. And his powers were yet weak. He could not yet control her as he would have to do. The satisfaction of his new body's sexual urges, whether with her or with others, would strengthen him, allow him to draw on that part of him still left behind, his connection to the Whole.

The minds of these beings were simple, almost feeble compared to those of his kind. As he solidified his channel of communion with his race over the barrier between the worlds, he would be able to draw on its power, project his will onto her and to others. The absorption of his seed by select individuals would strengthen his ability to control them, serve as a reagent of desire for him.

So far, he only used his power of control to silence the human female's voice and to stimulate her sexual needs. He had probed her mind, drawing on her knowledge of this world to facilitate his acclimation to it. He had learned much from her during the night, some of which the unevolved mind he was now forced to use still needed to process and interpret. But that would come easier as time went on.

For the moment, the man took the opportunity to revel in the physical pleasure his body experienced from the fact of being. The taste of the air his new lungs pulled in and out of his chest, the rushing of blood through his veins, the sights and sounds of this world. The air around him was slightly chilly and caused his skin to vibrate with need for heat. He felt the warmth being emitted by the female form lying beside him. He pressed his body closer to it, spooning against her, enjoying the sensation of the heat transfer between the two bodies where their skin made contact. He remembered the softness of her flesh, its roundness and malleability. He recalled the pleasure of his rigid, enflamed member being sunk within her, her passionate responses.

No other race he had experienced possessed such a strong need to repeat again and again the sexual act necessary for reproduction. The desire for pleasure and union with another was intense within them. Their emotions were very strong as compared to others. Anger, fear and sexual desire were strong, and he could 'feed' on any of them. Of the three, sexual desire was the strongest and easiest to channel. He could feel his own now as he experienced the female's physical presence so close to his, the beauty and voluptuousness his human mind perceived, the memory of their coupling. These beings had an expanded ability to experience physical pleasure; his new body yearned for it again. That was good. It would greatly facilitate his task of developing his powers.

The woman's long, pinioned, rust colored hair lay between them. He felt the silkiness of its surface on his skin. Although he knew he risked awakening the woman, he could not resist the temptation to run his hand over her naked shoulder, down her curvaceous torso and over her prominent hip. Her flesh was smooth, warm and satisfying to his hand. His male, human mind took great pleasure in the suppleness of the skin. He leaned his head over and took in a deep whiff of the woman's scent, detecting elements which made his loins stir. He felt the bittersweet pleasure of desire, the exquisiteness of the compulsion for union.

The day had just dawned and a faint glow of sunlight was emanating from the closed drapes. Outside the open bedroom door, the man could see the dissipation of the darkness from the light through the unobscured windows in the other rooms. He needed to explore. Safety was one issue. He needed to make sure his possession of his familiar was not threatened or interfered with by any other beings. And the other was his natural inquisitiveness, his eagerness to experience more of this new world.

He didn't want to arouse the sleeping female. He could anticipate her unhappiness at her seduction and his forcing of his will upon her. She would be greatly disconcerted and confused about the melding of her dreams and reality. Until he was able to bring her under more close control, he would have to be careful she did not try to escape her fate or try to harm him.

The man placed his right hand on the side of the sleeping scientist's head and concentrated his mind. Since she was already asleep, it was not difficult to nudge the part of her brain that controlled her unconsciousness and deepen her slumber. The woman moaned a meek protest as she slipped deeper into sleep. Her face wore a worried frown and then went back to rest. He would not have long until she struggled to wakefulness. He would return before she did.

Slipping quietly from the bed, the naked man stepped across the bedroom and entered the hallway. His gait was unsteady, like someone learning to walk on high heels. The body felt wonderful. He flexed his large, strong hands as he walked, reveling in their usefulness as tools and he thrilled at the sensation of propelling himself on his feet. It was a clever way to manage the need to cross short distances, but he saw immediately the drawbacks as tools of locomotion for any long time. Walking seemed ponderously slow and he was anxious to try out one of the concepts he had drawn from the woman's mind, that of running, or to run. But that could wait until he grew more adept at controlling his body's functions and his strength had grown.

From his vantage point outside the bedroom, the man could see into both the living room and the kitchen. In the living room, he saw fabricated forms which he recognized as chairs, a sofa. There were two electronic devices that he gathered were for the purposes of accessing information. He had discovered a concept the woman's mind seemed to classify as 'entertainment', but he would need to study that principle more before he could understand it.

In the kitchen, he saw a table, some chairs, and what looked like food preparation and storage units. He would need food soon. There was a bowl with colorful, round objects in it on the table. He picked up one that was a dullish red, but shiny and appealing. He stood for a moment and searched the information he had gathered from the woman's mind, not all of it processed yet, and he formed a recognition. This was an apple. The woman's mind had catalogued this object and ones like it as edible and pleasing. He assimilated her knowledge of how to consume it and placed it to his mouth. A little unsure of himself, he pressed his teeth slowly on the reddish sphere and pressed downwards on the stiff outer coating. As his teeth pierced its surface, a rush of the object's juice leaked into his mouth. His body gave out a sigh and his mind reeled with pleasure.

So this was what taste was like, he thought. It was remarkable. He finished his bite and tore a chunk of the fruit's meat into his mouth. He closed his eyes as he masticated it, reveling in its sweetness and its texture. When he swallowed the mashed pulp, his body expressed its appreciation for the delivery of such succulent sustenance.

He continued to eat the apple as he rooted around the kitchen. When he had consumed it down to its core, which he agreed, after a sample, was not edible, he placed the remnants on the table. Exploring the room's features, it took him a moment to figure out how to open a drawer. The doors to the cabinets were easier. He made only a cursory inspection, a catalogue of observations he would go back to later when there was more time. He noted the long, sharp objects meant for piercing or slicing and he made a note to keep the female away from them. In the refrigerator, he saw what he assumed were comestibles. He left them alone since he wasn't sure whether any of them needed processing or not before ingestion.

There was a carton of orange liquid which had a picture of a human child consuming some of it out of an open topped, clear, cylindrical object. "A glass," he noted. He had seen some similar artifacts in one of the cabinets. He went back and retrieved one and tried to open the top of the carton so that he could pour some in. The hard, green top wouldn't pull off and he was, at first, perplexed as to how to open the container. Then, by accident, the top moved to the left and he felt it grow looser. He kept turning it until it fell off and dropped to the table. He placed his nose over the opening on the carton and inhaled the pleasing scent of its contents. He poured some into the glass carefully, not wanting to spill a drop of the fresh looking, orange substance. He put the glass to his lips and tilted it back until his tongue could dip its tip into it. It was cold. A new experience. He dipped his tongue in again, enjoying the refreshing feeling. The taste was thrilling. He tipped the glass back further and took a small mouthful of the liquid. He closed his eyes, savoring the flavor. Again his body thanked him as he let it seep down his throat. He downed the whole glass, coughing and sputtering some of the liquid back up when he took it too fast. Some of it ran over his lips and onto his chest, giving him an uncomfortable feeling. He was amused by the body's reaction to the too quick consumption of the liquid. He finished the glass, slowly this time.

Having satisfied himself no one else was around, he was eager to see what it was like outside of the structure. He remembered the door in the other room and walked towards it. He recognized the handle and what it was for, but when he pulled on it, he got no results. He tested it further and realized it was meant to be twisted. But still the door would not open. The word 'locked' came into his head. Looking between the edge of the door and the frame, he could see the gleaming, brass plug that held the door fast. There was a knob across from it on the door and he turned it. The door sprung free.

For the first time, the visitor stepped out under the open sky of our planet. He felt the coolness of the air all over his naked body. He paid it little heed as his eyes took in the wondrous vista before him. The sun had not yet crested the heavy, looming mountains many miles away. The sky was spread with rays of yellow, red and deep orange across an underlay of grey, tinted by a soft hue of purple. The fields around the farmhouse were awash with deep browns, yellows, and oranges and here and there a hint of green. He could hear the rushing of the nearby stream, a shushing and gurgling that was a collaboration of amiable sounds. Up in the sky, circling in a wide arc around the farmhouse was what he recognized as a bird, a creature of flight. It looked graceful and harmonious with its surroundings.

The new man stepped carefully over the wooden porch and down the three short steps to the ground. The walkway to the house was made of cinder gravel and the sensation of placing his bare feet on the stones was sharp and painful. Another new experience. It was just enough to command his attention to the possibility of harm to his soft skin and he appreciated the value and purpose of the function. The house was surrounded by a fifteen yard wide carpet of grass and he stepped over to it gingerly. His feet felt comfortable as he trod on the soft, spongy surface. He looked carefully at the ground beneath him as he walked, observing the dewy drops on the pale green stalks and the tiny forms of life that crawled among them.

And then there was the brook. The water was running fast and clear. He could see the rounded rocks and stones beneath its surface. He marveled at the sight of the flowing, clear liquid. He looked up and down stream, considering the length of the waterway and seeing how it curved and snaked in parts, slowing as it rounded its bends, and then speeding up again as if it had caught its breath and was hurrying on. He lowered himself into a crouch and dipped his right hand into the water. It was cold, far colder than the air around him. Its touch was exhilarating. He placed both hands in and then, excited, stood and stepped into the rushing water. The cold ran all the way up his legs as his feet began to numb. He wanted to immerse his naked body in the water and he looked downstream to where he had seen the water pooling. He stepped over to it quickly and sunk into the cold liquid above his knees. The bottom was soft and sandy. He dropped to a crouch, letting the water rise up to his hips and then he leaned back and let it flow all over him.

The man rose from the water as if shocked. His long, black hair dribbled water down his back, his muscles contracted from the cold. "Ahhhhhhh!" he exclaimed. "What pleasures these creatures have!" He sank back down to his knees and leaned back again. This time, he stayed in longer. His body reacted instinctively as he closed his mouth and eyes. He waited, submerged, his body growing pained due to the 45 degree water, until he felt his lungs demanding air. He rose up, all at once, and leapt from the stream. His body was freezing cold, but his mind was racing with the pleasure of the experience. "What a delightful world!" he thought.

As if shaken from a dream, he suddenly recalled the human female he had left inside the structure. It wouldn't do to have her awaken and cause a fuss. She could lock the door again, keeping him out. His revelry in the experiences of his new world was threatening to destroy his purpose. He pushed his soaking hair back on his head and took long, quick strides back to the house.

* * * *

Kelly had finally struggled to awareness. When she realized she was awake, she panicked and half rose in the bed, turning to see if the man was still there. She was alone. Her upper sheet and comforter were twisted and disheveled. Her body felt like she had been through a bout with herself. Maybe it was all a dream, a horrible, frightening dream. But it felt so real. Her body shuddered when she recalled the pounding, soul shaking orgasms she had experienced. That meant that it had to be a dream, right? She would never experience pleasure from a man who had taken her without her consent. Rapists were cruel and brutal and took you ruthlessly, striking you and hurting you. And where was he now if he was real? Would a rapist just up and leave without tying her up or maybe even killing her so as to avoid identification, arrest and a long imprisonment?

But it had seemed so real. She could still taste the man's hot tongue in her mouth, feel the echoes of his manhood inside her. She remembered coming and coming and coming, the feel of his hard torso in her hands, his weight on her, the noise he made when he came.

Kelly shifted her hand down to her loins. She was surprised to find the dried evidence of passion in her pubic hair. She looked down at the mattress next to her. Was it her imagination, or was there a long, deep indentation there? Then she saw what sealed it. Lying on the bright, white sheet was a long strand of black hair. Her heart went cold. She picked it up. It was definitely not hers. It was definitely black. The man last night had had long, shoulder length, black hair.

Kelly leapt from the bed. Was he still here? She needed to get to her cell phone in the living room to call the police. As she rounded the edge of her bedroom door, she saw the door to her cabin was wide open. There, framed in the doorway, hurriedly walking up the steps, was the man, the man who had forced himself on her. He looked big and strong. He was naked, his body glistening just like in the dream, and he was very, very real.

There was just one chance. If she could reach the door before he did, she could slam it shut and lock him out. He might try and smash the windows to get in, but that would give her the opportunity to grab her cell phone and escape out of one of the kitchen windows. She exercised religiously and was in excellent shape. Maybe she could outrun him and hide in the woods. Or maybe she could grab one of the kitchen knives and keep him at bay until the police arrived. How she wished she had a gun. She hated them but would have given her eye teeth for one now.

Kelly sprang towards the door. The man had been looking down at his feet as he negotiated the steps as if unsure of his tread. He looked up at her just as she started for the door. Astonishment spread across his face. He reacted quickly, leaping forward.

The frantic woman got to the door first. She placed her hands on the door's edge and began to swing it shut, throwing her entire weight behind the effort. For a moment, she thought she had achieved success and a thrill of victory swept through her. But just as the door was reaching its closed position, she met an opposite, more powerful force.

"Nooooooo!" Kelly screamed loudly. Last night, she remembered, she had lost her voice, been unable to scream or protest. She found it now.

"No! No! No!" she yelled as she tried to dig her bare feet into the floor, leaning against the slowly opening door. "Stop! Stop!" she yelled, as if her imprecations would halt the man who had callously invaded her home and her body.

Slowly, but surely, the door eased open. When Kelly realized she had lost the struggle, she let go of the door and tried to retreat to the kitchen to get a knife or something to defend herself with. The man was immediately behind her. He reached out and grabbed a fistful of her long ponytail and pulled her back. She gave a loud screech at the pain in her scalp and in frustration and fear at having been captured.

Coolly, she remembered one of her moves from her self defense class back in college. She pivoted on one bare foot and swung her other leg out at the man's crotch. Instinctively, he released her hair to ward off the blow. To her surprise, he caught her foot in midswing. He raised it high and then kicked at her planted foot.

Kelly' body went topsy turvy and she fell to the hardwood floor of the hallway. She groaned as she hit the floor, but scrambled immediately back to her feet, her arms flailing, her fingernails scratching and tearing at the man's naked flesh as he tried to subdue her. "You bastard!" Kelly yelled at him. "Fuck you! Fuck you!" She tried to kick at him again, but he pushed her body flat against the wall, knocking a shelf of knick knacks to the floor with a crash. He had grabbed both of her arms and he pressed his bare flesh against hers. He was slippery and cold and Kelly managed to slide away from him. She kicked him in the right thigh, once, twice, bringing a grimace of pain to his face. He managed to take hold of both her thin wrists in one hand and then pushed her back up against the wall. Kelly thought he was going to strike her when she saw his other hand coming towards her face, but instead, he placed it over the side of her head and closed his eyes.

Immediately, Kelly felt her mind and body freeze. The sensation was not actually pain, but was as close to painful as you could get. Her body felt insulted, empty, kind of soured, all at the same time. She uttered "Uhhhhh!" as she felt her knees buckle. Something had come over her! He had done something to her! Her backbone felt like rubber and her brain felt sick. She gave the man a look in his cold, dark brown eyes. "Please, please, don't do this," she begged him with her glance, and then everything went dark.

* * * *

The man had been startled when he saw the woman rushing towards the door. It was exactly what he had feared and he reacted immediately. He was lucky to get there just before the door slammed shut. It took a great effort to stop the forward motion of the door and reverse it. He was bigger and more heavily muscled than the woman, but he was still tired from his journey. As he gained mastery over the door, he felt it go free and saw the female try and run away. He lashed out his hand and caught her hair, pulling her to a stop.

He had no experience at using this body in a fight. Physical combat did not exist in his world. He seemed to sense nonetheless what to do to bring the woman under control. His mind was quicker than hers, even at this early stage of his adjustment. She telegraphed her kick at his groin and he was able to move his hand to catch her foot. She had a fierce, angry look on her face. He was actually able to absorb her emotions as she struggled with him. Like an analytical computer, he saw she was poised, unstable, on one foot and he reacted quickly to bring her to the floor.

A more experienced combatant would have fallen on her, taken advantage of his weight and strength once she was on the floor, but his indecision gave her the opportunity to regain her feet, scratching and clawing at him. As his mind recorded the new experience of the pain of her nails scraping across his skin, he noted the raising of his adrenalin level. It felt good.

He determined to bring the struggle to a quick halt. It would absorb more of his limited energy, more than he wanted, but this was a desperate fight and if somehow the woman got free or disabled him it would be a disaster of the highest order. For without this human female under his control, available to strengthen him, to anchor him in this world, he would be lost. His body would, in a matter of hours, begin to dissipate and his essence would be lost. Later, when he was stronger and drawing sustenance for the psychic energy necessary to retain him in his current form, he would be able to go longer periods without using her. Now, she was all he had and was the one humanoid in this entire universe he needed.

He didn't want to hurt her and he was not angry at her resistance. Surprised, desperate, but not angry. The teachings of the Whole were clear when it came to the subject of administering pain to other beings, sentient or not. It was permissible only as a last measure and then only to creatures of significantly lower intellect and reason. These humans qualified in that category, and it was necessary. She might injure herself or him. It was also essential he not create undue interference with her brain patterns. The energy that flowed through her to him, his connection to the Whole, depended on the maintenance of the synapses and brain connections that existed at the time of his jump. Disturbing them might weaken or even break the connection. He had to be careful.

The alien was capable of delivering a literally agonizing amount of pain to the woman's system. He had, after all, access to her mind. Aside from the practical reasons not to inflict it, however, he knew that would be wrong, even if it did temporarily disable her and make her fear to oppose him. There were lesser measures which would suffice. When he laid his hand to her head, his mind entered hers and caused a mild disturbance in her cells. The feeling it would produce would be akin to extreme sickness, like a raging flue. He watched as her surprised eyes recorded the sickening discomfort. Her lips moved in a futile attempt to speak, she looked at him forlornly and then she collapsed.

The man was both exhausted and exhilarated from his combat with the human female. Some part of his maleness thrilled at the experience of physically dominating her. And victory seemed sweet. But he had expended a lot of energy. He would need to recuperate and revitalize himself. First, though, he needed to be assured the woman would no longer pose a threat, that she would be controlled until such time as he could utilize more sophisticated, subtle methods.

It didn't take a rocket scientist to realize her ability to use her arms against him needed to be suppressed and that she needed to be silenced. Her screams could alert other humans, even in this remote location, who would come to her aid. His mind went over the inventory of objects he had viewed in his quick survey of the house and combined it with images he had taken from the young woman's memories and experiences. An image of a ball of thick but soft cordage in a drawer in the kitchen came to his consciousness as did a roll of silvery tape. He saw from her mind how they could be used.

It took some effort to drag the woman's limp body over to the bed. He placed her on it, face down and went into the kitchen to gather his tools. He added to his list a sharp knife with which to cut the cord and scissors to cut the tape.

When he came back to the room, the woman was beginning to stir. She tried to crawl away from him as he sat down next to her. He placed his weight on her, pinning her to the bed. He acted quickly. He cut a 3' long length of the cord and, relying on images the woman had herself unknowingly given him, gathered her wrists behind her and tied them off together. He made several circuits with the cord around her joined wrists, sideways and over the top, in a crossed pattern. He fastened it with a firm, triple knot.

He tore off a seven inch long strip of the wide duct tape. Holding the strip in his hand, he turned her body over to get access to her face. He moved his leg across her torso and knelt on either side, straddling her. Her eyes blinked open; her face was a mask of fear. She was about to speak when he laid the top side of the tape over her upper lip. With his hands on either side of her face, her forced her chin up and her lips together with his thumbs and pressed the tape across her mouth, patting it down until the seal was complete.

Kelly had felt her arms being joined behind her back. She knew she should fight him, struggle to the very last, but was too weak to resist. When the man rolled her over and climbed on top of her, she wanted to speak to him, to negotiate, to plead for release. She whined with fright and frustration when the man imprisoned her lips with the silvery tape. She had lost what was in all probability her last, best chance at escape. Her mind reeled with fear of what he was going to do to her, how long it would last, what he would do to her when he was finished. Tears came to her eyes. She didn't want to cry, but a wave of sorrow passed through her. She had never thought her life would end like this.

The visitor watched the emotions pass through his captive's face. He could feel them emanating from her. They strengthened him. And the contact of his naked body with hers, the sight of her bare breasts, the thrill of his physical control of her, had excited his human body. His cock had grown hard. He placed his smooth, strong hands on the woman's soft, inviting breasts. It was strange to him how his body derived such pleasure from the feel of the plump mounds. She moaned her unhappiness at his touch. But once he began to send his signals of pleasure to her, her face began to soften and her breath eased from its rapid, panicky pace, to a long, soft sigh.

Kelly watched with fear as the man gave her breasts gentle, loving strokes. Warmth and pleasure seemed to flow through the strong, large hands that had engulfed them. She felt her desire begin to rise and she cursed herself for it. What kind of woman was she, she thought, that a mere caress of her breasts could so immediately and intensely drive her lusts. Unwillingly, she gave a long, deep sigh of passion. She thought of her naked and exposed sex. The fact that her lower body was restricted from her view, blocked by the bulk of the man's body, made it feel more exposed and vulnerable than it would have otherwise. It made her think of a phrase from a book she had read as a young girl, "…that part of her body that could be used independent of the rest." The book had made her, at the time, long for the release from responsibility for her desires. She had forgotten about it, put those feelings away as foibles of youth. But now it came back to her, how the men in the book had imposed pleasure on the pretty, young woman. It was what this man was doing to her now.

Kelly felt as if the man was transmitting some kind of drug or power to her body through his hands. What kind of man was he? Why had she dreamed of him? She did not believe in precognition or any such hocus pocus. But here he was, identical to the dream man of her visions. It just couldn't be happening!

He had still not spoken a word to her. His cold gaze belied the passion she knew her body raised in him. She could feel his stiff prick on her belly, his unsheathed sword with which he would soon penetrate her. How could he be capable of such strong desire, such raging lust that he would invade a stranger's home and violate her against her will and yet remain apparently so self possessed?

The man had been softly caressing her blood filled breasts for several minutes now. He stroked them slowly upwards, his large hands virtually surrounding them and then closing as they reached the tips, administering sharp pinches to the hard, distended nipples. Kelly felt as if every inch of her breasts were hotwired for sensation. The man's motions mesmerized her, caused her exposed pussy to burn. Her mind didn't want it, but her body relished the man's touch, each connection between their bare skins.

Having satisfied his hands' lust for her soft orbs, Kelly's tormentor slid his body down her torso, until his lips could reach her stiff teats. He took them in his mouth, one by one, savoring their hardness, sucking and licking at them. His hard prick lay along the puffed lips of her sexual opening, as if presaging its penetration of her. The heat of his tongue and lips sent tingles of pleasure through the captive woman's body. She moaned again, half in protest, half in pleasure. She tried to will her bound hands free, but the cords that held them, imprisoned them under her back, were tight and sure. He slid further down her body, forcing his legs between hers. She watched as his hand glided across her taut belly and over her upper thighs. She tried to push them together to deny her assailant access to her tender flesh, but the man had captured her right leg with his left and was pushing against her other with his right knee, forcing her legs wide apart.

Kelly's body shuddered as she felt the man's thick finger trace the line of her already moistened slit. Delicately, as if handling a baby bird, he stroked her there, drawing her deeper and deeper into her need. She felt the tender lips parted, felt the finger delve inside. It slid easily upwards until it made soft contact with her stiff pleasure bud, teasing it gently, circling it, rubbing it, sending her into a deep longing for release.

The impassioned woman felt the man's lips leave her breasts. She had closed her eyes, to shut out the vision of the callous man above her, to try and block out what was happening to her body. She opened them now and the man's eyes captured them. He was peering deeply into her, she could just feel it. It was like he was examining her soul. She waited for him to mount her, wanting him despite her dismay at her powerlessness to refuse him. She then realized he had no immediate intention to do so. He was going to bring her off with his hand. She was going to put on a show for him, she thought dismally: woman in the throes of an orgasm.

Kelly's passion grew higher and higher. Her mind disobeyed her desperate attempts to ward off the pleasure of the man's caresses and instead, shut out all else but the messages of passion the man's determined fingers were sending her and his mesmerizing, deep, dark gaze. When she felt her orgasm rising, she tried once more, feebly, to shut her legs, to drive the tormenting hand away. When the first, pounding, wrenching contractions of her pussy began, she gave up all efforts at denying the man what he wanted. Her body shook as the waves of pleasure engulfed her. She moaned staccato behind her sealed lips at each intense pulse of pleasure, "Mmm! Mmm! Mmm! Mmm!" Humiliated at the loss of control of her body, her eyes peered frantically at the man's, begging and pleading for him to halt the almost painful seizures within her womb.

Out of breath, drained by her climax, Kelly's body went limp as her orgasm subsided. She was grateful for the surcease of her passion. She thought she detected a hint of a smile of satisfaction on the man's face, his first expression of emotion other than desire. He took his hand from her loins and caressed her belly and her breasts, softly. He brought it to his nose, inhaling her scent. He then grabbed her by the hips and turned her over.

The vision of the female in the throes of her orgasm had been, in fact, very satisfying to the man. He had felt her energy enter him, working to solidify their bond. Now he had his own needs to satisfy. His body was hot with lust. He had learned the ABC's of coitus from the woman's mind and wanted to possess her from behind. He grabbed her hips and flipped her to her belly. He pulled her hips back until she was on her knees, her head on the mattress, her breasts pressed against her thighs, her legs spread beneath her. Kneeling behind the woman's finely shaped, taut, rear cheeks, he grabbed his stiff and burning cock with his right hand, maneuvered it to her dilated slit and pushed up and into her hot, tight canal.

The woman's body seemed to vibrate with pleasure as he pressed his thick manhood deeply into her still burning pussy. She uttered a deep, forlorn groan. Her bound hands twisted and writhed on her pale, curvaceous back. Her long, silky, auburn ponytail rested on the mattress beside her. He placed his hands on her hips and began to rock back and forth, first slowly, and then with more and more urgency. The female emitted a low, continuous moan as he traversed the walls of her cleft. She began to come again, almost immediately, and he could feel her fierce contractions on his heated pole. He felt his testes tighten, a tingle all along the shaft of his cock. His mind clouded over, receiving not only the throes of his own pleasure, but the woman's intense sexual passion. When his cock exploded and began to throb and pulse within the woman's sex, he grunted and groaned, pulling sharply at her hips to meet each one of his mighty thrusts. When the crest of his passion passed, he plunged his cock deeply inside her, holding it there, letting his cock feel the final echoes of his orgasm while fully encased in her flesh.

The man let his body drape across the kneeling, moaning form of the woman. He needed to sleep, to process her spent energies, to gather his strength. First, though, he needed to complete the female's securements.

Rising from her limp, exhausted form, he took hold of her knees and pulled her legs straight. She gave out another low moan as he manipulated her body. The roll of heavy cord was still on the bed and he cut another long piece. He crossed her ankles and tied them together, wrapping them several times horizontally and vertically with one end of the cord. He took the other end and, bending her knees, affixed it to the tie that imprisoned her wrists behind her.

He leaned back and appreciated the picture of the confined woman. Something inside him, some part of his human brain, was enraptured by the sight of her helplessness, her subservience to his control. The word 'hogtied' came to him, a word placed there by her mind, a vision of some picture she had seen or some description she had read. She had kept it there, at the upper levels of her mind, not buried deep in her subconscious, a level he hadn't reached yet. He wondered why.

The dark haired man pulled the unhappy woman's body to its side so her back was towards him. He took one more length of rope and, after securing it to the woman's bound hands, tied the other end to his wrist. If she struggled too much, or managed to slip off the bed, he would know right away and awaken. He laid down beside her, and fell immediately asleep.

CHAPTER FOUR

While her assailant slept peacefully behind her, Kelly agonized over her fate.

It had taken her a while to recover from the torpor that had seized her following the intense orgasms the man had inflicted on her, but now she was awake and alert. She could actually see her naked body, arched and helpless, in the mirror across from her bed. She could gaze into her own terrified eyes, the wide, silvery tape obscuring her mouth, see her exposed breasts, her naked thighs and the patch of furry hair that covered the object of the man's lusts. Having the man behind her was actually more perturbing to her than if he had turned her to face him. She wanted to study him, to try and decipher what his plan was for her. She wanted to know when he awoke so she could prepare herself mentally for his next assault. Having to stare at her bare breasts and belly so open and exposed to the now bright room was more discomforting than if she had been turned towards him, away from her reflected image.

She tested her bonds frantically when she first heard the man's evenly spaced, deep breaths signaling his loss of consciousness. She realized quickly, to her dismay, that the efficiency with which he had tied her barred any slippage of the bindings that would permit her to ease one of her wrists free of the cords. When she realized the hopelessness of her yearning for freedom, she began to cry in self pity. After a short while, though, her rational self took over. She was a scientist, a weigher of facts, an expert in logic and reasoning. She realized she would have to use all of her mental skills to develop some strategy to deal with her frightful and terrorizing new reality.

First, she had to outline what she knew about the man, what she could deduce from her observations. That he was real was indisputable. She was way past imagining she was still in a dream. His silence was disturbing, but it might very well be indicative of the fact he was not mentally deranged. If he were, he would likely have ranted and raved while he assaulted her. He had not shown any of the typical quirks or idiosyncrasies of the psychotic. He had acted coolly and efficiently and with definite purpose. He had not taken the opportunity to vent rage on her when she made her desperate fight to escape. So, to use the vernacular, he was probably not crazy.

She had noticed several other things. His piercing gaze was abnormal. It was as if he were seeing a woman for the first time. He had used her expertly, but the expression on his face when he had massaged and pleasured her breasts was one of wonderment. It was unlikely a man of his age, he looked to be in his mid thirties, would never have touched a woman's breasts before. His bringing her off with his hand had almost seemed like he was conducting some kind of experiment.

When she saw him coming up the steps outside the house, he looked wobbly, as if unsure of his feet. And what was with the parading around naked outside? His body and hair had been all wet, like he had gone for a swim in the stream. How weird was that?

The thing that was most inexplicable was how she felt when he had placed his hand to her head during their struggle. He had actually, somehow, disabled her body. Kelly knew the human nervous system well. There was no way he could have affected her body that way by a mere touch. She knew what an electric shock was like and a sudden infusion into her system of a high voltage charge could produce similar results, a loss of bodily control and unconsciousness. He didn't have anything in his hands. She had seen them during the fight. And she would have felt extreme pain at the point of contact if she had been zapped. The feeling she had when he touched her, the emptiness, angst, sourness, was more like a sudden, massive attack of illness. An injection of a drug could produce, perhaps, such a result, a nerve agent of some kind, but she experienced no after effects from his actions, no sickness or vomiting. Once she had awakened, she had been completely recovered.

And where were his clothes? Surely he didn't come to her house to assault her naked. He could have left them outside, but there would be no reason for him to do that. And why didn't he tie her up when he first assaulted her? Was he so sure he would be able to entrance her with his sexual skills that she would not try and escape?

The word 'entrance' triggered a whole new line of inquiry. She had been entranced. He had cast some kind of spell over her. She knew her normal sexual responses well and her reactions to his handling of her body were not consistent with her own history. For a moment, her mind swooned at the recollection of the passionate heights to which he had driven her. She felt a twinge of desire as she thought of it. Her body seemed to yearn for his touch. She recalled how quickly her heat had risen when he had massaged her breasts, as if he was transmitting some force into her through his hands.

Kelly realized she had raised more questions than supplied answers. What had happened to her, what she had seen, the evidence of the man's actions, defied logic. She needed more evidence, more facts. Miserably, she realized she would get them soon enough when the man awoke. She might learn things about him and his intentions she would regret knowing.

She lay motionless and confined for a long while, unhappily awaiting the man's pleasure. Her body actually shivered in fear. When she ran through the possibilities of her fate, her stomach quailed and she began to sweat. His unseen presence loomed behind her ominously.

Kelly's arms and shoulders began to ache from their forced extension behind her back. She tried to stretch her legs higher to relieve them, but only managed to bring soreness to her hips and her thighs. When she let the force of her body's natural desire to be at rest reestablish equilibrium between her limbs, it hurt worse than before. If the man would so cruelly tie her like this, what else might he do, she thought miserably. She realized that if she were to keep her sanity, she would need to think about something else other than the worst case scenarios of what he might have in store for her. Her mind drifted as she tried to calm herself.

So this is what it's like to be hogtied, she thought. In her wild days, she had been secretly intrigued by the whole idea of bondage, of surrender of control to a lover. The book she had read had instilled strange thoughts and feelings in her, something she had never talked to anyone about. She had never found the nerve to ask any of her boyfriends to tie her up, to use her as their sexual plaything. Once, she had spent an evening surfing forbidden web sites, marveling at the sights of the bound women and how they were treated. Her pussy had grown wet and her lust had risen while she carefully studied the faces and bodies of the women, imagining what it would feel like. She had never had the nerve to go back. Her feelings had shamed her. She was a modern woman, a feminist. Her mind told her it was wrong. If her current situation was different, if the man did not seem so strange, almost other worldly, she might be able to see these events as a kind of experiment, something to explore. But she realized the man's actions were no game. She had no 'safe word' she could give him to call it all off. She could not discern his ultimate purpose, but she had to consider the possibility he was a madman, perhaps sociopathic. He could kill her.

Suddenly, she felt as if she had been gifted with an inspiration. That phrase which had entered her desperate musings, 'other worldly', could there be something to it? Her rational mind fought against it. There had been a movie she had seen once, a science fiction movie her boyfriend had shown her. In the movie, the characters had conjured up creatures they referred to as "monsters from the id." They had acquired a super intelligence and were able to bring their emotions into reality. They created a physical presence that carried out their subconscious desires.

Could she have somehow conjured this man from her subconscious desires? The dreams she had been having were so strong, so realistic, especially the last one. The man sleeping behind her mirrored the image of the man she had seen in her dreams. Although his features had been obscure at first, they had become clearer and clearer as they went on. It was dark in her room when he had first assaulted her. She did not actually see his face until she had attempted her escape. When she had seen him ascending the stairs to her porch during her escape attempt she had recognized him immediately. How could she have known in her dream what he would look like in advance of actually seeing him? For his face in the dream last night was crystal clear. His body, his hair, the color of his skin was all the same. Even his height, tall, over 6', as Adele had suggested last night back at the lab, was consistent with his actual, now real, physical presence.

What did Shakespeare say? "There are more things on heaven and earth than are known to your philosophies." She was not super intelligent like the men in the movie, but she had a strong mind, and her desires were strong, albeit suppressed for a very long time. She had read many things in newspapers and saw stories on TV about allegedly inexplicable events. She had discounted them. But what would a sixteenth century scientist have thought of the ability to record brain waves, or to control madness with drugs? Television, radio and electricity would seem like magic to a primitive man. 'Science' had rejected Galileo, Keppler and Spinoza. It had scoffed at the very idea of bacteria. Even Einstein had been unable to decipher the 'unknowable', with his speculations about dark matter, a multidimensional universe and his fruitless search for a unified theory of physics. Experiments with subatomic particles had produced mysterious, inexplicable results.

Her theory, if you could call it that, would explain how the man was able to manipulate her desires, how he was able to assert such total control over her. He knew her inside and out. If he were the product of her own mind, that would explain it. She recalled Sherlock Holmes' dictum: If you eliminate the impossible, the answer that's left, no matter how improbable, is the solution.

If it were true, if the man was a product of her desires made flesh, then he would not hurt her. She had no desire to suffer pain, had no death wish. But she did yearn for sexual fulfillment. She did have a suppressed desire to be relieved of guilt for her needs. It all fit. It was a solution her psyche, if not her training as a scientist, could accept.

* * * *

There was a clock on the dresser on Kelly's side of the bed and she had watched the time move slowly. It was about 7 A.M. when he had left her to her own devices, hogtied and naked, and it was 8:35 when she heard the man stirring behind her. Her mind had kept wavering between a resolution to accept her situation as calmly as she could and absolute terror. Although she had given herself a mental framework to accept her situation, she was still afraid. She could be wrong. It did seem fantastic after all that he could be some sort of apparition from her mind. She would gaze at her reflection in the mirror, see the wide, silver tape he had placed across her lips and begin to cry. Then she would close her eyes, take a deep breath and try and bring herself back to a mindset where she could be calmed. It would last about ten minutes. Then she would open her eyes again, see the tape on her mouth, her naked, proffered body, her arms disappearing behind her back, her bent knees, and begin to cry all over again. She was fatigued from the emotional roller coaster she was on, but could not sleep.

Kelly's first notice the man was awakening was a tug on the cord that bound her connected hands behind her back to the man's wrist. Her heart went in her throat when she felt him stirring on the bed. She felt him untie himself from her. She jumped when she felt his strong but soft hand glide over her hip and along her thigh. She watched it run along her body in the mirror, a disembodied hand appearing from behind her. While it had been easy to propose to herself that she put away her fear, the reality of his touch made it clear to her how hard that would be. She had lain dormant for so long, she had almost forgotten she was tied. His touch reminded her she was defenseless against him and subject to his whims. She flexed her bound wrists and pulled at her ties with her legs, issuing a small whine from behind her gag. Her stomach fluttered with fear.

The awakened dream man was able to sense from his caress of the bound woman that she had begun to absorb the effects of his discharges within her. She would need much more to become fully acceptant of her new role as his familiar. He knew he could wash away her resistance with virtually a wave of his hand, but wanted to avoid direct disturbance of her mental processes as much as possible. There was plenty of time to accomplish his goal and no need to take drastic action. He read from her mind her efforts to come to terms with what had happened to her. The fact she had already begun to rationalize his existence and build a mental framework within which to accept it was a good sign.

He pulled the woman's body over so she was on her back. She gave a moan as he shifted her. She was laying on top of her bound hands and her legs were drawn up towards her torso. Her eyes widened in fear and apprehension and her breathing became sharp and strained. He pushed her knees apart, revealing her sex to him. He took a moment to appreciate her. His human mind was very satisfied with her body and he felt its appreciation in his loins. Her breasts lay gently on her chest, shimmering as she breathed deeply in her distress. Her face, although recording her unhappiness, was graceful, pleasing, well set off by her auburn hair. Her body tremored as he ran his hands down the inside of her thighs and she arched her back and whined from behind her taped lips. The feel of her skin and her helplessness before him fueled his lust. He moved his hand so it covered her mons and he began to stroke the length of the gap between her labia with his thumb. He watched as her visage went from fear and dismay to acute distress and then to passion. He could sense her efforts to resist him. But the energy he was conveying to her through his hand was too strong for her to overcome.

As soon as the man caressed the tender insides of her thighs, Kelly felt the telltale signals of her arousal begin to rise. She looked at him, disconsolately. He was going to fuck her again, and she realized, miserably, that she was going to succumb to another bout of lust. When he placed his hand on her sex, her body shuddered. She could feel her moistness grow as he began to tease her cleft. She strained at her bonds and moaned her unhappiness. He might be the product of her secret desires, but that did not overcome her conscious shame and belief what she was feeling as a result of his unwanted caresses was wrong.

Slowly, Kelly's resistance melted away. Her mind began to welcome the stroke of the man's finger. She shook and took a sharp inhalation of breath through her nose when the thumb began to stroke her hardened pleasure button. She tried to close her legs, to deny him access to her center of passion, but his strong arms kept them apart. Despite her struggle to deny it, she felt herself yearning for the man's cock to enter her.

The dimensional traveler sensed the woman's desire for coitus. It was what he had been waiting for. He eased himself forward and placed his hips between her outstretched thighs. His cock was stiff with his own heat and he ran its head along the length of the woman's gash, pushing aside the engorged love lips. She moaned as he did so and raised her hips invitingly. Her nipples were hard, her breasts taut. Her chest and face had a fevered look. Her body seemed to melt as he entered her. Her crevasse was tight and hot and the pleasure he felt spread throughout him. He began a slow, steady, rhythmic stroke within her. She moaned and squirmed, abandoning any effort to deny her passion. A part of him reveled in her helpless surrender to his power over her. None of his previous interactions with other races had been this intense. What creatures these humans are, he thought as he felt the strong pulses of pleasure emanating from his manhood. His cock's need permeated all of his flesh.

He could feel the woman's arousal grow higher and higher. Twice he stopped just before she came. She moaned and cried from behind her taped lips, begging him with her eyes to continue. He was poised above her, his arms locked and on either side of her torso. The only parts of their bodies that were touching were their loins, his hips and her thighs. When he resumed his cock's manipulations of her lusts, her body shook and she cried out from behind her sealed lips. His lusts had been rising too and he felt his sexual fluids cresting. Her pussy's first intense contraction triggered his climax. He groaned as he pumped his essence into her. She received it wantonly. His hips slapped against her thighs and she cried out at each stroke. His pulsing manhood sent him surge after surge of pleasure. Finally, his orgasm spent, he slowed and then stopped.

Kelly was finding it hard to catch her breath. Her heart pounded wildly in her chest. She couldn't remember ever having come like this. Her brain had been overwhelmed by the flood of pleasure. Slowly, as her pussy's convulsions ceased, she began to recover her consciousness of where she was and what was happening to her. Dismally ashamed at her acute arousal, her wild exhibition of lust, she turned her head to the side and closed her tear filled eyes.

The man eased himself out of the woman's place of pleasure. Part of him wanted to continue, to quickly rally his forces and resume their coitus. But for now, he realized, she had physical needs to be taken care of and, to his surprise, so did he.

Rolling the unhappy woman to her belly, he unfastened the hogtie and released the bindings around her ankles. She uttered a sigh of relief as she was able to relax her legs after so long a time. He gave her a minute to enjoy her partial liberation while he admired the graceful slope of her naked back, the roundness and firm flesh of her rear, the remarkable color of her long strand of hair. When he sensed her mind was functioning, he rolled her to her back and then pulled her up from the bed. He could feel the tenseness in her and he saw the frightened look she gave him. He regretted the need to acclimate her slowly to him. One of the Whole's primary teachings was the importance of respect for other life forms. He did not want to cause her unnecessary suffering. He looked into her eyes and ran his hand over her head in a gesture of comfort. He softened his gaze and tried to mimic a smile. It would be a while before he had learned to adjust his facial features to readily exhibit human emotions. He released just a tiny bit of his energy into her, enough to take the edge off of her fear.

Kelly saw and felt the man's gesture. A feeling of calm entered her. It was not enough to wash away all of her fears, but enough so she did not break out into hysterical crying. How did this man do this to her? How long would he keep her his prisoner? She had no idea what the man's ultimate purpose was. If only she could talk to him, she thought. His crooked smile did nothing to assuage her concerns that he might be deranged.

He took her by the arm and led her from the bedroom. She stumbled alongside him obediently. Kelly was surprised to see he was taking her into the bathroom. She looked at him anxiously to see if he was permitting her to use the toilet or whether he had something else in mind. She was relieved when he motioned to it. She sat down on it happily, spread her thighs and let a forceful stream of water flow from her. She didn't care that he was watching. His gaze was locked on the column of water that continued to empty out of her and its source. It was a stark reminder her body was under his control.

Raijamoon had absorbed much knowledge about basic human needs from the woman's mind. It was his initial, highest priority. It was essential to learn to function and to take care of the being whose existence was so vital to him. The transported alien was fascinated by this method of removing liquid wastes from the body. He watched intently as the stream of liquid seemed to fall from the woman.

When the flow stopped, the woman remained sitting on the toilet and looked up at him expectantly. It seemed there was something she wanted him to do although she was torn by her dependence on him to do it. He saw the roll of toilet paper on the wall and made the connection. He pulled a length of the paper from the role, folded it over several times and used it to wipe the woman's lower lips and the passage they surrounded clean. The woman stood up shakily and he tossed it into the toilet.

Now it was his turn. He had to give the issue some thought. He stood in front of the bowl for a few moments as an image in his mind informed him what to do. He took his long, softened manhood in his right hand and held it out over the yawning hole. With his other hand, he leaned over and lifted the seat, making his target bigger. He stood there waiting for his discharge to flow. Nothing happened. He waited and he waited. He knew his body needed to void and did not understand. He gave his groin muscle a little push, and then it came.

The man was surprised at the pleasurable feeling his body experienced as the flow of liquid ran down his cock. It was reminiscent of the ejaculatory response, but different. He closed his eyes and emitted a soft sigh. This is a wonderful body, he thought to himself. It was constantly surprising him with its capacity for sensual experiences. He almost wished the flow of water would never stop. But, after about ten seconds, the stream began to diminish and then halted. A lone drop of his discharge remained on the tip of his organ. He looked at it for a moment, unsure of what to do. He did not know where the idea came from, perhaps some instinctual function of his human brain. He shook his softened penis and the drop fell off, floating down to the bowl and making a ring in the water. He smiled in self satisfaction.

Kelly was gradually recovering her senses. It was strange watching the man piss. It was as if he had never done it before. She gazed at his cock with a mixture of hatred and desire. She was so confused. She wanted nothing more than her torment to end, but part of her reveled in the pleasures he had brought her. His strong, solid, manly flesh was everything she had desired in a lover. She desperately needed an explanation for what was happening to her. She wanted her hands back. She wanted her right to say no back. She wanted to speak. She wanted to hide her nakedness from this stranger who was so callously abusing her. At the same time, though, she found herself relishing her nearness to the man, admiring his flesh, wanting him.

When he had finished shaking himself off, the man stood looking at her for a moment as if trying to recall something. A flash of recognition came over his face and he stepped to the sink and washed his hands. Kelly was startled at his meticulous attention to hygiene. "If he is a maniac," Kelly thought, "he is a strange one."

Her calmness, brought on by the pedestrian and intimate nature of their activities together, was dispelled when the man took her arm and led her back into the bedroom. But he did not bring her to the bed. He was merely retrieving one of the cords he had bound her with. Once he picked it up, he led her into the kitchen. He sat her down at one of the straight backed chairs and used the cord to tie her feet to its legs. A chill went through her as she was reminded of his dominance over her. And her nakedness in her kitchen was disconcerting. It was more easily accepted in her bedroom and bathroom, where nudity was commonplace. To be naked in her kitchen, tied to a chair, her arms still bound behind her was well outside the realm of normalcy. It emphasized starkly her desperate plight.

The visitor knew both of their bodies required sustenance. But what form? He could remove the woman's gag and ask her, but it was important there be no verbal communication between them if they were to develop the mental connections they needed for his purposes. He needed to train her to receive his projections readily and to channel her mind's thoughts to him.

He opened the refrigerator and looked inside it. He had gained much strength from his absorption of the psychic waves sent off by the woman's lust and had processed much of the download from the woman's mind. He picked up a long, rectangular carton. "These are eggs," he thought. "They need to be cooked." He put them back. He saw a round container with a lid. He removed it and opened it. Inside was cooked animal flesh. "Meat," he said to himself. He put it back. He would not consume the flesh of any being. It was against the code of the Whole. And she would not either as long as she was under his control. He saw a large, translucent carton on the door and pulled it out. "Milk," he realized. It was liquid and white. He saw and understood the word on the label. This was ok.

He continued his search and removed bread, some celery and some cheese. This would have to do for now. Later, when the woman was fully acclimated to him, he might have to permit her to cook and produce meals. But he couldn't risk her using a kitchen utensil to harm him and so for now, he would manage what they would eat.

It took the man a few seconds to develop the protocols for the consumption of these comestibles. Recalling his exploration of this morning, he produced a glass and a knife and a large plate. He sat down at the table next to the anxious woman and poured out some milk. He placed the wedge of cheese on the plate and cut it into small pieces. He took out two slices of bread and placed them on the plate. He did the same with the celery.

Kelly watched the man with great interest. She was dismayed when she saw he had only taken out one glass and one dish. Was he going to feed himself and not her? She was famished and she could feel pangs of hunger in her belly. Then the man leaned towards her. He took one side of the tape that was over her mouth and began to pull it slowly. Once it was loose, he pulled it gently but steadily from her face. For the first time in many hours, Kelly felt her mouth liberated. He took up a piece of cheese and presented it to her mouth. Gratefully, she opened her lips and took it inside. She chewed it slowly, relishing the taste of the sharp cheddar. When she was done, he gave her another. She took it readily.

He seemed to be watching her for some sign of negative reaction from eating it. When he was satisfied, he took a piece of cheese into his own mouth. He savored it, chewing it slowly, a look of pleasure on his face. After they consumed a few more pieces, he picked up the glass of milk. He held it to her lips and watched her drink it. He poured it too fast into her mouth and it spilled over her chin and onto her breasts.

Realizing his mistake, he poured it more slowly and then drank some himself, with the same expression of discovery and pleasure as when he had eaten the cheese. Next came the bread and then the celery.

It was odd, being hand fed like she was a small child. Every time he put food to her lips, Kelly was reminded of the fact she was bound and powerless. As she ate what he gave her, her appreciation of the opportunity to fill her stomach's void was tinged with sadness at her plight. She looked at the kitchen clock. She had intended to go back to the lab this morning to check on some experiments. If she didn't go soon, it would be too late. And then she realized that if the man killed her, she would lose all of that, everything that she wanted to be and to do. There would be no more Dr. Kelly Jameson. All her thoughts and ideas, her memories and her experiences would be gone with her. She had a moment's panic. Her eyes grew wet. She looked at the dark, naked stranger. Was he from her dreams? He had the long, flowing black hair, the strong jaw, the fine features of the dream man. But if she had conjured him, wouldn't she have conjured him whole? Would he have to learn how to use the toilet, what foods to eat and how? It didn't make sense, but how could she talk about sense when she was considering something that was totally beyond any understanding she had of the basic realities of existence?

The man seemed to sense her discomfiture. He gave her the same gaze he had given her in the bedroom a little while ago. As if by magic, she relaxed and calmed down. "He's feeding me," she rationalized. "Why would he feed me if he was going to kill me? He seems tender and concerned about me. He doesn't seem to be the kind of person who would harm me." As he fed her another morsel of celery, she smiled at him hopefully.

When he was satisfied they had eaten enough, the man put the remnants of the food away and placed the dishes in the sink. He grabbed a paper towel and, after wetting it, wiped Kelly's face and breasts and then his own mouth. He looked around the room thoughtfully and then opened the cabinet under the sink and threw the dirty napkin away.

Kelly was amazed at his apparent ability to intuit what to do. It was clear he had no experience at it, but it seemed to come to him when he gave it some thought. She had hesitated to say anything to him up to now. She didn't know how he would react if she spoke and she didn't want to interrupt their meal, such as it was, but she wanted to try before he decided to gag her again. She might not get another chance. She mustered all of her courage to do so.

"P-please," she said haltingly in a low, supplicative voice, "who are you?"

The strange man looked at her with concern. He stepped toward her and placed his hand on her naked shoulder.

Looking at the woman, the man knew he would have to punish her for speaking. It was the only way she would learn it was not permitted. He had taken her voice last night and he could do it again, but he didn't want to interfere with her brain patterns. He would not give her the same level of discomfort he did before. That was during a fight and he had little control over his powers at that time. Now, he was stronger and his ability to control them was more refined. He reached out and touched the woman's skin. He sent a small flow of energy into her.

As soon as their flesh connected, Kelly felt a wave of sickness pass through her. It wasn't pain, but it might as well have been for its effect on her. Her body sagged and she gave a low moan. Every cell in her body seemed to swoon. Her heart began to thump hard in her chest, her breath grew short and she began to sweat. It was like he had done to her before, this morning, although not as intense. Still, it was strong enough to make her want to have it go away immediately, as soon as possible. She looked in the man's eyes, her face a mask of misery. Then he removed his hand and it was gone.

Kelly's mouth formed a frown and she gave a little whine. She bit her lip and started to cry. What was this power the man had? How could a mere touch bring such nausea and unhappiness? She closed her eyes, grateful her physical misery had ceased. She fought back her tears. She needed to be strong, keep her wits about her. Seize any opportunity to escape.

The dream man watched the tears form in the woman's eyes. She would not do that again. He didn't want to discomfort her, but she had to learn. He crouched at her feet and untied the bindings on her ankles. Now that they were refreshed, there was more work to do.

Kelly watched unhappily as the man released her legs from the chair. Docilely, she let him raise her from the chair and lead her back to the bedroom. When she saw the disheveled bed, the scene of her prior ravishments, her tears began to flow anew. She knew what was going to happen. She wanted to beg him not to use her again, but she knew better than to speak. He had made the consequences of any form of verbal communication to him clear. She knew she had no choice but to succumb to his demands.

Laying the woman's body on the bed, belly down, the man untied the bindings which had secured her wrists. He brought them above her and tied them to the ornate, brass headboard. He left a little slack so her body would have freedom of movement and then turned her so she was on her back. Her pretty, blue eyes looked up at him apprehensively.

Sitting on the edge of the bed, he ran his hands up the woman's graceful, naked legs and over her thighs. His touch had an immediate calming effect on her. Her body, which had been tense, relaxed. Her eyes softened. He lightly caressed her hard, toned belly and her breasts, his hands loving the feel of her skin, the heft of her ample globes. He wanted to discover every inch of her. He lowered his head and placed his lips on her belly, just above the small thatch of hair that sat above her sex. He savored the salty taste. He let his lips play over her skin, washing her with his tongue. He seized one breast with his mouth and then the other, suckling them gently. The nipples were hard and he enjoyed the sensation of them in his mouth. His left hand was on her thighs, softly stroking them. Leaning over her torso, he dragged his lips along her chest and up to her neck. He nuzzled it, kissing her delicately, letting his rough tongue scour its surface.

As soon as the man placed his hands on her, Kelly felt desire spread through her body. It washed all of her fear and apprehension away. What was she afraid of anyway, she thought. His use of her seemed natural, caring. Her whole body felt thrillingly alive. She relished his lips and tongue as they excited her. His mouth on her breasts, gently tugging on her nipples, generated a soothing, welcome warmth. When he kissed her neck, she let out a sigh of desire. And then he placed his lips upon hers. She parted them to receive him. His hot tongue danced with hers while his hand rubbed her belly and breasts. Her hands tugged at their bindings above her. She wanted to embrace the man's flesh, pull his hard, strong body on top of hers. She spread her thighs unconsciously, her sex burning with need.

Raijamoon savored the woman's lusts as they grew. His cock was hard with desire. It yearned for the woman's heat and soothing moisture. But he would wait. He wanted to drive her desire higher first.

He drew his lips from the woman's and began to retrace his mouth's journey down her body, kissing her hardened teats one by one and then descending down her belly. He placed his hand between her parted thighs and took possession of her hot sex, probing it, caressing it. Her hips thrust back at him as she moaned. When his tongue dragged across her skin, she shuddered. And when her pulled her thighs up and apart and began to kiss their inner surfaces, her body began to writhe beneath him.

Kelly knew what the man intended. She wanted his hot tongue on her sex. Her mind anticipated the feeling of his lips on her moist crevasse and a wave of pleasure flowed through her. When they made contact, when she felt his tongue slide down the gap between her nether lips, his arms circling over her thighs, his torso on her belly, she groaned with pleasure.

The smell and the taste of the woman's loins were intoxicating to the man. He plunged his tongue between them, lashing at her pussy's walls. Her thighs pulled at his grip as her body recorded his efforts. "Mmmmmmmmmmmm," she moaned as he explored her inner surfaces. When he placed his lips over the hard button at the apex to her cleft, teasing it with his tongue, she groaned, "Auuuuuuurh!"

The gentle, hot sucking at her clit drove Kelly wild with desire. Her breathing was deep and labored. Wanting to press the man's head deeper into her loins, her hands strained at their confines. She dug her heels into the bed and arched her back. "Oh, god! Oh god!" she thought as she felt her lusts rising to overflow their banks. She bit her lips and tensed as her pussy burned. Its first contraction made her whole body jump. The pulses of pleasure came again and again and again. The man's tongue was lapping over her pleasure bud, driving her on and on. She felt like her whole body was going to explode. "Ahhhhhhhhhhhh!" she moaned, "Ahhhhhhhhh! Ahhhhhhhhhhhhh!" while she came.

As her orgasm gradually began to fade, the man's lips abandoned her clit to lap at her oozing fluids. She felt her body relax as the tongue soothed her. But when the mouth again took possession of her pleasure bud, sucking at it gently, flicking it with its tongue, she felt her lusts begin to begin to build once more.

Her second orgasm was as wrenching as her first, making her moan and writhe with pleasure. Her body was covered with sweat and still shuddering as her spasms finally began to calm. But there was more that she wanted. She wanted the man's thick rod inside her. Her pussy was yawning with need to be filled. She bit her lip to forestall a verbal plea for the man's cock, but her mind reached out to him, sending him her desperate desire.

Her dream lover had received her emotive, almost frantic message. From behind his own lust, he acknowledged in his mind this crucial, first step in the intertwining of their psyches. He needed to possess her almost as much as she needed him and he maneuvered his body between her outstretched thighs. He poised his rigid pole between her distended, engorged labia and pressed himself into her. His cock reveled in her heat as he felt her pussy's walls close around him. Lowering his body onto hers, he extended his arms, taking her bound hands in his. Her hands gripped his tightly as he pressed his burning lips on hers, parting them with his tongue and delving inside. She greeted him and they exchanged their lusts. She groaned when he began his motion inside her fevered cleft. Their bodies bucked like beasts, their mutual passions overwhelmed them. When he came, her legs intertwined his and she pulled him deeply inside her womb.

Kelly felt the man's hot seed splash into her and the throbbing of the man's cock in her electrified channel. Her pussy exploded in response. It felt good. It felt right. His semen seemed to flow directly into her bloodstream, sending an intense stimulation throughout her body. She felt her electrified pouch grab at the thick, rigid, pulsing pole as if milking it. The wrenching pleasure of her pussy's convulsions as she came made her mind rejoice. When his motions slowed and then stopped, and his body went limp atop hers, she sighed and let her body melt underneath him.

The otherworldly visitor let himself revel in the post coital warmth and satisfaction of his human body. He knew that he and the woman needed to rest, to recover their energy, but he did not want the intermission to their lovemaking to last long. He knew his seed was seeping into the woman's pores, entering her very cells, germinating what would eventually be an overwhelming and irresistible desire for his flesh and his essence. They had taken an important step; there was more work to do.

He let his still hard cock slip from the woman's hot canal. She moaned as she felt it leave her and she looked deeply into his eyes. Her fear had left her. He could see that. He placed his hands on her graceful, thin hips and urged her body over so she was lying on her belly. He pushed her knees up under her and raised her until her spread legs revealed her delicate, soft cleft. His human mind absorbed pleasurably the erotic view of her slender hips, her graceful back and the sight of her bound, helpless hands stretched out above her head. Her long, auburn ponytail lay askew around her neck and made her skin seem pale and vulnerable. Running his hands over the smooth, tender skin of her back, he slid his cock up and into her again.

Kelly meekly submitted to the man's manipulation of her body. He could do what he wanted with her. When she felt the thick, hard cock slide once more into her soft canal, she sighed with pleasure. "Yes! Yes!" her mind exclaimed. "Do it again! Again!"

CHAPTER FIVE

It was dark outside now. Kelly was kneeling on the floor of her living room, her head between her knees, as he had left her after their latest round of lovemaking. They had been at it all day. She couldn't remember how many times she had been driven to ecstatic completion of her passions. He had come in her more than a dozen times. She had experienced frenzied lust for his touch, craved to be possessed by his relentless cock. But now, she was completely at peace. A sense of well being was suffused throughout her body. Her fear of him was completely gone. When she gave it any thought, she knew her reactions were contraindicated by her circumstances. She just didn't care.

Her hands were bound behind her back and, earlier, after he had satisfied himself inside her once again where she now knelt, he had tied her feet to her hands. It was not the disabling, confining hogtie of this morning. There was suf-ficient play in the soft cord that connected her ankles and wrists so as not to cause her any discomfiture. He merely wanted to ensure she would stay where he had left her, that she wouldn't rise and stumble, dazed, around the small, but comfortable cabin.

The man was outside, gazing at the stars. She could see him through the open door when she raised her head, sitting on the steps to the porch, his head turned upwards. She looked up from time to time to make sure he had not wandered away. The inexplicability of his arrival made her fearful he would leave just as suddenly, without explanation, without reassurance of his return.

She was satisfied to wait for him. Movement without his direction seemed purposeless.

Their bouts of manic copulation had been separated by rest, small meals consisting of whatever he could scrounge from her refrigerator and his fascinated exploration of her little world. She was aware she had undergone some form of transformation. It wasn't as if she were drugged or hypnotized. She remembered everything very clearly. And she was still the person she had been before he had sprung from her consciousness. The things that were important to her then, her work, her friends, family, they were all still important to her now. She had lost none of her ambition or intellect. She was just different. It was as if the man had added to her personality, not taken anything away.

She tried to recall when she had realized that her self was being altered, supplemented. It had been clear from the beginning he had some kind of power over her. His ability to affect her moods, her responses seemed to grow and grow.

It was in the middle of the afternoon when she sensed she had crossed some dividing line between what she once was and what she was now. She had been kneeling on the kitchen floor, her hands bound behind her. Her body was erect, her knees apart. She was watching the man attentively. He had no need to gag her since she had learned well to resist the impulse to speak to him.

They had already made love many times. The man was examining minutely the contents of every drawer and cabinet in the kitchen. He went through her pots and pans, seeming to weigh the function of each of them. He removed the utensils from the drawers and turned them in his hands. He looked carefully at the plates, the dishes, the canned goods, the cereal boxes, the cleansers. He even perused the cook books, seeming to read carefully several of the recipes.

He had been at it about half an hour when he came to the other side of the kitchen table and sat in one of the straight backed chairs and looked at her. He had picked up an apple from the table and was eating it with relish. His eyes wandered over her naked form, measuring it, savoring it. He had earlier unpinned her long, wavy, reddish brown hair and brushed it lovingly. It lay about her shoulders now, free and flowing.

Kelly's mind had been wavering between rebellion and acceptance. She knew she should abhor what he was doing to her, but her body was so satisfied, his touch was so compelling, she felt herself sliding into a deep desire for him. She was pleased he appreciated her form, proud that he admired her ample, round breasts, her slender waist, her well toned thighs. As she received his gaze, her body started to tingle with arousal. He seemed to be calling her, inviting her as he had in her dream. But this time she was to come to him.

Kelly slowly, uncertainly, rose to her feet and stepped closer to him. His legs were spread wide, laying his softened sex open to her gaze. He was waiting for her to act on her desire, proffering his manhood to her. She was suddenly seized by an urge to please him, to bring him to pleasure as he had brought it to her. She sank slowly to the floor, her eyes locked onto his. When she was again resting on her knees, she let her gaze drift down his pleasing body to his loins. She leaned forward, arched her back and spread her thighs. As if in a dream, she brought her mouth to his sex, brushed against it with her lips and then took it into her mouth.

The sensation of having the man's cock in her mouth sent a wave of pleasure through her. She suckled on it gently, relishing the thickness and taste of the flesh. Her breasts hardened and her pussy began to burn as she felt his manhood start to fill with blood and take form. She ran her tongue over the tip and under the circumcised head. For a moment, she wondered at this detail. She hadn't given it any thought before. But if she had conjured up her dream man, it made sense to her that his cock would have been circumcised. She had never slept with a man with an uncut penis. Her medical training told her it was unhealthy to leave the foreskin intact.

Naturally, her perfect man would conform to her image of him.

Her thought was fleeting. The cock was hardening and she moved her pursed lips tightly down its shaft. The man sighed with pleasure at her efforts, bringing a sense of joy to her. Her mind gave full focus to the meat within her mouth as she gave it earnest, loving caresses. She felt like she was feeding at him, drawing sustenance. The hard flesh between her lips sent a current of desire through her. She began to understand why it caused her pussy to burn so when it was within her. It seemed to radiate an energy that coursed through her whole body.

Slowly, gently, she coaxed the stiffened pole to completion. The man had placed his hands lightly on her head and it was if she could feel his pleasure emanating through them. The whole world around her seemed to disappear. There was just her body and the cock that filled her. She bobbed her head back and forth, drawing her tight lips the length of the shaft, suckling the meaty head and then descending again until she felt its soft tip press against the back of her mouth. Her bound hands behind her back strained with the need to take hold of it, to possess it. She could feel her naked, heavy breasts sway beneath her. She moaned as her passions grew higher and higher.

She sensed the man begin to echo her motions with his hips, slowly pressing his hot prick across her lips, drawing it back, pumping into her mouth. His body stiffened and a deep groan emerged from his throat. His grip tightened on her head. When she felt the first throb of his climax, her heart jumped. It was if she could feel his pleasure. His body's thrill at the sensations of his ejaculations passed through his fingers to her brain. It was as if she was coming too. Her burning pussy shuddered and spasmed with pleasure. Groaning, she welcomed the splash of his warm essence against the back of her mouth, savored the flavor as it coated her tongue, thrilled to feel the pulsing of the meat against her lips. She sucked on the throbbing rod hungrily. She wanted his cum inside her, wanted to feel it assimilating within her. It was like he was granting her his life force, feeding her. She was drinking at a font of ecstasy. When his spasms slowed, she kept her mouth on him, her lips surrounding the bulbous tip, relishing each drop that oozed from his softening cock.

Now, as she knelt in the living room gazing at the naked form of her dream lover through the open door, the recollection of that moment sent a twinge through her loins. She wanted to do it again.

Raijamoon was peering up at the heavenly canopy above him. He sensed the woman's thrill at her recollections. They had made much progress. He could feel her contentment flowing from her mind. He closed his eyes and sent back to her a small message of pleasure as a reward. He heard her responsive, soft moan behind him.

It was the stars up above which were engaging him right now. Where he came from there was no concept of night and day. His universe, his dimension, followed different rules. Their reality was a wholly different construct, one he could not express through the limited capabilities of the human brain. Being human now, having taken on its aspects, he could appreciate the beauty of the vast, black sky above him dotted by the points of flickering light. It made him feel at once alone and connected, part of the sprawling universe in which he found himself and yet, somehow apart from it.

The cold air began to chill him. Watching the distant headlights of a car chugging along the road some half mile away, he was reminded that tomorrow they would have to prepare for his entry into the world. The woman would have to be conditioned to accept him as part of her everyday life. His body's chilliness made him realize he would need clothes. He wondered what it would feel like to be covered in fabric. Other than a protection from the elements, as a concession to social norm, he could not conceive of wanting to interfere with the exposure of his wonderful body to the sensations of the environment around him.

His mind wandered to the task he had ahead of him. He would need much information. He had not yet accessed the woman's electronic devices, but they would be useful in gathering data he could not possibly draw from her knowledge or recollections. He believed that her laboratory would be very useful. He needed to know more about the substances she utilized there and their properties, and he would undoubtedly have to add to her raw materials. The processing methods were primitive, but he was sure he could construct what he needed once he obtained or made the basic components.

His mind also reviewed her staff of employees. They would present no problem, even be helpful to him. He saw the figure of the chief assistant, Adele. His male mind appreciated the woman's visual image of her. She was a vibrant, outwardly healthy, attractive female. She had an apparent, very strong desire to serve and please her employer and friend. The woman, his familiar, projected a warm feeling towards the younger woman in her mind that seemed to be returned. He would need to explore it for its usefulness.

The visitor's human body was tired. He understood that these life forms needed extensive periods of dormancy in order to function properly. He would need his energy for tomorrow. And so would the woman.

Raijamoon rose from his perch on the stoop and turned to walk into the house. He could see the woman, kneeling where he had left her, framed by the outline of the door. She was looking at him anxiously. He had been outside for about half an hour and it had been the longest period and distance of separation between them since he had arrived. Although he had made much progress in molding her, he could sense some slippage. He would need to reinforce her bond to him.

He stepped into the house and closed and locked he door behind him. He turned to face the prostrate female. Her reddish brown hair was spread like a corolla over her back and shoulders. She had raised her torso and was sitting on her heels. Her heavy breasts peered at him invitingly. He knelt down before her and took her soft mounds in his hands, caressing them. He took the woman's mouth with his lips and brushed her tongue with his. The woman's body responded easily to his attentions.

Sensing the female's desires, he parted from her lips and, placing his hands on her shoulders, gently guided her torso down. He raised himself on his knees so his manhood was proffered to her lips. Without the need for encouragement, she slid her lips over the already rampant cock and took him inside her mouth.

Kelly had grown uneasy at the man's distance and lack of attention to her. A twinge of fear had reentered her mind. All of what was happening was so unnatural. Her contentment at kneeling bound and naked in the middle of her living room floor started to worry at her. When the man placed his strong hands on her breasts, kissing her fervently, all of that passed.

As he gently eased her down so her face was even with his loins, she wondered at how readily he had gleaned her desires. She had been thinking about and reexperiencing her oral caresses of him earlier that day, and had been longing for the taste and feel for him in her mouth. He had somehow intuited that desire and had presented his stiff manhood to her. She seized his distended and rigid cock hungrily with her lips. A wave of pleasure coursed through her body as she felt its heat and hardness within her. She was grateful for the opportunity to please him, to let him enjoy her obeisance to him.

Raijamoon's male mind swooned as the heat of the woman's mouth engulfed him. What had happened earlier that day had been the woman's idea. He had merely read her inner compulsions and encouraged them. He had had no idea that the feel of her mouth on his cock could be so pleasurable. It was a relatively effortless and extremely satisfying way of transferring his essence to her. And the direct contact of his manhood with the extensive nerve endings in her tongue and mouth facilitated the communication of his life force to her, bringing her pleasure and strengthening their bond.

The eager lips and tongue excited his rigid pole. This afternoon, she had caressed his pole lovingly, with tenderness and wonder at the joy it was giving her. Now, she was serving him passionately, lustfully, as if she realized the need to reinforce her mind and body's connection to him, to restore the feelings of contentment and comfort that had ebbed. He could hear her moaning as she pleasured him and the sight of her bound hands on her arched back writhing and flexing with passion drove his lust.

As the female's head bobbed on his cock urgently, he could feel his fluids rising, the flow of pleasure through his scrotal sac as it prepared to release his essence to her. He placed his hands on her arched back to steady himself and to allow some of his pleasure pass through him to her. When his cock started to spasm and jerk in her mouth, she gave an excited groan and her body shuddered.

Kelly felt driven to accomplish her task. The heat of the man's tool emanated throughout her. When he came, her burning pussy exploded into orgasm. "Mmmmmmmmm! Mmmmmmmmmmm! Mmmmmmmmm!" she moaned as the copious discharge of the man's prick flooded her mouth. She had never known a man to come so much or so often. He was incredible. She drank his spunk joyously, savoring its flavor, welcoming its absorption by her body.

When his flow of essence ceased, Raijamoon slid his manhood from the woman's lips. He raised her by her shoulders and kissed her mouth, rewarding that part of her body that had brought him so much pleasure. He felt her soft breasts crush against his chest as he embraced her body with his arms. He felt her press against him, seeking contact with his flesh. "This race is so passionate," he thought as the woman moaned into his mouth. He eased himself away from her, stroking her long, free hair with his hand and looking her in the eyes. She was his now. He would need to continue to reinforce his link with her regularly, but she was bound to him, bound to his will. She would devote herself to him, need his approval, his affection, seek his pleasure.

Although his intelligence in some ways compared to hers as hers would to a dog or a cat, she was more than what a pet would be. The bond was so much stronger, and he could never disregard her nature as a sentient being. In some ways, their relationship would be like a child to a parent. She would accept naturally his dominance and want not only to please him, but to receive his adulations and praise. Like a parent, he was obliged to see to her needs, her happiness, and, from time to time, he would have to make decisions that would displease her, that she would resist, fight against. For he had not deprived her of will. That would have disturbed the mental patterns so necessary for his survival, his connection to his native world. She could still choose.

Which was why he had continued to keep her bound when the necessity for it had, if not passed, been attenuated. He had the ability to read her human mind, but his understanding of her race was not flawless. And there was much of her nature that was hidden, covered over by the experience of millions of events in her life, perhaps billions. Each little act she took in her daily life, hundreds of thousands of them a day, added a little to her memories and her psyche. He would have to be careful with her, guard her.

He sensed that the bindings would continue to help assuage her inner revolt against losing control over her emotions and her destiny. When her body was confined, her hands unable to attempt to fend off his caresses, when her feet were unable to provide her with the mobility to escape, or even to move away from him, she could relieve herself of blame for succumbing to his demands, to surrendering to her own inner desires, the desires he had found in her and which he had fueled.

Now it was time to prepare for the extended rest period. He untied her bound ankles and the rope that connected them to her wrists and brought the female to her feet. Her gait was unsteady as he led her to the bathroom. He had decided he would bath her and himself, to remove the excretions of their energetic day. He allowed her to use the toilet and then used it himself and then turned on the water in the shower. Although the cabin was small, the bathroom was spacious and well appointed. There was a large shower with ample room for both of them at the same time. He waited for the water to come to what seemed to be an appropriate temperature and unbound the woman's hands from behind her back prefatory to leading her in.

Kelly was pleased the man was going to permit her to wash away the sweat and grime from her body. She usually washed her hair every morning. Several times during the day, when she had been able to concentrate on anything other than sex, she had regretted the sensation of her unclean hair. It was her pride and joy and, although a shorter cut would have been more conducive to a business like appearance, she was not inclined to change it.

The experience of having her hands unbound was disconcerting. She almost didn't know what to do with them. She had wanted so much to touch the body of the strange man who had brought her so close to him. Now that they were free, she reached out and tentatively placed her right palm on the man's broad, well toned chest. A feeling of warmth and belonging surged through her. She could feel something flowing through her hand up her arm and into her body from the contact with his skin. She had never desired anyone so much, felt such an affinity for their flesh. It was unnatural, she knew it, but the experience of being close to the man, of having contact with his body was so pleasurable, so fulfilling, she had cast away her reservations.

Seeing that she had become dazed at their contact, the man led her gently into the shower. He slowly urged her body under the steady, hard stream of water. When her head was under the flow, the water cascading over her and down her body, she closed her eyes and gave a sigh.

The sensation of the hot water drenching her body was mesmerizing to Kelly. She raised her face to receive the stream directly on it. Her hair became slick and her body shiny as the water flowed over her. She raised her hands and drew them over her face and up over her head, smoothing her hair. When she opened her eyes, she saw the man standing in front of her, carefully observing her. The confined space of the shower was filling with steam and it reminded her of her dreams of him. "Could it really be true?" she asked herself. She was clearly involved in something outside the realm of human experience. To some extent, the impact of the hot water on her body had shaken her from her strange enchantment with the man and brought her back to her rational self. He had clearly done something to her, had powers beyond human understanding. Where had he come from, what was his purpose? She couldn't fathom it. He was watching her as if he had never seen or experienced a shower before, didn't know what to expect from it.

Suddenly, she wanted him to feel the pleasure of having the hard, steady stream of hot water caressing his body. She wanted to watch him experience the comfort and relaxation it brought to his muscles and his mind. She stepped from under the water and, taking his arm in her hand, guided him in. He was hesitant, at first, and balked slightly as she urged him under the flowing stream. But when it began to strike his chest and slide down his body, his eyes lit up with surprise and pleasure. He relaxed and let her pull him fully under the shower head.

Raijamoon's body welcomed the heat from the water and he nearly swooned with delight. He let the hot flow cover his head, wetting his long, black hair and compressing it to his skull. He felt some kind of energy from the hot stream and he again wondered at how many diverse, pleasurable experiences his body was capable of.

Kelly saw the man become enthralled by the sensations of the hot water covering him. It was clearly a new experience, a fact that added to her clinical study of him. She guessed he did not know how to wash himself and she decided to take the opportunity to explore and discover the attractive, fit body that had all day explored hers.

Taking a large, round, natural sponge from the wall and wetting it, she squeezed some liquid soap into its middle and worked it until it had developed a nice frothiness. She stepped up to the man and, checking with her eyes for his permission, applied the sponge to his well developed, hairless chest. She began to rub his skin softly, working the sponge in large, round circles over his pectorals. She ran the sponge along his strong neck, over his broad shoulders and down and under his arms. She was holding the sponge with one hand and, with the other, she was feeling his skin, exploring his muscles, the thick bones of his frame.

The experience of being so close to the man and freely exploring his flesh was delightfully sensual to her. When she had finished his chest and stomach, she used her hands to turn him around so she could have access to his back. She refreshed the sponge with soap and began to wash the broad, muscular expanse. She loved the feel of his coffee colored flesh. It was everything she had ever thought about. Although he had mastered her, brought her under his sway, she felt, nonetheless, that he somehow belonged to her. She had conjured him from the ether, hadn't she? She had dictated his looks, his mannerisms, even the color of his skin. Although she had made into flesh a construct of her dreams that was stronger than herself, he was a part of her and her a part of him. It was like an idea that sprung from your mind so original, so creative it took a life of its own. It was still yours, wasn't it?

Having finished washing the man's back, Kelly lowered herself into a crouch so she could wash his rear and the back of his legs. A wave of pleasure flowed through her as she placed her hands on the strong muscles of his buttocks. Her breath began to become heavy as the feel of his taut skin in her free hands delighted her. She rubbed the soft sponge over his rear, even separating the cheeks so she could clean the space between them. Then she lowered her hands to wash his thick, well defined thighs. These were the thighs that had pounded against hers as the man plowed her cunt, she thought. They were strong and powerful, just as she had imagined them.

Her sex had begun to burn with need, clouding her mind. But she shook herself from her reverie and urged the man to turn around once more. She was startled to see his loose cock and heavy balls so close to her face. For the moment, she ignored them, washing down the front of the man's thighs and his shins. She lifted each foot and washed between the toes and under them.

Now there was one place left to wash. Kelly hesitated before addressing herself to the man's loins. Mist rose around her and the steady drumming of the streaming water highlighted the tension and strangeness she felt. Her body was drenched with the flow cascading off of the man's body. She was crouched down in a squat and she felt herself swaying, losing her balance. She lowered her knees to the hard tile and spread them, giving herself a good base.

She felt like she was about to pay obeisance to a god. The man's instrument had pleasured her so thoroughly, so many times throughout the day it seemed magical, almost sacred. The fact that she had not been permitted to touch it other than with her mouth and tongue and her lower place, gave it a mysterious quality, like some forbidden totem. She was no school child and had fondled and explored men's loins before. She had never been embarrassed or coy about it. She had enjoyed the heft of their soft sacs, the fleshiness and, ultimately, after she had fondled them to hardness, the strength and firmness of their cocks. Somehow this felt different. The man had used his manhood almost as a magical wand to entrance her, to drive her to delirious pleasure. When it had been in her mouth, she had been overwhelmed with its radiant heat. She looked up at the man's face. He was staring down at her with anticipation. She felt like she was seeking his blessing to adore him in this way. His eyes were soft, comforting. He ran his hand over her head and she felt goodness and peace flow from it.

Gathering her courage, Kelly spilled a dollop of liquid soap into her hands. She fixed her gaze at the source of her anxiety and raised her hands towards it. She softly positioned them under his leathery, soft sac and placed her palms on it. The skin seemed to welcome her as she made contact. She was dizzy with passion as she gently worked the lather around the man's soft balls, caressing them softly, enjoying their vulnerability, their strange feel. The man had spread his legs and she heard him moan with pleasure as she massaged the tender stones. She brought her hands up and circled them around the man's long, thick shaft. It began to harden as she worked the soap along it, caressing it between her palms.

As the tool filled with the man's hot blood, Kelly felt her lust rising. The man's energy seeped from his sex and through her hands. Placing her left hand on his strong right thigh for balance, she began to stroke his soft appendage slowly. She gazed with longing at her own hand as it rode the thick, now stiffening pole. She was exhilarated by the sensation of his flesh in her palm. Her slow, steady pumping of it, lubricated by the sweetly smelling soap, enchanted her. It seemed to her that giving loving and deliberate pleasure to him with her hands was the most personal thing she could do for him.

Raijamoon had reveled in the woman's attentions to his body. The combination of the heat of the pleasing water, the delicate roughness of the sponge and the feel of her hand exploring his flesh had immersed him in delightful sensations. He had felt her mind hesitate before devoting her attentions to his sex. He had stroked her soft hair, passing a message of encouragement to her. When her hands had cupped his testes, he had felt a surge of pleasure go through him. When she circled his tube of flesh with her small, soft hand, he had felt his sexual hunger rise. Each loving stroke brought a charge of pleasure to his brain. He could not have anticipated the varied ways his human form could find pleasure. He had never experienced this intensity of sensation from any other alien form he had inhabited. What a world he had discovered! And this was just the first day. There were many to come and he delighted in the thought of the plethora of pleasurable experiences ahead of him.

When she heard the man sigh and sensed his body sagging, Kelly knew his discharge was imminent. She felt a deep craving for the man's seed and she placed her lips around the bulbous tip of his cock so it would not be wasted. His manhood began to throb and spasm in her hand. She reached her free hand under his scrotal sac and began to massage the soft stones that produced his delicious essence. As the salty, viscous fluid spurted over her tongue, she heard the man groan. He placed his hands on her head for balance as the sensations of his orgasm appeared to overwhelm him. Her mind exploded with joy at the taste of his discharge and the feel of the powerful pulses of his manhood transmitted to her hand.

It took Raijamoon a while to recover from his spent passion. The woman continued to gently suckle his softening rod. When he had regained his composure and the echoes of his pleasure had died away, he bent down and lifted the woman from her knees. She looked at him contentedly as she licked her lips and smiled. It was his turn to explore her flesh and he bent down and retrieved the soft sponge from the floor of the shower chamber. He soaped the sponge and began to rub it softly over her body.

The dream man tenderly soaped her soft, malleable breasts, her belly and the gash at the apex of her graceful legs. He ran his hands down her supple but firm lower limbs and cleaned the inside of her thighs. He took his time, savoring his contact with her flesh. When he leaned over to wash her feet, he felt her soft hands on his back, steadying herself. He could sense her delirious absorption of his attentions to her body. He rose and turned her so he could wash her back and the back of her thighs. Her back was soft and smooth. He rubbed the gently scouring sponge over her shoulders and down and under her arms. How different their bodies were, he thought. His was muscular and hard, emanating strength. Hers was soft and pliant, inviting. He ran his empty hand over her firm but welcoming buttocks as he sponged them with the other. He cleaned the gap between her rear cheeks.

As he passed his hand over the small circle of her rear aperture, he sensed a slight jolt of pleasure flow through the woman. It was commingled with shame and embarrassment. Her response intrigued him and he passed his finger over it once again, lingering this time over the dainty hole. The female shied her body away from him, but he detected a flush of excitement in her mind. He decided to explore the matter further.

He dropped the sponge and circled his arm around the woman's waist. Holding her still, he pressed his finger forward until the tip had just entered her there. He sent a signal of pleasure through his hand and heard the female draw in a long, deep breath. She began to struggle at his grasp and put her hand behind her and on his wrist to try and deny him access to this secret place.

Kelly had never experienced anal sex. As a doctor, she frowned on the practice as unsanitary. As a woman, she had always felt that a man's use of a woman's ass was degrading. But some part of her had always wondered what it would feel like. She had heard tell some women enjoyed the use of their smaller portal, but discounted that as improbable or the result of some disturbed fetish. Although, once or twice, she had felt a compelling desire to try it, she had never had the nerve to suggest it to any of her boyfriends. One of her lovers had placed his finger there during oral sex and she had felt a twinge of pleasure as he teased the opening. It had not gone beyond that.

When the man's fingers brushed across the small ring as he washed her, Kelly felt the energy from his hand flow into her. It had been brief, just an instant of delight. When the finger returned, she had felt the pleasure again, but her mind revolted at the touch. When the point of his digit pressed past the tiny opening, she began to panic. She didn't want him to use her that way. She tried to squirm out of his grasp and push his hand away. It was the first time in many hours she had even thought of denying him his pleasures. When she felt his grip around her waist tighten and the finger circle the soft anal tissue, she realized if he wanted to pierce her there, she was powerless to prevent it.

Raijamoon felt the woman's incipient revulsion at his exploration of her rear opening, but he also felt the lines of pleasure that had flowed from there to her brain. He took his hand and stroked it several times down her watery back, soothing her, sending her a calming message. When her mind accepted his mesmerizing energy, he returned his fingers to her small orifice and continued his exploration.

Kelly's anxiety about the man's penetration of her bowels melted away. He was doing this to her, affecting her brain, she knew that. She had felt the soothing signals passing through the nerves of her back and flowing within her. When the hand returned to her secret, private place, and the man's thick finger entered her once more, slipping past the tight ring of flesh, she experienced a strange, exotic pleasure unhindered this time by her apprehensions.

Slowly, gently, the man's finger explored the opening, sending messages of pleasure through the young woman's body. When his second finger entered, she gave a gasp and leaned against the wall, placing her hands on it above her head to steady herself. When the third finger was introduced, stretching the membranes of the little ring, she moaned.

The dream man drew his long, thick fingers back and forth across the sensitive tissue. This use of the woman had not occurred to him. He saw now that the possibility was something she had repressed, buried deep in her subconscious. His cock had stirred at the thought of entering her there and it was now stiff and hard. Raijamoon realized this method of intercourse would help him cement his mastery over the woman. He would be overcoming her shame and humiliation at this form of use and introducing her to a pleasure she had never experienced. He could very easily remove all of her inhibitions towards it, but he felt it would be better she experience it as a continuing source of both shame and pleasure, a reminder of her subservience to him and his dominance over her. It was important that no part of her be secret from him, that her whole being be bound over, compelled to join with him, to obey him, to want him, to please him. He would develop her desire for this form of copulation until she willingly proffered it to him despite her humiliation and shame at her need.

He sensed his penetration of the small entrance would tear at her tissues until she became acclimated to this form of use. He sought a form of lubrication to ease his way and he spotted a jar of moisturizing cream on the shelf near the shampoo and conditioner. He released the woman and opened the jar, gathering a dollop on his fingers.

When the man's arm released her waist and his hand left her rear, Kelly hoped he had abandoned his exploration of her. When she heard him open the jar of cream, she knew he had not and that he would shortly seek entrance to her bowels with his thick, hard member. Her stomach fluttered and her heart grew heavy as she dreaded his invasion. She knew what she would feel when his cock parted the small circle of flesh. She knew its power to drive her lusts. He would make her pant and shudder with passion. Everything in her wanted to push the man aside and rush out of the shower. Maybe she could make the door to the outside before he recovered. Maybe she could grab something and smash him with it. But her mind ached at the thought of separation from him. Her body needed his touch and his nearness. And she had not the courage to put her frantic impulse to flee into action. One touch of his hand to her flesh and he could send her into convulsions of discomfort and sorrow. She had experienced it twice and it was the most awful thing she had ever felt. It was worse than pain, a combination of intense loneliness, despair and physical illness. She dreaded ever experiencing it again.

Raijamoon felt the woman's urge to flee and her desperate unhappiness. He knew they would soon pass. He spread the cream liberally over and inside the tight hole and then presented his rampant cock to it. Placing his hands on the woman's buttocks, parting her cheeks, he let his energy flow into her. Immediately, her body relaxed, her tenseness ebbed away. The ring of flesh between her buttocks, which had contracted and tightened at his approach, loosened and relaxed. He pressed the head of his cock forwards slowly, enjoying the pressure of the small circle of flesh on his shaft. The woman moaned with pleasure and pain as his thick piece scraped across the ring, stretching it to its extreme. He reached around her torso and took hold of her breasts, caressing them, emitting signals of warmth and pleasure to them as he eased himself deeper and deeper. Her bowels transmitted a murky warmth to his cock, a strange, exhilarating contrast to the tightness of the entrance. When his penetration reached its apogee, he moaned with delight. He would not let the female deny this experience to him, he thought. It was wildly exciting and pleasurable. He transmitted his approval of her obedience and compliance to the woman and he heard her moan with pleasure. When he began to draw his cock back and forth over the rim of her rear orifice, the woman's body shuddered.

Once the discomfort of the man's invasion has passed, Kelly let the waves of pleasure roll through her body. She arched her back and spread her legs wider to ease the man's penetration. She could feel her pussy burn with lust as he slowly, deliberately plowed her ass. Her breasts felt afire with the feverish energy that passed through the man's hands. He was possessing her as no man ever had. He was bringing her a form of bodily delight she had never fathomed. A part of her was shamed by her enjoyment of this deviant form of intercourse, but she had no will to fight it. She knew she would never again try to refuse this use of her body to the man. She felt that it was his right to possess her at any time and in any way he wanted. She had innocently thought she was the owner of his handsome, desirable flesh. But it was he that owned her, he that controlled her pleasures and desires. She would serve him willingly in any way he wished.

When the dream man came, Kelly came too. Her pussy pulsed and contracted and she howled her pleasure in the shower chamber, her voice echoing off of the glass and tile walls. Her body was still being pummeled by the hot stream of water from the shower and the steam around her made her feel her body had entered a strange, new plane. The man grunted his pleasure as his semen washed into her bowels. When he was done, he leaned against her for a moment, caressing her breasts softly.

The man afterwards washed himself clean. He then poured shampoo onto her head and washed her hair. His hands massaged her scalp gently, making her sigh with pleasure. He made sure all of the strands of her long, reddish brown hair were covered with suds. He rinsed her hair thoroughly, added crème rinse and then rinsed it again twice.

Kelly's captor crouched in the shower while she returned the favor. Her body was warm with satisfaction at her pleasing of the man. She cleaned his hair with all the love and caring she could give it. She was glad she was fully opened to him, glad he had brought her to pleasure there. The small orifice he had entered still reverberated with the echo of his presence. Her reticence and momentary revolt against him was all but forgotten. When she had finished rinsing his long, black locks for the third time, she crouched down behind him and pressed her body to his, circling his torso with her arms and kissing his neck.

The man dried her body with a large, soft towel. He brushed the tangles from her hair and even used the hair drier to remove the dampness. She happily did his. Her body felt warm and refreshed. She brushed her teeth and handed him an unopened package containing a new, fresh toothbrush she had bought the other day and he followed her example. She showed him how to bind her now dried hair into a ponytail behind her back. When he had done it, he turned her body around and gave her a deep, soulful kiss. She ran her hands over his broad, strong shoulders and arms as she pressed her body against him.

When they parted, he retrieved the cord which had bound her wrists behind her for most of the day. Her joy turned bitter when she saw it in his hands and she took a tiny step back from him. She didn't want to be tied. Her shower with him had been an idyllic, liberating interlude. She had felt, for a little while, like a willing, almost equal partner with the strange man.

Kelly's visitor saw and felt her disappointment and sorrow at the prospect of being bound again. It was a sure sign his work with her was not yet complete. Her very thought that she had a right to the use of her body in any way other than as he desired it proved the need for her confinement. He placed his hand on her head and sent her a strong message of her need to obey him, to serve him, coupled with a small signal of punishment for her effrontery.

Kelly felt the man's energy pass through her. She remembered at once her duty to him even as the sensation of his displeasure caused her body suddenly to cringe and ache. Her physical misery lasted only a few seconds, but her sorrow at disappointing him caused it to echo throughout her after it passed. She was ashamed she had made him angry. She recognized her punishment as deserving. She started to cry. She had spoiled it. She looked at him despondently. She wanted to tell him she was sorry, that she would obey him, that she existed only to serve him. She was afraid he would leave, abandon her. Her lips trembled. What had happened to her that she needed him so? She didn't even know who he was, where he had come from, his name? She was a respected scientist, a self determined, free woman. Yet every pore of her body felt drawn to this man's flesh, to his will. She felt like she should fall to his feet and beg his forgiveness.

The dream man saw his familiar's acute discomfort and unhappiness. It was unfortunate she needed to be punished, but he saw she had benefited from it. He sensed there would be other bumps and detours along the road to her ultimate submission. He caressed her breast with his hand as a sign of his forgiveness for her sin. Her face calmed as her body received his warm, comforting energy. She wiped the tears away from her face with her fists and gave him a little smile.

He urged her with a motion of his head to turn around and she complied happily. She presented her crossed, delicate, pale wrists behind her back and he tied them off.

The dream man led Kelly directly from the bathroom to the bedroom. She watched patiently as he reassembled the bed into proper order. Their seemingly endless bouts of passion on it had scattered the sheets, pillows and comforter all over. When the bed had been made, he seemed to have an intuitive understanding at how to do it, he drew back the covers and had her lay face down on the mattress, her head on a pillow at the head of the bed. She felt him bind her ankles together and then raise them to join them with her wrists. It was a loose, comfortable tie that left her able to draw her feet some distance from her hands.

He left her there for a few moments while he made his rounds of the small house, extinguishing lights, checking the door and windows. When he returned, he pushed her to her side so she would be facing him. He turned off the small table lamp on the nightstand, plunging the room into darkness, climbed in the bed and, before drawing the sheets up over their bodies, ran his hands over her proffered breasts and belly.

Kelly felt oddly secure and comfortable in her bindings. She rationalized he would not confine her so if she were not important to him. She felt pleased to have succumbed to his will for her. When darkness fell in the room, she sensed her dream man bring his body close to hers. She welcomed his hands on her body, reveling at his touch. When he drew the sheet and the heavy comforter over them both, she let her body and mind relax. In a very short while, she was asleep.

CHAPTER SIX

The morning, at first, brought to Kelly a continuation of the previous day's idyll. When she awoke, the drapes to her bedroom were still drawn closed and the emerging sign of day glowed through them, illuminating the room with a soft, diffused light. The clock was behind her on the dresser and she could not turn to see what time it was, but she guessed it was about 7:30 or so.

She had been startled for a moment on her awakening by the fact of her bound hands and legs, but when she saw the sleeping form of the man before her, it had all come back to her. She immediately felt a deep, almost painful longing for him. He was lying on his stomach, his powerful arm crooked under the pillow, his face turned away from hers. His long, jet black hair lay across his broad back. The quilt that covered them both reached just up to a few inches from his shoulders and she could see the form of his tall, heavy body underneath. "What a pleasing picture we make," Kelly thought, ironically. "A scene of domestic bliss." For although she was helplessly bound, her body too was concealed under the covers and all an observer would see was a man and woman in bed, the man sleeping, the woman lovingly casting her eyes on his form.

Something had happened to her in the night. She had had intense, disturbing dreams, mostly involving her strange visitor. In one, she had been lying on her back in a huge bed with her arms affixed to the headboard as they had been a number of times the day before. Her legs were spread, her vulva open and yearning. A crowd of people surrounded the bed in which she picked out her mother, Adele, the girls from the lab, an old boyfriend or two and numerous strangers whose faces she could not make out. The man stood at the foot of the bed, naked, with his manhood rampant. He was speaking some foreign tongue. Not Spanish, as she might have anticipated, but a language whose guttural sounds and variable pitches and tones seemed other worldly. And although she could not decipher the words, if they were words, she knew he was addressing her, ordering her to prepare her body for him. Her pussy began to burn and its juices started to flow as if on command. Her nipples became taut and her skin began to tingle with delight. She raised her hips in invitation to the tall, brooding, dark haired man. As he began to approach her, climbing on the bed from its foot, crawling across the sheets, she became aware of the crowd of people staring at her, judging her. But as unhappy as she was at their disapproval and contempt for her need, she could only react by spreading her thighs wider, hungry for the man to fill her.

Kelly awoke from this dream with a start, panicked. Darkness covered the room like a sea of black ink. She frantically tugged and strained at her bonds. Her eyes tried to pierce the blackness. She was desperately afraid the man had abandoned her. Then she heard the telltale sound of his deep, regular breathing. She almost broke into tears at her relief. She edged her face closer to his body so she could feel the heat rising from it. The man stirred, as if he had sensed her discomfiture. His hand reached out and caressed her hip and thigh. She felt a wave of reassurance pass through her and she went back to sleep.

This had been the most disturbing of her dreams. The others, from what she could recall, involved her standing in the mist her lover had arrived in. She was looking across the field which the man had floated across and the mist kept rolling in steadily towards her body. When it reached her, her body seemed to absorb it. Somehow, she felt she was receiving energy from another world, acting as a conduit for it to enter hers, a depository, perhaps. It was strange, as if it was filled with some highly energized substance intended for the man that she would transfer to him when he awakened.

Kelly watched as the man's head turned in his sleep. His face became visible to her and she took the opportunity to study his peaceful features. He had a long, strong nose and wide apart, large eyes. His eyebrows were black and full and tapered off to within an inch of each other above his nose. His lips were full and manly. His chin was strong. She noticed he had grown a forest of tiny black whiskers on his face. She made a note she would have to shave him. Since there hadn't been a man around her house for a long, long time, he would have to use the razor she used on her legs.

The man's eyes fluttered and his tongue darted out across his lips. "What does a dream man dream about?" Kelly thought. Was he dreaming of her? Of his other world? Did he have any consciousness of a time before appearing in her bed, his hot prick immersed in her fevered slit? The scientist in her yearned for information, answers. Her legs unconsciously tried to stretch out to their full length and she felt the tug of the rope that connected her ankles to her wrists tighten and pull on her hands. It was a stark reminder of the fact he had decided to keep her bound and helpless, that he controlled her, owned her in some way. It sent a shiver of lust through her to think about it. She squeezed her thighs together and bit her lower lip as she felt her passion for him commence to rise. Her body yearned for contact with him, her hands yearned to touch him, her voids craved to be filled. But she dared not wake him. Her life now, she realized, would be ruled by what he wanted, what he needed.

But how would that work out? She had a career, a laboratory she was responsible for. There were people in her life, people she was obliged to like Adele and the young girls who worked for her. And then there was her project itself. She didn't want to abandon it for a life of blissful slavery to this man. At the same time, however, she never wanted to lose the feeling of belonging and of being needed the man gave her. When she closed her eyes and concentrated, she could feel the energy passing between their bodies as if they were joined somehow. When she concentrated on it, her mind was flooded with a sense of well being and happiness she could not explain.

If only the man would awaken and fill her once more. She had so much she wanted to give him that she felt like her body was set to explode. She knew that when his essence flowed within her it would wash away all of her concerns for anything but him. His radiant cock sent electrical charges through her which made her feel in total communion with his will. The orgasms he brought her left her in a state of utter contentment and calm.

Raijamoon's eyes slowly opened to see the adoring face of his familiar staring at him. Her pretty, blue eyes were wide apart with wonder. Her graceful, full, round breasts seemed to be thrust out to him in invitation for his touch. Her lips were open and trembling as if in need.

He sensed she was in need. During the night, the sea of fluids he had deposited within her had assimilated fully into her system. Her lust for him was strong. He recognized the essence of the Whole that had seeped into her during her dreams, her body serving as a vessel for the lifeblood of his existence in this realm. He would need to feed on her, to draw it into himself, to make himself stronger. His strength would intensify his powers and they, in turn, would allow him to absorb and receive sustenance from her emotions and passions and that of others like her. For there would be others, minds he would have to control, bodies which would become his servants. The dream man the woman had conjured had no inclinations which would allow him to commune with males as he did with females and he would not be able to establish the sexual bond needed for such use. He would be able to influence and, to some extent, control male minds, but it was nothing compared to the connection he could establish with female thoughts and emotions.

Somehow this day he would need to make preparations for his entry into the world. His first priority, however, was to relieve his familiar of the burden she was carrying. The energies that had passed into her during the night would have supercharged her body with lust. Like a vessel about to burst, he needed to drain her passions, allow her to release the forces that had built up in her.

Raijamoon smiled at the distressed woman, rubbing his hand on her cheek to assuage her troubled mien. He threw off the covers and, leaning over her, unfastened her ankles from her wrists. He unbound the wrists as well, only to affix them to the headboard above her.

His cock was hard as the woman's sexual energy conveyed itself to him through their strengthening bond. He placed himself between her widespread, inviting lower limbs and stroked her tender flesh, her belly and her breasts, her hips and her inner thighs. He needed to convert her sexual longing to sexual excitement. When he saw her lips parted and pursed, her breasts hardened with blood, her hips gyrating with need, he placed his cock at the entrance to her womb and slowly entered it.

Kelly sighed deeply as the man's thick, hot rod pressed into her. It was like all she had dreamed of in life had come true. She felt the man place his weight upon her. Electricity passed between their skins. His chest crushed her breasts and his legs circled around the outside of her knees locking themselves around her shins. The man used his strong legs to pull hers wider and wider until his pelvis bone was shoved up against hers. His hands slowly caressed her arms until they joined together with hers above her head. His mouth covered her lips and his tongue slipped between them, establishing his hot, fevered presence in her mouth. She felt like every inch of the front of her body was in contact with his electrifying skin.

Suddenly, she felt herself coming. Her pussy wrenched with repeated hard, almost unbearable spasms. Her imprisoned hands gripped his fiercely as if to a lifeline. As she came, she felt the powerful, inexplicable force which had amassed within her flowing from her body to his. It was like she was emptying herself. Her body shook and her heart pounded in her chest.

The dream man was in ecstasy as the energies of the Whole passed into him. He felt the female's pussy clench his enflamed cock tightly at each of its powerful convulsions. Her tongue sought union with his and she cried and moaned beneath him. It would be like this every morning now. They could never be apart for very long, a few days at most. If he could manage it, they would never be apart for more than 24 hours. His existence depended on their closeness and physical intimacies. Separation from him would cause her intense, excruciating anxiety. It would be difficult, though, to bring her on his quest. He needed to be able to move about surreptitiously, and she would be like a walking signpost to his enemy.

She would need to be well cared for when he was away. It was one of the reasons he needed servants.

The female took a while to recover from the draining of the Whole's essence from her. She lay listlessly on the bed for about an hour, her hands still bound to the bed frame, the man's soothing fluids seeping into her. Raijamoon took the time to begin to explore her living room, testing the communication devices. The television fascinated him. It had a great volume of information, none of it valuable, but it presented its content with all the earnestness of a camp meeting preacher. The computer was another story. He learned to connect to the Internet and was able to access a number of news records that were informative. There was a vast supply of scientific information, some of it spurious, but here and there he found a kernel that would be important as he solidified his base and prepared to complete his mission.

He made love to the female again after she had recovered from her stupor. She received him enthusiastically, moaning with rapture as he stroked his cock this time into the small hole between her rear cheeks.

* * * *

She was kneeling dreamily in the kitchen when it happened, naked, her hands bound behind her, eating the small spoonfuls of peanut butter he was feeding her and drinking milk. There was not much of it left.

The telephone rang.

Kelly jumped as the jarring sound echoed throughout the small house. It took her a moment to realize what it was. When she had recovered enough to realize it was the phone, a deep feeling of uncertainty ran through her. It was the outside world on the other end of the line. The world she had almost forgotten about. Her conflict about her future came back to life. Today was Sunday. Tomorrow was Monday. What would happen then? And how would she deal with whoever was calling her? Would the man allow her to speak? Was the ringing of the phone the death knell for her bond with her dream lover? Would he leave now that the inevitable intrusion of the reality outside of her four walls had come closer? If he was a madman, and had somehow drawn her into his psychotic world, was her doom now sealed?

The telephone rang four times and then the answering machine kicked in. The man stared at her while her voice cheerfully spoke, "Hi, this is Kelly. I can't come to the phone right now so please leave a message after the beep and I'll get right back to you." There was a few seconds pause and then the machine went, "Beep!"

A bright, young, female voice came on the line. "Hiya, Kelly, this is Adele. I guess you're in the shower or something. I'll be there about twelve for lunch. Don't worry about making anything. I'm picking up a quiche from the New Age Deli and some salad. And I'm gonna bring a big bottle of wine, so don't plan on doing anything else for the rest of the day. See ya soon!"

The man and the woman both looked up at the kitchen clock simultaneously. It was a little after 10:30. Adele would be there in an hour and a half, sooner, if she was early.

The man looked back at Kelly the same time she looked back at him. He had a stern, almost angry look on his face. Kelly had forgotten all about Adele and the tentative date they had made on Friday to get together today. She had planned to make her excuses and had then filed it away somewhere in her mind. As she suffered the disapproving glare of the dream man, she realized she had somehow sinned in his eyes. Was he angry because she hadn't told him about it or because Adele was coming? Somehow, she sensed it was the former. But how could she tell him if she wasn't allowed to talk? He seemed to have the ability to probe her mind, to know what she knew, what she wanted, what she was thinking. By not thinking about it, she had hidden it from him

Kelly realized her sin consisted of storing this information somewhere he couldn't find it. How was she to know? She hadn't even met him until many hours later. Even as she thought that, she knew his possession of her had deprived her of the right to keep anything from him. She would, hereafter, need to scour her brain for every little detail that might be important to him, open her mind up to him entirely.

Her mind took the next step. "Adele!" she thought. "She's in danger!" What would he do to her? How could she stop him? How could she warn the happy go lucky Southern belle who would be walking into the nefarious control of her dream man? For she realized at that instant that that's what it was, nefarious. He was controlling her, doing things to her for some mysterious, perhaps evil, purpose. It was too late for her, she knew that. Somehow, he had taken control of her. She could not resist him. She needed him more than she ever needed anyone or anything. But Adele! She had to do something, anything to save her!

All at once she realized that the man had read every one of her thoughts. She saw his angry reaction right in his eyes. She had diverted her will from his and, if only for a moment, consciously plotted to oppose him. He was going to punish her! She knew it! Suddenly, mind wrenching fear swept through her. Tears of dread and self pity came to her eyes.

Raijamoon watched the female's body sag as she began to cry. He read her fear of him. She was right to be afraid; he was angry, angry with himself as well as her. How had he missed it? He was reminded that his ability to read the woman's mind was not unlimited. Unless he drove deeply into her psyche, an action that might prove counterproductive since it would certainly disturb the very mental processes he needed to preserve, there would always be more to discover about her. He had been overconfident, had failed to take full advantage of the tools of persuasion and seduction he could use. He had been distracted by the exciting sensuality of his new existence.

This was the second time, the first being yesterday when he had frolicked in the stream oblivious to the fact that the woman was waking. That had been a close run thing. He would not make this mistake again. He was in a strange and ultimately hostile world, surviving only through the lifeline of the female's existence. What if the next time it was something worse than the mere fact someone was coming over, someone he could easily deal with?

He rose from his chair and stepped over to the kneeling, sobbing woman. She was right to be afraid. She had sinned grievously, both by failing to reveal to him her friend was expected and then by trying to oppose his will, to consider taking action that would frustrate his ability to contend with the pretty, young girl who was on her way. She would have to learn a severe lesson.

Kelly tried to shy away when the man's hand reached out for her shoulder, but his mind had frozen her in place. At the instant his flesh made contact with hers, a feeling of deep, bitter unhappiness came over her. Every cell in her body seemed to fall ill. Her insides seemed to twist and turn sickeningly. Her mind begged him to release her, to remove his hand from her, to stop the flow of misery into her, but it kept going on and on and on. It was a deeper, harder feeling than he had inflicted on her before, more personal, as if intentionally cruel. She looked at him, her face a mask of misery, and tried to speak, to beg surcease, but was only able to muster repeatedly the bare beginnings of a single syllable, "Pluhhhhhh! Pluhhhhhh! Pluhhhhhh!" The sounds came from her like the monotonous tones from a scratch on a warped record, jumping back and releasing the same wavy, distorted sound again and again. When the miserable feelings inside her intensified, she understood she had committed another sin by attempting to speak. Even pleas for mercy were outlawed.

Raijamoon withdrew his hand when he realized he had continued the woman's punishment longer and far harder than he had intended. His human brain had taken control of him. Anger was not an emotion his race was familiar with, at least not in their domain. They had put it aside eons ago. He felt shame that he had violated one of the precepts of the Whole. He had harmed beyond justification a sentient being. The woman needed to be punished, it was clear. However, the purpose of punishment was to teach, not to cause pain. The female didn't know any better. She was still evolving as his familiar and had many steps yet to take. The very subordination of her mind to his limited her ability to anticipate what he would want from her. Her psyche had been filled with what was to her inexplicable feelings and desires so strong they had pushed aside her ability to think beyond the moment.

And yet, her lack of understanding of her obligations to him did not vitiate the need for punishment. She needed to be deterred whenever she went down a wayward path and to understand clearly that for her errors she would receive a stern and deserved retribution. Nor did it justify or explain her revolt against him. He would need to explore this, calmly, rationally, without rancor or ill will. She was not a prisoner to be tortured or abused when the whim or fancy struck him. That was not the way of the Whole. She was a primitive, albeit sentient creature, entrusted to his care, who needed to be instructed and guided, even if from time to time it meant she would suffer unpleasant, unhappy consequences.

The woman looked up at him with fear and misery. He would have to undo the damage he had done. She needed to feel his warmth and caring for her. It was not only his responsibility as a superior being, but it was vital to the process of maintaining and strengthening their bond.

Raijamoon knelt down in front of the distraught woman and placed his hands on the side of her head, locking his gaze into hers. She resisted him, as he knew she would, but she quickly succumbed to the messages of comfort and desire he sent to her. He probed her mind and soothed the disturbed parts of it. He took her lips with his and kissed her tenderly, lovingly. He conveyed to her his sorrow at hurting her, his promise to care for her, his assurance he would not harm her friend.

Kelly's mind revolted when the man took his position in front of her. She knew what he was going to do. He was going to control her. She tried to back away, but a feeling of ease and peace quickly flooded her brain through his large, strong hands. She felt his mind entering hers and was surprised when she detected his remorse at what he had done to her. She was stunned he would reveal himself so. It was his first, direct, specific, psychic contact with her. The authenticity of his emotion overwhelmed her. No one had ever cared for her like this. She was ashamed at her rebellion against him. Even as his lips pressed against hers and his tongue entered her mouth, she began to cry again, this time not in pain, but in sorrow. She felt responsible for his outburst of anger and bitterly regretted causing it. She wanted to put her arms around him, to hold him, to express her devotion to him.

The dream man sensed the strong, vital need of the woman for emotional release. He reached down behind her back and freed the cords that bound her hands. He felt her gratitude at his concession to her needs. She placed her head on his shoulder and her arms around him and began to sob heavily. Her chest heaved with the strength of her unhappiness. He could feel her mind reaching out to him, straining to make him believe her earnest sorrow at her wrongs. His hand stroked her long, silky, auburn hair. He felt her tears flowing down his shoulder. He had become acquainted with the word 'heartbreaking' in the process of learning the woman's language, but he had not understood what it meant. He understood it now. The woman's sorrow was heartbreaking to him, to the human part of him. The same part of him that had produced his unfortunate anger filled him now with a profound ache.

Slowly, the woman's sorrow began to turn into an intense need to express her union with him. She lifted her head from his shoulder and placed her hands on his face. She seized his lips and probed his mouth hungrily with her tongue. He let his energy flow into the woman through his mouth. She began to kiss him fervently, stroking his body with her hands. She placed them on his chest and firmly urged him down to the floor on his back. Her need for union had turned to lust. She flung her bare leg over his and straddled him, her knees on the floor to each side of his hips. She took hold of his stiffened manhood and guided it eagerly to her hungry, lustful envelope. It slid over him easily and she moaned into his mouth as his rigid prick scoured the walls of her hot, moist crevasse and filled her.

Kelly was beside herself with desire. Her whole body burned with the need to have the man within her, to feel his heat, to have him come inside her. She rocked her hips up and down, riding him like she would a stallion. His cock sent wave after wave of concentrated pleasure through her. She rubbed her hard bud against its length. "Oh god! Oh god!" she thought. "I need him! I need him!" She could feel his lust flowing back at her through his thick meat. Her whole being centered round it. When she came, she gave a loud cry. She could feel his mind wrapping around hers, rewarding her for her lust, heightening her pleasure. When her spasms ebbed, she didn't stop. More! She wanted more!

Raijamoon lay still underneath the woman, letting her bring them both exquisite physical and mental delight. His eyes rolled back as his cock took in her heat, her desire. Their separateness as individual beings ceased to be a barrier to the exchange of their emotions, their thoughts. All at once he understood the reason for the woman's rebellion. It was love, love for her friend. And it was her love for him she was expressing now. The emotion was foreign to him, he did not possess it. But he sensed the strength of it in the woman's soul. She wanted to protect her loved one from harm and had been willing to sacrifice herself for that goal. He sent to her, amidst their passion, his forgiveness and his acceptance of her devotion towards him. He would use her friend, yes. He needed to. Nothing was more important than his mission, not even her, his familiar. But he would do all in his power to protect her friend and all others he would use from harm. He promised her that.

When the man came inside her, Kelly felt a rush of exhilaration. His seed spread throughout her womb like a soothing salve. Her hot cleft expressed its welcome to his orgasm by delivering a series of hard, tight contractions sending sharp signals of pleasure through her body and causing her to jerk and moan.

Her frantic exertions finished, the female laid her head on his chest, her hair spreading over him, and surrounded his strong, thick neck with her arms, clutching him tightly. He could feel her heart beating wildly within her chest as it echoed on his. He caressed her, granting her waves of soft, gentle pleasure as her reward for giving in to her passions. Her mind was finally at rest, savoring their sweet afterglow.

Raijamoon took a few moments to savor the aftermath of the woman's lust and then looked at the clock. Twenty five minutes had passed. He would have to hurry to be ready for Adele.

The woman was still dazed from the effects of her emotionally wrenching experiences, the lows of her intense, dreadful punishment and the exhilarating high of their bout of passion. His cum was assimilating inside her, increasing her sensations of estrangement from her former self. He would need to bring the woman deeper into her bindings to him so she would passively accept what next had to be done.

He drew her to her knees and kissed her, sending strong signals of his will into her. She was limp and docile as he handled her, but responded acceptingly to his kiss. The cord which he had released from around her hands was on the floor next to them and he picked it up and showed it to her. A quick look of sorrow crossed her face and then, resignedly, she smiled at him accepting his will. Without instruction, she crossed her hands behind her. He leaned his bare chest against her torso, crushing her naked breasts, and circled his arms around her. He was far taller than she was, even kneeling, and he was able to watch his hands as they worked the soft cord around her compliant wrists.

When the woman was bound, he led her into the bedroom and placed her on the bed on her side. He lay down next to her, facing her and maneuvered his body so his loins were opposite her face. He presented his tumescent manhood to her lips, sending to her mind her a message of invitation. He placed his hand lightly on her head, transmitting feelings of peace and contentment. The woman shuddered with longing and took his cock between her lips.

He lay there side by side with the woman for about forty minutes. She sucked lazily on his meat, her legs drawn up, her head lying on a pillow he had brought her. Her long, wavy, reddish brown hair flowed down her back. Her naked breasts were pressed against his thighs. The vision of her soft, rounded figure, her lightly pinkish skin, her bound hands resting peaceably behind her was stirring to the man. She had closed her eyes and her face was a visage of serene satisfaction as her pursed lips surrounded the source of her pleasure and the subtle movements of her jaw recorded her gentle suckling at his pole.

It was not passion he sought from her. He wanted her to lose herself in the radiant energy of his sex, to absorb slowly but steadily his psychic essence until her whole body was intoxicated with feelings of happiness and pleasure. He could sense her muted, almost slothful joy as she ran her tongue lazily around it, slid her lips slowly up and down the thick shaft. After about twenty minutes, he allowed himself to come, a low, lazy, throbbing ejaculation that sent a steady stream of his viscous fluids into her mouth. She moaned as she received it, her closed eyes fluttering, her breasts pressing harder against him. Her throat pulsed as she consumed it. When his pleasurable spasms were done, he placed his hand on the woman's head, urging her to remain at her task and sending a pulse of his approval of her as a reward for her compliance and affectionate, loving attentions to his sex.

To Kelly, nothing had ever seemed so right as the sensation of the man's soft, pleasantly textured, hard meat in her mouth. The taste was luxuriant and she could feel rays of his power seeping through its pores. As she sucked at him, she realized the man could not only control her, he could regulate her, either keeping her lusts on a slow, steady, languorous boil as he was now, or compel her to a frantic, mind blowing need for completion, for union with him. She had put all thoughts of Adele behind her. Something would work out, she thought. He wouldn't harm her. What could she do anyway? How could she resist the man's allure? How could she suppress her need to bend to his will? When he came, she drank at his essence, relishing the warm effusions of his seed as it flowed into her. When he allowed her to continue, she blessed his munificence.

After he had come for the second time in the woman's adoring mouth, Raijamoon drew her up from the bed. She was in a kind of stupefied state. He guided her out to the hallway outside the bedroom and eased her to her knees. He left her there for a moment while he retrieved the cord he had been using on her ankles. He came back to her and tied her ankles to each other after crossing them. He then tied the woman's wrists to her ankles. This time, he tied them together tightly, causing the woman to arch backwards and spread her knees. There was a pipe ascending the wall behind her and he affixed her bindings to the pipe, locking the naked young woman in place.

The dimensional traveler did not want any interference with his dealings with Kelly's friend and employee. This would be his first effort at total control of a human being and although he had great confidence he would have no problems, he didn't want to take the chance his familiar's love for her friend would cause her to distract him or his quarry at a crucial moment.

Kelly knelt where she had been positioned, dazed and confused. The man's semen was seeping through her. The long period of contact between the man's cock and the nerve endings in her mouth and tongue had made her drunk with his psychic essence. She had felt his will stroking her mind, settling her into a comfortable, listless place.

From her position in the hallway, Kelly could see the door to the outside of her house directly opposite. The hallway was the meeting place for the four main rooms of the house, the bedroom, the living room, the kitchen and the bathroom. There was a spare room off of the kitchen she had intended to equip as a guest bedroom but had never gotten around to it other than buying a small, single bed. From her perch, the bound woman could see into all four of the principal rooms. She could see the entire living room and kitchen, a small sliver of the bathroom and about a third of her bedroom. The long mirror on the bedroom wall that backed up to the wall of the living room gave her a clear view of her bed and almost all of the rest of the room.

The man made sure the outside door was unlocked and then retreated into the kitchen. He took a seat at the table and proceeded to leisurely peel and consume the last orange in the now empty, fruit bowl.

The house remained utterly quiet while the couple awaited the arrival of their guest. It was ten minutes to twelve. Twice, the refrigerator turned itself on, its compressor whirring for about thirty seconds or so and then shutting down. The gas heater kicked in, sending warm air through the house's ductwork. It had dropped to 45 degrees over night. Once or twice, Kelly issued a low moan of recalled pleasure as the almost hour long, continuous contact of her mouth with the man's loins reverberated through her. She had risen to semi-consciousness once or twice, and dulsatorily struggled at the bonds that held her so tightly to the pipe behind her. But her mind quickly sank back into her reverie of devotion and love for her dream man.

Raijamoon was sitting about ten feet away from her in one of the strait backed chairs. His elbows were on the table and his shoulders slouched as he nonchalantly stripped the orange and plunged little wedges into his mouth. He loved the taste of fresh oranges. They had finished the orange juice this morning, but the "freshly squeezed" promise of the carton did not compare to the juice fresh from the fruit's pulp. He spit out the little seeds, plucking them from his lips, and placed them on a small plate on the table.

The quietude of the residence was intruded upon by the sound of a small engine car climbing the slight hill to the house. Kelly, startled for a moment into semi-awareness, felt a twinge of unhappiness as she realized her friend was here. Her mind was so hazy with satisfaction and desire for her controlling lover, that it barely reached the surface of her consciousness. But it was there.

The visitor sensed her feeling of fear for her friend right away. He put the last wedge of orange in his mouth and stood from the table. He had placed the role of silvery duct tape and a pair of scissors on the table next to him and picked it up and carried it over to his bound thrall.

The woman was startled by his sudden, quick movement. She looked at him dolefully. He detected her fear that he had arisen so he could punish her for her wayward thought of concern for her friend, but he had no such intention. He could not punish the woman for her love for her friend nor her fear for her friend's fate.

In fact the emotional bond between the two women would prove useful. And he did not want to make an automaton of his familiar. He could squeeze all concepts out of her mind except for her need to obey him. But he didn't want that. In fact, he couldn't have that if she was to maintain her mind in the proper state to receive the transmissions of his energy from across the dimensional divide. An automaton could not express devotion and desire, the key to his binding of her to him, the same way a free mind could. The female's mind was free. That's what made his management of her somewhat problematical. She chose to adore him, chose to give in to her desires, chose to surrender to his will.

The fact that he stoked her emotions to impel her in those directions, rewarded right thinking and behavior with delirious, addictive, virtually irresistible pleasure, didn't change the fact that she had made a conscious decision to surrender to him. The workings of his seed in her, of which he had now supplied her with copious amounts, and which was now integrated with her every cell, opened her receptors to his energy, accentuated her physical need for it. If her will was strong enough, if she could muster supreme inner strength, she could oppose him, for a while at least, but he did not intend to give her any immediate, direct reason to do so. His subversion of her personality would be gradual, almost imperceptible, until she would hardly remember anything else more important in her life than him.

The dream man gave Kelly a caress of her face to calm her and to reassure her he meant no harm to her. He would tolerate her affection for others. In fact, her emotional needs were to be left untrammeled. The more she depended on her emotional side, the easier it would be to maintain and strengthen their psychic bond.

Raijamoon cut a six inch long strip of duct tape from the roll and, placing the roll and scissors on the floor, presented the strip of silvery material to the woman's lips. He did not want her to be tempted to cry out any warning to her friend, although he doubted she was capable of doing so in her current state. More importantly, he wanted her to be totally immersed in her role as an observer of events. That was why he had positioned her so she could witness her friend's subjugation. She needed to know the extent of his powers, what he could do. She needed to see the contrast between her relationship with him, how he dominated and controlled her, with how he would assume control of her pretty, blond haired friend.

After silencing the still woozy woman, Raijamoon returned the tape and the scissors to their storage places. He took up a position in the living room out of the direct vision of anyone coming in the door. Adele would see her bound and gagged friend first, and then him.

A car door slammed outside, and a few seconds later, Kelly heard the thud of heavy soled shoes striking the wooden steps and then the porch. Adele never used the door bell. She usually knocked on the door as a courtesy and then walked right in. Kelly never kept her door locked in the daytime. There was no reason to.

Three sharp reports of a small fist striking the door echoed through the house. "Kelllllleeeee!" a pleasant, lyrical, woman's voice called out. Kelly saw the handle to the door turn and then it opened.

"Ke-el...." the voice began to yell as a woman's body came through the door frame. Adele was dressed in tight, navy blue, denim jeans, high, sparkly sandals that tied over her feet in large, sky blue bows, a baby blue, cashmere sweater that had a deep 'V' neck which left exposed the inner sides of her large, round breasts and their serious cleavage, and a pea green, fall jacket, left open, with a brass zipper and yellow piping around the collar and over the pockets. Her hair was loose and short, a blond shag. Her face was, as usual, perfectly made up, with dark lines over her eyes, mascaraed eyelashes, a medium blue eye shadow and bright red lips. She wore large, bright, diamond, post earrings, a present from an executive over at Delran Corporation. The torrid romance had ended after about six weeks when the man had returned to his wife, but Adele had been happy to keep the diamonds. "They're a girl's best friend," she had told Kelly jokingly. She wore them almost all the time now as a sort of trophy.

Adele had a large, flat, round object in her left hand inside a bakery bag and a plastic grocery style bag dangling over her wrist of the same arm. In her other hand, she carried a long necked bottle of a golden hued wine. The bottle had little drops of condensation on it, indicating it had been chilled. Adele's large red and gold pocketbook, without which she went nowhere, was dangling on her right wrist.

Adele had halted in the middle of her usual ceremonial announcement of her presence. What she saw before her eyes she could barely credence. Her friend was kneeling naked on the floor. She had a broad strip of silver tape across her mouth. Her knees were spread wide and her arms were pulled behind her back. Although Adele's mind screamed, "Danger! Danger! Danger!" she could not resist the impulse to come all the way into the house and take a closer look at her friend's predicament. "Oh, god, Kelly!" she exclaimed. "What's happened to you? Are you okay? What's going on?"

The pretty woman was acting oblivious of the fact that the woman was gagged and only half realized her questions would have to remain, at least temporarily, rhetorical.

She was three steps into the house, her shoes clacking on the hardwood floor, when she sensed something over to her right. She looked and her face fell. There was a tall, well built, Latino looking man with long, black hair down to his shoulders standing there, staring at her. He was naked too. He was broad chested and fit. He looked old to Adele, who was after all, all of 23. He was obviously strong and he had a determined, fearsome look on his face. "Oh!" was all Adele was able to say.

Raijamoon took a moment to appraise his familiar's pretty, young co-worker. When she peered into his eyes, he struck. A signal of mind numbing power arced across the room invisibly and into Adele's head. She froze in her tracks.

Her thoughts became scrambled. She looked like she was trying to say something and had forgotten what it was. Her body conveyed a state of indecision as to whether to take a step away from or towards the man. Her hands held her packages out in front of her foolishly. She managed to eek out two small syllables of sound, "Ah...Ah...," when Raijamoon transmitted another strong surge of his energy towards her. Her mien changed from one of indecision and confusion to simple disbelief.

Kelly witnessed her friend's stupification with sorrow and astonishment. The man hadn't touched her at all! He had stopped her in her tracks as if he had shot a bolt of lightning into her. Kelly's mind was still dazed with the aftereffects of her long oral tryst with her strange, silent lover, but she was still very conscious of what was going on around her. The dream man had captured her friend effortlessly. She had grown used to the idea of his ability to control her, to infuse her with his will, but the thought that he could do the same to other people was a terrible revelation. She looked over at him fearfully. Who was he? What did he want from them? What was he going to do to her friend? Was he going to reduce her to a state of eager subservience like he had her? But he had never used his powers to paralyze her. There was something different about his treatment of the other woman.

He slowly stepped over to Adele, keeping her locked in his gaze. As he walked behind her to the door, her body swiveled to keep him in her sights. She was still holding her packages out like some kind of offering to him. When he had closed and locked the door, he took the paper bag containing the quiche and the bottle of wine from her hands. He placed them on the coffee table in front of the dark brown, cloth couch. He then relieved the startled looking young woman of the bag that contained the salad and her pocketbook. He placed them on the coffee table as well.

Adele was watching the man's hands as he removed her burdens from her grasp as though they were strange, pre-hensile claws. When he turned to her again, her eyes locked back into his and she licked her lips nervously. She looked at him, a fearful inquisitiveness on her face. "Ga…" was all she was able to say. The sound was not the precursor to any full word the young woman could think of, it was just the only sound she could get out of her mouth.

Kelly watched as the man took his hand and stroked the side of Adele's face. Her big, blue eyes widened and her mouth formed a circle as if she was recording the fact that the man had inserted something into her head. "Ga…" she said again, softly.

The man circled behind the tall, blond woman. This time, she stayed in place. She was facing Kelly and she looked at her quizzically, as if seeking an explanation. The man took the lapels of her light, green, fashionable jacket and drew it back over her shoulders and down her arms. After placing it over one of the tall backed, plush chairs Kelly had gotten at the auction, he stepped back from her. He took his time in admiring her form. Adele's breasts pushed her tight sweater out brashly. Her hips were slender but her slim torso managed to curve inwards just enough above them to give her a delicate, distinctively feminine look. Her face was a little long to be called perfect, but her features were spread across her face pleasingly, with a thin, well proportioned nose, fleshy lips and remarkable eyes.

Kelly watched as her dream lover assessed the girl's hands, taking them up one by one. Adele was a manicure junkie and had had her longish nails colored with a blue lacquer interspersed with tiny, gold designs meant to represent stars. Her toe nails were polished similarly and were prominently displayed in her open toed sandals. The fact that it was getting cold out did not deter Adele from showing off her pretty, slim feet and the fine decorations on their ends. It had cost almost a week's wages and she would be damned if she was going to put shoes over them until they were all chipped and faded.

The man placed his right hand on Adele's head again and this time she winced slightly. Her gaze flitted from Kelly, to the man, to Kelly and then back again, as if something had happened to her. When Kelly's dream man stepped back from her, Adele licked her lips nervously. She had a grim determination on her face and her eyes were slightly teary. And then, moving suddenly as if she had made some decision, she crossed her wrists in front of her waist and lifted her soft, pretty, blue sweater up over her breasts, over her head and then down her arms and off.

Adele handed the sweater to the man. She was wearing a lacy, white bra that covered her breasts well over her nipples. The lace was thick and delicate and hid her teats, although it thinned out as it projected about an inch and a half over the top arc of her areolas. Adele hesitated for just a second and then reached behind her with both hands and unclipped the delicate bra. She curled her shoulders and let the straps fall forward over her arms, freeing her heavy, round, large breasts. Kelly had been after her for a while to start wearing more supportive bras. "You're not going to be 23 all your life, you know," she had warned her. But Adele was Adele and she would rather risk a little sag later on for the pretty presentation her more stylish lingerie made. "You never know," she always answered Kelly when they discussed it. She was, of course referring to the always hoped for opportunity to delight a newly found, handsome, wealthy lover.

Adele's breasts were admirable in their fullness and shape. Her nipples were long and thick and her areolas were wide and dark on her pale skin. The long and expansive, but firm, fleshy orbs swayed slightly as they dropped from their confinement. Adele handed the bra to the man and immediately started to undo the thin gold belt she wore with her jeans.

When it was undone, she looked at the man and seemed to think for a second. Before proceeding further in removing the rest of her clothes, she crouched down and removed her sandals one by one. She tossed them to the side of the room and then stood up and unfastened the button that held the waist of her jeans together. She quickly lowered the zipper and then put her hands on her hips. The jeans were very tight and she had to shimmy her hips, as slender as they were, to get the jeans to descend to her thighs and then below her knees. She had grabbed the elastic band of her slim, maroon thong at the same time and it worked its way down her legs together with the denim slacks. When the pants were below her knees, she bent over and carefully stepped out of one leg and then the other, almost losing her balance as she tugged them over her feet. She handed the commingled blue jeans and underwear to the visitor and gave him a small smile of accomplishment which quickly changed back to a confused, apprehensive look.

Raijamoon looked on with admiration and lust at the beautiful, young woman's body. Her breasts delighted him although he still had not figured out why the human male mind placed such emphasis on them. It was undeniable that it did and he had felt a pulling in his loins whenever he had touched or looked on the pleasing, round breasts of his familiar. He reached his hands out now and cupped the ends of Adele's heavy mounds. He had edged himself closer to the dazed woman and he could feel the heat of her body next to him. She could feel his too, and he used his pores to let a glow of his essence flow between them. The blond woman's lips pursed and she shifted on her bare feet. When she felt him massage her more than ample orbs, she gave a little moan.

The bound and imprisoned Kelly watched as her lover seduced her friend. She had a view of his broad, muscled back and his bulk obscured her vision of her friend's now naked body. She could feel his body's radiation of lust from where she knelt and it sent a tremor through her, making her pussy tingle with incipient need. She saw her friend's delicate, long fingered, blue tipped hands rest on her dream lover's hips and their bodies move even closer. Adele tilted her head back and raised her lips. Her mouth joined with that of the large, well built, dark skinned man. They kissed.

Kelly immediately felt a surge of lust in her loins. She writhed her bound hands behind her and moaned behind her taped lips. Seeing her friend kiss her lover was compellingly erotic. She knew she should be fearful for her friend's fate and part of her felt jealous of his attentions to this other woman, but the room was flooded with the man's psychic discharge and she felt it wash over her, driving her passions.

She watched as Adele's long arms circled her lover's back, grabbing on to him intently. The pale skin of her graceful arms was in sharp contract to his tawny skin and his broad, firm muscles. The blond girl moaned, rubbing her body against the man who had pierced her mind. The man turned their bodies so Kelly had a side view of them. She could see their locked lips. Adele had her eyes closed as she consumed the man's mouth with hers. Kelly had never seen her friend naked and she could not help but admire her lithe, attractive form, the pale beauties that were her breasts, her firm, taut rear.

Raijamoon had turned his body so his bound and gagged familiar could get a better view of the enthrallment of her friend. He was actually surprised at how easy it was to make the woman succumb. He had established a firm presence in her mind and even as they kissed, he was transforming it, changing the overwhelmed young woman's idea of reality and of herself. He could sense the sexual energies of his familiar building behind him. He was drawing strength from the flood of need flowing from both women.

The man took his hands and pressed them on Adele's slight, round shoulders. They broke their passionate kiss and the woman's eyes widened even as she began to sink to her knees. Kelly could see there was still a part of her consciousness that was confused and upset at what the man was doing to her. Her mind cried out for her friend even as her body exhilarated in the strong waves of passion that filled the room. When the dazed, blond beauty reached her knees and saw his rampant cock in front of her, she frowned and a tear came to her eye as if she realized that the moment she put her mouth on it, knowing full well that she would, something terrible was going to happen to her. As if entranced, she reached her hands out and stroked the man's powerful thighs. The contact with his skin sent a shiver through her. A hunger came across her face. She closed her eyes as if entering a state of bliss and eased her plump, red lips over the head of the strange, enthralling man's cock.

At first, Adele seemed to freeze as the powers of the man seeped into her lips and tongue. She uttered a deep, soulful sigh. Then, slowly, as if testing the hard wand of flesh for its flavor, she tightened her lips around the stiff pole and inhaled it fully into her mouth.

Kelly watched, her gaze cemented on the erotic tableau before her, as her friend serviced the dream man's cock. The blond woman's hands were circled around the base of his sex. Her eyes were clamped shut and Kelly could see the movements of her jaw and cheeks reflecting her energetic servicing of the man's rampant wand. Kelly's lusts were over boiling as she yearned for the feel of the man's flesh across her own lips. A part of her was shamed at her pleasure at watching the man fill the young, blond girl's mouth with his thick manhood. His hands were on her head, intertwined with her short, mop like hair. His back was arched and his neck was bent back. He had closed his eyes so as to better relish the pleasure the new mouth and lips were giving him. His body had sagged slightly and his knees were bent. Adele was pumping her head over his manhood frantically now, moaning her lust. Kelly saw the man's body stiffen and sensed his arousal and imminent explosion of lust in every pore of her body.

Adele moaned loudly when the man came. Kelly came too, her pussy sending deep convulsions of pleasure to her body.

Raijamoon sent out intense waves of pleasure to the bound woman. He wanted her to share complicity with her friend's transformation. He transmitted the exquisite pleasures of his own orgasm to her. To the woman on her knees in front of him, he sent his will, his desires. As he came, his fluids flowed into her body, initiating a bond she could never break.

Adele's body shuddered in post orgasmic bliss. She held the man's meat in her mouth as she panted for breath, unable to break the connection without her overlord's consent. Finally, he released her and brought her to her feet. Her face registered her confusion about what had just happened to her. Raijamoon gently led her to the bedroom. He would need to complete his mastery over and transformation of his new servant.

Kelly's heart sank as the couple walked past her into the bedroom. She watched in the bedroom mirror as the man led her friend onto the bed, guided her to her back, spread her thighs and entered her. The young blond woman gave out a loud moan, "Ahhhhhhhhh!" and circled her long legs and delicate arms around him. Within seconds they were engaged in a frantic, energized fuck. The man had ceased sending the energy of his lust to Kelly and she felt empty, deserted. She was shamed at how she had orgasmed while her friend was being enslaved. In some way, it made her feel responsible for the poor girl's fate. What would he do with her, she asked herself frantically. Would he make her a highly sexed zombie to serve his will? Did he consider the younger, prettier, blond girl as a more suitable repository for his lust than her? What would happen if he shifted his compelling, sexual attentions away from her? For although he was fucking her friend, her loins still burned with desire for him, her lips yearned to caress him.

Kelly knelt helpless in her bonds as the man pummeled the flesh of the impassioned, young, blond woman. She watched in the mirror, obsessed, as their bodies seemed to consume each other. She saw Adele shake and quiver with prolonged, intense, sexual satisfaction, watched the man's body tense and heard him groan as he pumped his essence into her. They shifted positions several times. Adele no longer seemed the entranced automaton who had sucked the man's cock in the living room. She was growing increasingly vocal and energetic in response to the man's attentions. "Oh god! Oh god! Oh god!" she heard her yell as she came again, bent over on her knees, the man entering her from behind. And when he caressed her loins with his lips, she kept shouting out, "Yes! Yes! Yes!" At one point, she began to take the initiative, gleefully pushing the man over and delving her mouth between his thighs. "Gimme that cock!" she said lustfully as her lips descended on his pole.

Finally, the pair of lovers had exhausted their forces. Lying together intertwined, they fell asleep on the bed. Kelly, despondent at what she had heard and seen, bent her head and cried.

CHAPTER SEVEN

It was about an hour later that Kelly heard bodies stirring in the bedroom. She thought she heard her young friend giggle, but discounted that as impossible. She was surprised when she saw the naked body of the young, blond woman scooting by. "I've got to pee!" she announced in a gleeful voice. She padded into the bathroom and Kelly soon heard her water spilling into the bowl. She turned to her left and saw the man standing in the bedroom doorway. He was looking at her intently. Kelly felt a surge of hunger for him and, at the same time, a wave of despondency flow through her. Would she now learn her fate? The toilet flushed, she heard water running, and then Adele came scurrying back out of the bathroom. She pressed her body up to the man's and, standing on her bare toes, gave him a soulful kiss.

"Ooooooo, baby," she said when their lips parted. "You're too much." She looked down at the disconsolate Kelly. A soft, caring look came over her face. She bent over, her large, soft breasts swaying out from her body, and caressed Kelly's tearstained cheek, saying sweetly, "You're so lucky, honey." Kelly looked back at her, unsure what reaction she should have to this unusual statement. "I'm starving," Adele then added merrily as she brought herself back to full height. "I'm gonna heat up the quiche."

The happy, blond girl dashed into the living room and returned with the food she had brought. She swept unheedingly past the kneeling, naked, bound and gagged Kelly and went into the kitchen. A few seconds later, Kelly heard the microwave spring to life.

For a moment, Kelly felt like she had entered some bizarre, new world. Didn't her friend see her all trussed up and naked, tied to a pipe in the hallway of her own house? Hadn't the dream man just forced his will on the pretty blond girl and enslaved her? What was going on? Was she mad?

Raijamoon saw the frantic confusion on the kneeling woman's face. She was looking up at him dolefully. She was a vision of delight to him. Her naked breasts pointed up to him invitingly, her pretty, frantic eyes begged him for relief. Her graceful, well toned, widespread thighs and her open sex made her seem frail and vulnerable. Affixed to the pole, her pretty lips hidden by the silencing, silvery tape, her arms and ankles crossed and bound together behind her, she was helpless, utterly dependant on him and defenseless against his will.

He sensed her dismay and uncertainty. He needed to reassure her. He crouched in front of the auburn haired, distraught female and placed his hands on her head. He sent waves of comfort and affection to her through them. He shifted his hands and stroked the pleasure center of her mind as he caressed her sensuous, bare breasts lovingly. He felt the bound woman's body relax, her mind calm as his energy flowed through her. He stoked her need for him and felt the strength of their bond reassert itself in her. He dropped his hand to the center of her widespread thighs and stroked her labial lips until she was panting and had lubricated. He leaned over and suckled the stiffened teats of her breasts until the woman moaned, twisting her pinioned arms behind her.

In the meantime, Adele continued the preparations for their repast. Through her mind fogging reverie at her lover's attentions, Kelly heard Adele exclaim, "Okay, come and get it!"

The dream man untied his familiar from the pipe and released her wrists from her ankles. Kelly groaned as she was raised to her feet. Her muscles had stiffened during her long confinement. Unsteady, dizzy from the man's stimulation of her lusts, she allowed herself to be led into the kitchen. The square, wooden table had been set for two. The steaming, yellow quiche was sitting in the middle of the finely polished, dark brown table, together with a large bowl of green, fluffy salad. Two of Kelly's round, long stemmed wine glasses sat next to yellow, woven, cloth place mats and matching folded napkins. There was silverware and salt and pepper and salad dressing, all set in convenient reach for the prospective diners. Adele smiled as she saw the dazed and sexually excited Kelly being led into the room.

"It's a good thing I didn't get the Swiss cheese and ham quiche," she said. "Ramón doesn't eat meat."

Kelly looked at her friend. "How did she know his name?" she asked herself incredulously. She looked at her lover. "Was that his name? Ramón?" Her lover smiled and sent a wave of pleasure to her. Kelly moaned and her knees sagged.

Adele ignored Kelly's display of lust. "I've got a place for you over here, honey," she said, her natural, eager smile still on her face. The young, blond woman had set the plates next to each other, separated by the corner of the table. She had taken the little, plush, deep orange rug Kelly kept in front of the sink to soak up spilled water and had placed it on the floor between the two settings. She took Kelly's other arm and helped Ramón guide her to it.

"That should be nice and comfy, honey," Adele told her concernedly as Kelly sank her knees onto it. "Just rock back on your heels and you should be all right."

Kelly's back was to the kitchen window. The early afternoon sun cast a shadow in front of her of her restrained form. The man she now knew was called Ramón sat to her left. She was perched at the corner. He reached down and caressed her left breast, sending a tingle of pleasure and a wave of calmness to the upset woman.

Kelly had been trying to come to mental terms with the vision of her naked friend fluttering around the kitchen, her large breasts swaying and jumping as she moved. If Adele was mind controlled, she sure didn't look it. She had all the mannerisms and quirks of the friend she had known and worked with for a year and a half. Nothing was unusual about her except for her incongruous acceptance of Kelly's plight. "Maybe I am mad," Kelly thought, just before she felt Ramón's hand give her breast another gentle squeeze and passed a warm flow of his energy to her. Her concerns faded as she enjoyed the dream man's comforting gesture.

Adele stood next to Kelly with the golden yellow wine bottle in her left hand. She had one of Kelly's plastic cork screws in her other, the kind that come apart into two pieces and then reassemble to make a screw with a tiny handle. She had peeled away the plastic covering at the top of the bottle and was struggling to turn the screw into the cork. Kelly wanted to tell her about the larger, more efficient cork screw she had in the bottom drawer to the left of the sink but then chided herself for succumbing to the deceiving naturalness of the setting: two young women and a dark, handsome man about to enjoy a Sunday brunch. Quiche, salad, a nice wine, what could be more normal? Except the man is some kind of dream man or alien, one of the women is tied up, kneeling on the floor, naked, with a gag over her mouth and the other woman, who is also naked, has developed some kind of psychosis which makes her act as if this scene was not eminently unusual.

And then Kelly's mind paused. She had described the dream man as an alien. Was there something to that? It was as good an explanation as any. She decided she would have to mull that possibility over in her mind during one of her infrequent bouts of sanity. She looked at Ramón, as she now knew he should be called. He was looking at her. Did he really know what she was thinking? If she worked out that he was an alien and she was right, would she get some kind of reward for being so smart? Or would she be punished? Just the thought of being punished again by the man made her cringe. The man reached his hand out for her head and a well of panic and fear rose up in her. But when he touched her, a warm, comforting force was released that was so strong it almost made her faint.

Meanwhile, Adele was having problems with the cork. "Damn this thing!" she said in her sweet, Southern voice. Kelly turned her head to see Adele tugging and pulling at the cork. All of a sudden, the God of Wine decided to allow them to partake of his essence and the cork slid quickly out. "Pop!" it went. Adele's large breasts shook as her right hand pulled the cork free. A splash of wine emerged from the now open top and spilled over her bare chest, rolling down the crevasse between her mammaries. "Oooou!" she yelled out, giggling. She looked down at herself, noting the dribble of wine rolling down her cleavage. "Oh, well," she said, looking up and smiling, "waste not want not!"

The happy woman scurried over to Ramón still holding the wine bottle and the now impaled cork in her hands and, arching her back, leaned over and presented herself to him. She used the heels of her hands to spread her breasts apart. "Would you like to sample the wine?" she asked merrily. Ramón looked at her with what might be called amusement. He saw the line of liquid slowly descending between the woman's pretty breasts. "Why not," he thought and he leaned his head forward and plunged his face into the deep valley. He dragged his tongue its length while massaging the tips of the naked woman's breasts with his hands.

Adele's eyes rolled back and she entered a mild swoon. "Ohhhhhhhh!" she moaned. He was sending his energy through her, a message of intense pleasure. Her adjustment to the alignments of her brain had gone better than he ever would have thought. He wanted to reward her. When he released her breasts, Adele's body swayed and she took a small step backwards. "Oh, my," she said dreamily. It took her a moment to recover her equilibrium, but then she smiled at the man and proceeded to pour several inches of the golden hued liquid into his rounded wine glass. She stepped around the kneeling Kelly and poured some into her own. She sat in her chair and brought the glass into the air. "First one today," she said, grinning, and she took a deep sip.

Ramón mulled over the wonderful flavor of the liquid. He picked up his glass to sample some more. He noted the intoxicating nature of the beverage. He made a note not to consume too much. But the mouthful he swallowed brought a myriad of flavors to his palate. He did not know how to describe them; they were combined in both subtle and not so subtle degrees. It was another amazing discovery for him. He smiled at the pretty, blond woman.

Adele started to slice the quiche. "I got the wine at Caravaggio's. The old man behind the counter said it was good," she said as she lifted a steaming slice and put it on Ramón's plate. "You know the place, Kelly, don't you? Well, if I got a nickel discount for every time he looked at my tits, I would have gotten it for free." She was concentrating on her task of slicing and serving the quiche and did not look at the kneeling, naked woman or wait for a response.

"They were out of the ham and cheese quiches. It's a good thing, too, for Ramón here. This is cheddar and broccoli." She put a piece on her own plate. Ramón watched her as she took her fork and cut into it. He followed suit and when he put the forkful of food into his mouth, was immediately lost in the wonderful, warm flavor.

"Don't forget to have some salad," Adele said as she scooped some out of the bowl for herself. "Try the mustard vinaigrette dressing, it's real good. Kelly turned me on to it. I was always one of those creamy dressing types, with all those calories," she said, the last phrase in a whispery, conspiratorial voice. "But I like this stuff."

One of the reasons Kelly liked to have lunch with Adele is that she rarely really had anything to say. Adele's mouth went a mile a minute and her conversation wandered aimlessly from subject to subject without pause. Kelly could let her mind drift and put her worries away for a while. Her mind began to drift now as she took in the younger woman's easy to listen to tones.

"And, its low cal, too," Adele continued. "I mean it's not one of those diet things, but it's real good for you. I hate that diet stuff. It never really tastes right. I don't drink diet sodas or use Splenda or any of those things. In fact, I heard that Splenda....." She had turned to look at Ramón, who was sniffing at the open bottle of salad dressing and caught the kneeling, naked, Kelly from the corner of her eye. "Oh!" she exclaimed. "I'm being so rude!" She put a dramatic emphasis on that last word. She pushed back her chair and knelt next to her friend. "I forgot all about you, honey," she said to the astonished Kelly. "Let's get this silly thing off of you," she continued, referring to the woman's shiny, silver gag. Adele looked up at Ramón as if to see if it was okay and then began to tug the edge of the tape free from Kelly's cheek. "I have to do this careful, honey. I don't want to hurt you," she said.

The naked blond girl leaned against Kelly's body as she slowly tugged the tape free. Kelly was embarrassed at the contact as the blond woman's bare breasts rubbed against hers. It didn't seem to phase Adele one bit. Kelly's eyes watered with tears as she realized her friend would never help her escape. She felt, suddenly, as if she was trapped in some kind of nightmare. It was like the Mad Hatter's tea party and she was Alice. She knew she could never escape from the man on her own accord. Her need for him, like some highly addictive narcotic, bound her to him too strongly. But if she had help, someone who would rescue her and find some kind of cure for her madness, that was something else. Maybe a day or two away from the man would make his spell wear off. Clearly, though, Adele would not be the one to free her from his clutches.

When Adele had finally exposed her friend's taped mouth, she looked at Kelly's upper lip. "Oh, it's all red and splotchy!" she said. She was obviously distressed. She looked up at Kelly's eyes and, misinterpreting the source of her tears, said solicitously, "Don't worry, Kelly, I'll get you something for it." She looked up at Ramón with a mild scowl on her face and said somewhat petulantly, "Men really don't know anything, do they?" She turned back to Kelly and gave her an affectionate kiss. "You'll be okay," she said, smiling.

Kelly was startled by the woman's kiss. Not that they hadn't kissed before. They often pecked at each other as they parted or as a gesture of greeting. But this was something different. Adele's mouth had been open. Her lips had been soft, pliant. She held them against Kelly's just long enough so the other woman received an almost imperceptible taste of her hot breath. She had placed her hands on the sides of Kelly's head, mooshing them in her soft hair. When their lips separated, Adele smiled at her friend tenderly and then got up and resumed her seat.

Kelly was comforted somewhat by her friend's physical demonstration of affection, but was calmed even more by the hand of her keeper as he stroked her head several times, giving off strong messages of well being to her. It actually made her a little dizzy. "I'll be all right," she thought as the hand left her head. "Everything will work out."

During the meal, Adele fed herself and Kelly alternatively. She would turn and give Kelly a small forkful of quiche or a leaf of lettuce, holding her other hand under it so nothing would spill on the floor. Her large, naked breasts swayed from her torso as she leaned over and presented the food laden fork to the kneeling and bound woman's lips. She even gave her some of the wine to drink, although she consumed most of the two glasses she poured herself. She continued, uninterrupted, her soliloquy. She told Kelly who she had met up with on Friday night, how some girl tore her dress in the lady's room, about the guys they met and why they were idiots. She apologized for not calling on Saturday since she got really wasted the night before and almost, mind you, almost, let this guy talk her into going to a motel with him, and then she had to go see her cousin Melody so she could see her other cousin, Whitney's, baby, how cute it was and why she would never want one. And so on. She looked at Kelly happily as she prattled and at Ramón, when telling him something Kelly and she had done together or said to each other at this or that occasion.

Kelly was happy to receive her first real sustenance since Friday. She chewed it slowly and leisurely. The wine gave her a warm, comfortable feeling and she realized that the alcohol was probably affecting some of the same receptors as the energy the man sent her from time to time. He continued to caress her and stroke her throughout the meal. He was obviously enjoying his repast, tilting his head back each time he took a sip of wine, holding it in his mouth and savoring its flavor. Each time, he would smile and give Kelly a little stroke as if to share his pleasure.

While he worked on his second piece of quiche, Kelly began to realize that the man's treatment of her was sort of like a favorite pet, a pet you could fuck and which would suck your cock. Was it his intent to domesticate her? And what would Adele's role be, caretaker? And how long could they maintain their little idyll before the landlord came to ask for the rent? Would the dream man or alien or whatever he was mind zap him too? And the Sheriff's Department when they eventually came to investigate, the state police, the Army, the United Nations? But each time Kelly had started questioning what was really happening, the man would caress her and send her such a pleasant, deep seated sense of contentment she would lose her train of thought and have to start all over again after she had regained her sense of place and time.

For a while, she watched her friend, amazed at how she just continued on as if there was nothing abnormal about her kneeling there so naked and silent, her arms tied behind her back. The man had obviously altered her mind so that she accepted her own and Kelly's domination without a single pang of conscience or rebellion. She actually looked happier than Kelly had seen her lately. She had been worried about her inability to meet 'the right guy', whether she drank too much, money, her folks wanting to know when she was going to get married, settle down, have a family. Now she looked and sounded as carefree as a bird, oblivious to the changes the man had made. Why hadn't the man done that to her?

Why did she have to be tormented, Kelly asked herself, with her struggle between her desire to be a free, independent, successful woman and the need to submit to the man's irresistible will and lust. Wouldn't it be better, if you had to be a slave, to be a slave and not know it, like Adele? Or if you could believe all of your actions and desires were of your own free will, even if they weren't?

The end of the meal was signaled when the man dropped his utensils on his plate and slid his chair back from the table. Adele poured back the last drops of her second glass of wine and did the same. Kelly's stomach was warm and satisfied from the wine and the food. She leaned back on her heels, closed her eyes and took a deep breath. There was silence in the room for a few minutes while the three savored the after effects of their meal.

Suddenly, Kelly sensed that the eyes of the man and her friend were on her. She opened her eyes and looked at them. Adele was just smiling at her affectionately, as if she were conveying her happiness for her. The man had a deeper, more intent look in his eyes, one that Kelly well recognized. As if on his signal, her belly began to burn with desire for him. He was beckoning her, and she knew she would be unable to resist him. Her nipples grew tight and her pussy began to tingle. She felt ashamed at her lust, but her hunger for his flesh began to grow stronger and stronger. She looked up from her knees at her blond friend. She saw in Adele's eyes that she was aware of her gnawing passion and her face transmitted approval and delight. "You're so pretty," she said to her in a soft, kindly voice. She reached out and stroked her silky, long, auburn hair. She said, "You go ahead, honey, don't mind me."

Despite her friend's reassuring words, Kelly was torn by conflict between her lust and her shame. Up till now, her physical obsession with her dream man had been private, something only she and he knew about. Now Adele was obviously was aware of it too. She didn't want to display her wild lasciviousness before the younger woman who respected her and looked up to her as a kind of mentor. But the pull of the man's loins was too strong. Kelly bit her lip to silence a moan. "Why is this happening?" she thought desperately. "Why is this happening to me?"

Finally, Kelly could stand it no more. With tears streaming down her face, she edged her way over to the waiting man. He had turned his chair and his thighs were spread expectantly, proffering his cock to her. She moved off the soft rug Adele had considerately placed down for her and she felt the hard, stone tile surface of the kitchen floor on her knees. She did not have far to travel. The man's cock was not hard, but turgid, in a state of semi-erection, as if it was readying itself for her. She looked up at the man. His eyes were piercing, demanding. He placed his hands on her head and a wave of lust passed through her body. She gasped and her mind forgot all about Adele, her shame, her resistance. She moved forwards the final few inches so she could have ready access to the man's sex and then leaned over and took it between her lips.

Kelly felt like she had seized a wonderful, precious object as the man's energy radiated through her mouth. She sucked on the stiffening pole as if taking in a long, cool drink of water on a steaming, hot day. Pleasure rippled through her brain and she moaned low and long, "Mmmmmmmm!" as her bound hands writhed behind her. Slowly, she moved her head up and down, swirling her electrified tongue over and under the fat, round head. She moved closer so she could force her head down into the man's loins, bringing the tip of the hard meat to the edge of her throat. Ramón had kept his hands on her head and she could feel his energy and the sensations of his own pleasure flowing through them to her.

Suddenly, she was conscious of her young friend's warm body next to hers. She had forgotten about Adele, and now her passion was so far gone she could not muster the will to rebel at her close presence. She felt the woman's soft hand stroke her back, felt her put her lips on her skin. She pressed her body into her, rubbing her soft, round breasts against Kelly's arm. When she felt her soft hand begin to gently stroke her breasts, she moaned again. The woman was kneeling next to her, at her side, and she stroked and caressed Kelly's passion hardened breasts softly with her left hand while her right hand slid slowly and gently down her back, over her bound hands and proffered rear and under her, between her legs. When the hand found her hot, burning mons, Kelly felt her lust surge.

Ramón watched he tableau in front of him. The blond girl was pretty and he would fuck her again. It was as if he was a high priest and the pleasing blond woman was his acolyte, assisting him in making holy the vessel he had chosen. The mouth of his familiar was well trained to his needs by now and the bond he had established made their passions run a loop between them. It was like a large particle accelerator in which their lusts ran round and round, getting faster and faster, building up their energies to a critical mass.

The first time Kelly came, she gripped the man's cock tightly with her lips, unable to move until the powerful contractions of her pussy's walls began to ebb. Adele's hands seemed to know just what to do and when the long, thin, sensitive fingers of her gentle hand began to stroke the distended lips of her labia again, began to tease the hard nubbin at their apex, the bound woman quickly felt her lusts rise once more to critical proportions.

When Ramón's hard prick began to throb and spasm, jetting his cum out in powerful spurts, Kelly came again. Adele was caressing her clit with impassioned fervor and squeezing her breasts and nipples tightly. Kelly received her dream man's cum with bliss while Adele leaned her mouth next to her ear and whispered softly and slowly to her in a low, husky voice, "Ohhhh, baby, take a good, long drink. Take it all inside you."

Strangely, to Kelly, the presence of her friend's body next to hers, the fact she was displaying her manic, irresistible passions to her, seemed natural and good. She would not be alone with her obsession any more. Adele would accept them, help foster them, facilitate her surrender of her will to the dream man.

Adele helped Kelly lean back once the man's ejaculations had ceased. She was intoxicated from the effects of the man's cum. Adele took her by the shoulders and gave her a long, loving kiss, her tongue washing the inside of Kelly's mouth, lingering there until both women gave out low, passionate moans. Adele pulled her head back and looked earnestly into Kelly's eyes. "I'm going to take good care of you, Kelly," she said. She leaned forward and kissed her again, her hand on her auburn haired friend's breast, cupping and massaging it lovingly.

Adele then leaned back and patted Kelly on the head. "I've got to get going," she announced matter of factly. "Just leave the dishes, I'll get them when I come back." She rose to her feet and dashed into the living room. Through her haze, Kelly could hear the sounds of her friend getting dressed, especially her huffs and puffs as she pulled her tight jeans up over her hips. Her hard soled sandals made sharp clicking sounds when she returned to the kitchen.

"I need some measuring tape, honey, where do you keep it?" Adele asked innocently. Kelly looked up at her. Her heart froze. Was she permitted to speak to her friend? Would she be punished for even thinking about it? Ramón looked at her sternly and then at Adele. She seemed to recall something and then said apologetically, "Oh, sorry. I'll go look in the bedroom."

Kelly would have told her to look in the bottom drawer of the bedside table on the right. She was glad she hadn't. Unhappiness seized her as she wondered whether she would ever be able to speak to her friend again. Would she ever be allowed to resume normal human, oral, verbal communication? Or communication of any kind whatsoever?

Ramón was pleased his familiar had resisted the natural urge to answer her friend's question. He placed his hand on her shoulder and gave her a surge of pleasure as a reward. Kelly's eyes closed and she swooned. When she opened them again, Adele had returned and had a long string of paper tape in her hand. "Found it!" she announced proudly. Ramón stood away from the table and the blond woman proceeded to take his measurements. She measured his neck, his shoulders, his arms and his waist. She knelt before him and took a measurement of the top of the inside of his thigh to his ankle. When she looked up, she noticed his flaccid sex hanging in front of her. She seized it with her lips and began to suck on it hungrily. The man let her continue until his piece was long and hard and then he gently pushed her head away. Adele was out of breath and her face was flushed. "Wow!" she said. She looked over at Kelly. "Save some of that for me, honey," she said smiling. She took a deep breath and bent down to measure the man's feet. "These aren't feet," she said, "they're boats!"

The thin, shapely, blond woman rose from her knees and wrote all of the measurements on a little pad Kelly kept for taking notes by the telephone. Kelly's pocketbook was next to it. Adele rooted around in it until she found Kelly's wallet and then pulled out her credit card. She looked at Kelly. "Sorry, honey, I'm all maxed out." And then to Ramón, "I'll be a few hours. I've got a lot of stops to make. I'll bring home Chinese."

The happy, blond woman gave Kelly a little wave and then proceeded into the living room and out the door. Kelly heard her car engine roar to life and pull away.

They were alone again. It felt strange to Kelly. The house was so silent. Adele had come and gone like a whirlwind. It was odd. She had been humiliated and ashamed for her friend to see her in her naked vulnerability, had cried when she was compelled to give in to her insatiable lust and mouth her dream man to orgasm while she watched. Now that she was gone, she missed her. She had brought a light, airy presence to the house and now she was left with the foreboding, silent man who had enraptured her. Still kneeling near the end of the kitchen table where the man had left her, she nervously tested her bound wrists as she fretted about how she and the man were likely to spend the next few hours. He was standing there watching her, stroking his excited member almost idly.

Ramón was very satisfied at how well things had gone. He had spent a lot of time working on Adele's mind when he was fucking her and the results had exceeded his expectations. He had intended the blond woman become his sexual auxiliary for the female he had bonded with, but getting down on the floor and stroking the bound woman to orgasm had been the blond woman's idea.

Kelly gave a little moan when the man approached her and took her by the arm. He lifted her from the floor and led her to the bedroom. Her pussy was already watering when he laid her down and fixed her wrists to the head of the bed.

When he spread her legs, raised her knees and entered her, her body shuddered with pleasure.

* * * *

Adele didn't return until after seven o'clock. She had been gone about five hours. The man had made love to Kelly several times in the interim, each time coming in her at least twice. For a long time, after first driving her to a body wrenching orgasm, he had left her kneeling on the bed with her legs spread wide, her hands tied before her to the shiny brass headboard, her forehead pressed to the mattress, ready for continued use when he deigned to return. Her loins burned with the expectation of him. She kept her eyes closed, trying to deny her growing lust, her aching, blood filled breasts. She could hear him wandering about the house, looking into closets, opening drawers. Her whole body tingled with expectant desire, both yearning for and fearing his return. Her proffered orifices yawned with need. She was like a cannon, ready to explode. When she felt the bed behind her sink as he climbed on it, her stomach fluttered with anticipation. When he entered her from behind, and she felt the thick, hot cock spread her inner passage, her orgasm erupted instantly, as if he had pulled her trigger.

When she heard Adele's fifteen year old Mercury climb the hill outside the house, she was crouched on the man's lap on the brown couch where she had often watched TV while working on her laptop. She was facing him, her knees raised on either side of his chest, her feet on either side of his hips, and she was impaled on his manhood. After their most recent bout of lovemaking, he had brought her to the living room and started examining her laptop. She knelt on the floor, her hands bound behind her, watching. She was amazed at the speed with which he ran through her research notes and the stored versions of her various papers. She had downloaded a number of technical journals and he raced through them as well. After a long period of watching him, her need for him began to grow and she bit her lip and moaned. He messaged for her to come and be near to him and she crawled up on the couch and settled next to him on her knees. She leaned against him while he worked, absorbing his pleasurable energies through the contact between their bare skins. One thing had led to another and he had pulled her onto his lap. She had stroked him passionately with her pussy, raising and lowering herself feverishly until they both came and had then settled to rest on him as she was now. His cock, true to form, was still hard, and, after her thrilling climax, she had closed her eyes and leaned her head upon his shoulder.

For the last 20 minutes or so, the man had held her body close to him with his strong, right arm while gently and affectionately stroking her long, burnt orange hair with the other. She had remained in place, peaceful and satisfied, in a state of semi-consciousness, dozing on and off, her soft breasts pressed against his chest, her arms bound behind her, while she laconically absorbed his cock's mesmerizing energies through the walls of her soft, satisfied sex.

This time, Adele entered the house without the ceremony of an announcement. She burst through the door, her arms full of bags and packages. When she saw the lovers joined and ensconced on the couch, she came to a halt and whispered, "Sorry." She quietly carried her treasure trove of goods into the bedroom and the kitchen. She had to make three trips. When she had gone back to the car the first time, Ramón had started a gentle probing of Kelly's lush gash, moving his cock almost imperceptively with his hips. By the time Adele returned from the car with more packages, Kelly was moaning with pleasure and was responding by slowly raising and lowering herself over the man's thick, hard pole, clenching her pussy's muscles around it firmly each time she ascended, and then softening them to ease her descent.

When she returned the third time, Kelly was stroking Ramón's cock enthusiastically, on the verge of her crisis. Her face was to the door and through her lustful haze saw the blond girl stop in her tracks and gaze at her and the man longingly. Adele carefully placed her packages on the floor and then sat on the edge of the easy chair that was turned to face the couch diagonally near the door. Her face was a mask of admiration and lust while she watched the lovers couple. When she started to come, Kelly moaned loudly and buried her face in Ramón's strong left shoulder, turning away from the disconcerting gaze of her blond friend, blocking from her mind the picture of her female admirer, as the warmth of the dream man's discharge flooded her womb.

As the lovers came to rest, Adele got up and sat down next to Ramón on the couch, snuggling against him. He turned his head and kissed her, a deep, passionate kiss. When their lips parted, Adele asked him hopefully in a low, saucy voice, "Got anything left for me, sailor?" Ramón signaled his assent and the blond girl got to her feet and started stripping off her clothes, throwing them around the room wildly. She eased the dazed Kelly off of the man's lap and had her kneel on the floor where she could watch. She climbed on Ramón's lap and pushed her pussy down over his still solid rod.

When she had engulfed him fully, she gave out a loud sigh, bent her head back and shook her mane of shaggy hair. "Ohhhhhh, yes!" she moaned. "I've been waiting for this for five hours. I think the front seat of my car is all wet," she said gleefully.

The lithe, young, blond woman roared to orgasm quickly and Ramón sent her a copious stream of his essence. Kelly was still stupefied from her own lovemaking, but the sight of the thin blond girl bouncing up and down on her dream man's lap, her large, pale breasts dragging along his chest, excited her. Adele was very vocal, and when she came, her screams echoed through the small room.

Adele and the man rested in their coital embrace for several minutes before either one of them stirred. Adele's pale skin melded well with the man's dark brown hue. When Adele came to life, she climbed slowly off of Ramón and gathered herself before announcing that the Chinese food was getting cold. She rushed into the kitchen and Ramón followed her, leading Kelly by her arm. There were six grocery bags on the table and Kelly knelt on the little dark orange rug Adele had placed there for her earlier and watched while the naked young woman rushed to put things away. She had bought more fruit and milk, several kinds of canned beans, a wide variety of cheeses, vegetables, nuts and whole grain cereals, among other healthy things. It was quite unlike Adele, who liked barbecue, bacon, hot dogs and potato chips. When she produced the ice cream, she lifted it and said "Ta ta! This is for after dinner."

Dinner went quickly. The seating arrangements were as before. Adele tried to show Ramón how to use the chopsticks. She was unsuccessful and so he ate with his fork. The blond girl maintained a pleasant, diverting monologue, laughing and giggling while the others ate, turning to Kelly continuously to proffer her a piece of this or a piece of that. Kelly felt like a baby bird feeding in its nest as Adele angled above her the long, flavorful lo mein noodles. She would bend her neck back, peering up hungrily at the worm like object and suck it down greedily to her friend's repeated amusement. Kelly was happy to have her second, warm, satisfying meal of the day. Adele and Ramón kept up a steady stream of caresses to her while she ate, keeping her lust on a slow burn. Although her lips were free, and Adele kept throwing rhetorical type questions at her such as "Do you remember when...?" or "Wasn't that funny that time....?" and, "Did you ever wonder....?", the contented, aroused woman was not tempted to reply. Adele served them each a single scoop of dark, rich, chocolate ice cream afterwards. Kelly watched as Ramón luxuriated in the flavor, his eyes closed, a smile on his face, as he let the cold, satisfying substance melt in his mouth.

Adele did the dishes. Before doing so, she brought Kelly to her feet and moved the orange rug close to Ramón's chair. Ramón had turned it towards Kelly expectantly. Adele guided Kelly to her knees and, while Adele cleaned up, the respected research scientist, overwhelmed with lust and pleasure, slowly suckled Ramón's cock until he released a lazy, long discharge of his hot essence into her.

The trio adjourned to the living room when Adele had finished the dishes. After placing Kelly on her knees, Adele announced she wanted to show off the goodies she had purchased. She ran into the bedroom and ran back, her pretty, large breasts swaying and jumping. There were several large, plastic bags marked "Wal-Mart" and a smaller bag with no printing on it whatsoever. Adele knelt next to Kelly and reminded her, "I told you I was going to get something for your lips." Kelly recalled gratefully her friend's solicitous concern at the irritation to her upper lip when she had eased the infernal duct tape off of her mouth earlier that day. Adele reached in the bag and produced a short thin, brown leather belt. The belt widened in the middle and a thick, long, wide plug of leather stuck out of it. Kelly's heart dropped when she realized what it was. It was a gag! Her friend had bought her a gag! She couldn't believe it. The blond girl's benign and seemingly scatter brained treatment of her suddenly seemed ominous. Her friend had revealed herself not only as an enthusiastic witness and facilitator of Kelly's captivity, but as an active accomplice, a co-conspirator in her debasement.

The distraught, bound woman moaned with dismay as Adele presented the obscene object to her like she was making some kind of offering. She looked up at the man, who was following Adele's actions with great interest. He was looking at her sternly, as if warning the young woman not to be disobedient. There was no doubt in Kelly's mind that everything Adele did was at this man's command or, at least, done consistent with his approval and in his interests. Why did he want her to feel so unhappy and degraded, she asked herself miserably. She had done everything he had wanted. She was completely in his power.

Adele presented the object to Kelly's mouth. "Come on, honey," she said almost sympathetically. "Open up and let me put this in. You don't want that nasty tape, now do you?"

Kelly pressed her lips together and started to cry. She wanted to shout out her protest at her treatment, wanted to shake her friend out of her macabre eagerness to assist the man in turning her into a sex crazed slave. But, in addition to her terror of the man whose gaze was piercing her, she knew her entreaties would be useless.

A tear escaped her right eye and rolled down her soft, pale cheek. Although she knew it was what the man wanted, what he demanded, she couldn't bring herself to voluntarily submit. Adele placed her hand on the side of Kelly's head and stroked her wavy, reddish brown hair. "Come on, Kelly," she said. "It's not so bad. I tried it on at the store. You don't want Ramón to punish you, do you?"

At this last comment Kelly felt a stab of fear go through her. No, she didn't want to be punished. Her body shivered at the mere suggestion of it. It wasn't just the intense misery she would feel, it was the unhappiness she experienced at the thought of his disappointment in her. She wanted to make the man happy. Why did he want to inflict this on her? She had been quiet; she would stay quiet.

Ramón watched his familiar struggle with herself. He regretted her unhappiness. It was important she understand her role as a completely controlled entity. Tomorrow, they would be going into the outside world. She would have to obey religiously his dictates with regard to her behavior. She had to discard entirely any idea she had any right to independent thought or action. She would make no communication with anyone without his express permission which would, once the appropriate adjustments had been made to her working life, be given sparingly, if at all, and then only when it was absolutely necessary. And so she had to be silenced now. And, like the bonds that held her arms behind her back and made her hands useless, the gag would be a forceful reminder of her isolation, her new singleness of purpose, to serve him. She was his creature now and would depend on him for everything. Only their relationship, their bond should matter to her.

Kelly saw the determination on the dream man's face. Slowly, meekly, she parted her trembling lips. She watched Adele's face as the pretty blond woman slid the thick wad of soft leather into her mouth. She looked pleased at Kelly's acquiescence. She leaned over and buckled the ends of the belt together behind her head. As she did so, her large, soft breasts pressed against Kelly's chest. Kelly could smell the aroma of the woman, a feint, flowery perfume, a hint of sweat, the earthy odor of skin. Suddenly a shocking thought occurred to her. Had the man done something to her? She and Adele had spoken many times about their aversion to girl on girl sex. "I'll never fuck anything that doesn't have a cock attached to it!" was the way Adele had put it. And yet the aroma of the other woman's body sent a quiver of pleasure through her.

When Adele pulled back, having fastened the gag securely in Kelly's mouth, she brushed away the miserable young woman's tears. Kelly was horrified at the reaction she had had to her younger friend's body. What had the man done to her? Would she now crave all female flesh, or just Adele's? Was it due to some alteration the man had made in her psyche, or was it something that had been buried deep within her, waiting to be liberated, like his use of her small, rear opening, a place he had used several times today, making her moan and cry out with pleasure as he spilled himself in it? Was the man doing it or had she done it herself, as a corollary to her newly found sexual liberation? What was happening to her?

Kelly looked up dolefully at her lord, her reason for being. As she did so, she unhappily explored the invasive presence in her mouth. She realized at once that the long, thick, hard probe of soft textured leather was, and was designed to be, reminiscent of a male member, even to its shape, which terminated in a soft, bulbous head. While she wore the infernal apparatus, she would be constantly reminded of the experience of the man's cock in her mouth.

Sucking the man's prick was an overwhelmingly passionate experience for her, the energies emanated by his tool radiating through the sensitive nerves and receptors there directly to her brain and then throughout her body. And now, as her mind recalled his manhood's shape and form, and her mouth recorded the penis-like presence, her body began to reverberate with incipient arousal. She hated herself for it. What had she become? She gave a heavy sob, which was muffled by the obstruction between her lips. She pulled futilely at the cordage around her bound hands behind her and squeezed her bare thighs together in an effort to deny her body's rebelliousness.

Raijamoon, the otherworlder, now known as Ramón, sensed the woman's unhappy reaction to the presence in her mouth. It was something he could have done, redrawn the synapses of her brain to derive lust from the offensive device. She had done it naturally and now he sent her a surge of his energy to reinforce it. He didn't like to fool directly with her mind, but it had made the connection on its own and it was an easy thing to do to amplify it. And he could lower it or raise it at will. The object would become a kind of totem to the woman, an object that had acquired a life of its own, sending wrenching pulses of pleasure to her or, alternatively, sending her into a trance like obsession with its taste and feel.

The dream man was sitting in one of the easy chairs and the women were on their knees in front of him. He leaned over and gave Kelly a comforting stroke on her head. He watched as the woman's frantic displeasure at her mouth's confinement melted away. There was no purpose of his to be served by her unhappiness.

Adele had her arm over Kelly's shoulder. She seemed pleased, too, at her friend's reaction to the sex store novelty. "It feels just like a cock, doesn't it," she asked her friend rhetorically, her voice sweet and friendly, like she had given her a new hat or a necklace to wear. "I thought so too. I nearly creamed when I put it in. I think the man at the store thought I was some kind of nut or something. And I got some other stuff too," she continued. "I'll show it to you later. I wanna get our man all dressed up first."

Merrily, Adele began to draw clothes out of the Wal-Mart bags. She tore open a package of colored men's mini briefs. She pulled out a small, dark blue pair with a white band that had small red and blue stripes around it. She handed it to Ramón who looked at it and turned it in his hands as if it was some strange, alien artifact.

"Clothes," the man thought. "What a shame to drape this superior body." He knew it was necessary. He looked at Adele as if seeking guidance on how to put it on.

The happy, blond girl looked at him teasingly. "You're going to have to put them on one leg at a time just like every other swinging dick in the world," she said. She giggled at her joke. She edged herself nearer to the man. "Here, let me give you a hand." She manipulated the soft, dark blue garment over first one foot of the man and then the other. She then pulled it up to his knees. "You're going to have to stand up, honey," she said, looking up at him.

Ramón brought himself to his feet and drew the garment up over his knees and up to his waist. He took a moment to consider its feel. There was something comforting at the way his testes and his long, thick manhood were secured together and held gently in by the material. Adele patted his now covered loins playfully with her hand. "That's quite a package you've got there," she said, a lustful, seductive look on her face. Her other hand was rubbing the back of the man's strong, muscled thigh. She spent a moment or two in reverie and then brought herself back to her task.

"Let's try on the blue jeans," she said, grabbing another bag. She produced a long pair of deep blue Levi's. "I got the tapered ones. I think they'll fit you real good."

Kelly watched, dazed and confused from her simmering lust, as Adele dressed the man bit by bit. He struggled a little with the pants and had to lean on the blond girl's shoulder to finish pulling them up. Adele had bought some colored t-shirts, and, when he tried one on, the man's chest filed it out admirably. She gave him a pair of white socks and a pair of Reeboks and he slid them on his feet. She had bought him a slim, gold chain, and she draped it around his thick neck, pressing her bare breasts against his broad chest. And there was a gold plated watch that she circled around his left wrist.

"The watch and chain were on sale, honey," she said to Kelly, reassuring her she hadn't gone hog wild with her credit card. Kelly was far gone from caring. She couldn't suppress the thought of the man's cock in her mouth. She was so energized with lust that she moaned piteously. Ramón, who had been distracted by his assumption of human habiliment, noted her discomfiture and used his energy to turn down her brain's reactions to the faux penis. He left it at a low boil.

Ramón walked across the room, testing the feel of the shoes and clothes. Adele had done a good job and they fit him comfortably. They would do for now. The cloth felt odd on his body, as if it covered it and enhanced it as well. He went into the bathroom and looked at himself in the mirror. He had, of course, no real standards to go by as to how his visage compared with other men other than through the eyes of his two thralls. The alien was in no need of self assurance on his looks. He just needed to be sure his appearance would suffice as that of an ordinary human male. It seemed to him from the pictures he had seen on the TV and the Internet that he would do just fine. He walked back into the living room.

Adele was gathering up the detritus from the fashion show. "I'll get this stuff put away," she was saying as she scooted the extra underwear and t-shirts into the bags. "There's a nice fall jacket and a sweater. We'll have to make some room in one of Kelly's dressers. I also got you some throwaway razors and some cologne. It'll make you smell real nice. Tomorrow, we can go to the men's store downtown and get you some nice shirts and a suit or two, if you think that you need them. I...."

The blond woman had been looking down while she put the items back into the bags. She looked up to see the dressed man posing in front of her. It interrupted her thoughts. "Well," she said, giving an exaggerated emphasis to her drawl, "put yourself between two slices of bread and let me eat you up! You better not let too many girls get a look at you, honey. We'll have a line outside the door."

The kneeling blond woman put her arm around Kelly's shoulder. "Watta ya think, Kelly? Doesn't he look good enough to eat?"

Kelly agreed with her friend. She was overcome with lust for him. "God help me," she thought, "I need to fuck him." The lust generated by the gag in her mouth had abated somewhat, yet her loins still burned for him. She chewed on the leather plug in frustration.

Ramón, satisfied at the women's reactions, shucked off the clothes and dropped them on the chair. He needed to reward his acolyte. She had done well. He knelt in front of the blond woman and took her mouth, pressing his lips firmly against hers. He held her large, pillowy breasts in his hands and sent her a message of pleasure through them. Adele moaned with delight and reached her hand down and placed it around his growing cock. She stroked it until it was hard. Ramón broke their kiss and, taking her shoulders in his hands, urged her to turn her back to him and then to bend over forward and place her head and arms on the floor. He rubbed his strong, sensitive hands over her long, thin, curved back and over her taut, rear globes. He directed his thick cock to her golden moss covered sheath and pressed himself inside. Adele gave a deep moan and her body shuddered.

Kelly watched, her own passions boiling, as the man plowed her friend's sex. Adele's large breasts swung back and forth under her as the man's thighs pounded against her rear. Her face grimaced and strained as he sent wave after wave of pleasure through her. "Ohhhhhhh! Ohhhhhhh! Ohhhhhhh!" she cried out as her passions built to their peak.

Kelly felt like her heart was going to break as she watched her lover spend his lusts in the other woman. She needed him desperately. She started to cry when the man's body stiffened and he emitted a heavy, deep groan from his throat. Adele's exclamations grew louder as she started to come again. She raised her head and arched her back, returning the man's thrusts with her hips. She gave one, last loud cry and then put her head back to the floor. The man slowed his hip's thrusts against her and stopped.

Ramón knew of the other woman's need. He could satisfy them both. One of the first things he had done was to make adjustments to the body he possessed. He was not a god who could make the impossible possible. He needed to work within his powers and what was permissible according to the laws of this dimension. He could affect the natural processes of his own flesh and he had increased its capacity to produce and his ability to deliver the elixir that so entranced the women. His resources were not unlimited; he could not literally fuck all day long. He could, though, come many times during the day and produced a large quantity of discharge. He had enough left over for the distressed, bound and gagged woman.

Kelly swooned when the man put his hands on her. She let him turn her until her pussy was presented between her widespread thighs, her forehead on the floor in front of her. She moaned as she felt the hard shaft slide smoothly up her lush canal. And when the man began his thrusts, her mind went blank, blocking out all else other than the stream of intense pleasure from the dream man's cock.

After he had joyfully jetted yet another load of his essence into her, Ramón let his cock languish inside his familiar's hot, happy pussy. Tonight, while she slept, his cells would continue the process of modifying hers. He rubbed her small, plump rear cheeks, sending warmth and comfort to her, deepening her mesmerized state. He had more research he wanted to do before he went to bed, although it was getting late. He rose from his knees and gave mental instructions to his blond acolyte who was still kneeling head down next to her friend, enjoying the aftermath of her fucking. He had not given her nearly as much of his fluids during the day as he had his familiar and he didn't have to. Her control was more direct and he didn't need to form as strong a bond with her to control and instruct her. But it did her good and reinforced his ability to command her to have his cum mixing with her cells, cementing her carnal need for him. Having received his message, she slowly rose to her feet. While he resumed his place on the couch in front of the laptop, she assembled the clothes and bags that were still strewn around the room and brought them into the bedroom. When she came out, she went into the kitchen. He heard the microwave give a little roar for a few minutes and, a few minutes after, she came into the room with a mug of hot, decaffeinated, orange pekoe tea.

Ramón had instilled in the young blond woman an overwhelming desire to serve and please him and had deepened and broadened her affection for her employer and friend. Except when he gave her a direct command or prohibition, he only needed to give her a nudge of guidance as to what he wanted and she would realize on her own how best to serve him. Her mind had not been harmed in any way, so she could think independently and creatively as to what might please him. Adele had thought about the tea all on her own. She had bought the gag all on her own. She would cooperate in everything he wanted and she would bring love and affection to his familiar, caring for her, making her adjustments easier. He would not be able to devote as much attention to the female he had enthralled in the days ahead. She would need her friend to cope with that.

The man had not really enslaved Adele. She was more a sort of devotee. He just made her want the things he wanted her to want and made her perfectly comfortable in doing so. When she put the tea down on the coffee table, she smiled at him. He had brought her perfect joy, a purpose in life. She wouldn't give a thought to where he came from, what his purpose was or why she found such pleasure in serving him. She knew Kelly was important to him, and she was clearly overjoyed over the liberation of her hidden feelings about her friend. She had watched the older woman work so hard and worry so much that something inside her had always wanted to just reach out and comfort her.

He had let Adele feel his caring affection for her friend and know that he would never harm her. She was aware he needed to use her for some important purpose and that sometimes he would need to make her friend unhappy. And, from time to time, she would have to do it too. She had done it tonight. Kelly was so joyful when she fucked him and when she took his cock in her mouth, that it would more than balance out in the blond girl's mind. Everything would be accepted as being for the greater good. The blond woman would perform her tasks happily and without regret.

Having brought her lord his tea, Adele knelt down next to her dear friend. Kelly was still bent over, luxuriating in the echoes of her orgasm. She could feel the man's seed as it merged with her, giving her a warm and pleasant feeling. It took her a moment to notice Adele was softly whispering her name and rubbing her back gently with her small, soft hand.

"Come on Kelly," she said sweetly. "I'm going to give you a bath."

Kelly docilely let the younger woman bring her to her feet. She followed as she led her into the bathroom. There was a large tub there she hardly ever used. She was always in too much of a hurry. The idea sounded nice now as she watched the hot water fill it. It was an old style tub with old fashioned, brass handles near the single spigot. It sat on gnarly, club feet and was a dark cream, almost beige color. Adele knelt next to the tub while it filled, testing the water. When she was satisfied it was perfect, she rose and, taking Kelly by the shoulders, turned her around. She loosened the rope around her wrists. Kelly felt joyful that her wrists were unbound. It was just so nice to see them and to watch them move that she didn't object when Adele tied them together again in front of her. Adele looked at her and said, "Sorry, honey, Ramón prefers that you be kept tied up."

The blond girl helped Kelly step over the lip of the tub. The water was hot and Kelly placed first one foot and then the other gingerly into it. She took a moment to acclimatize herself and then slowly lowered her bottom with Adele holding her hands for support, until she felt the hot surface of the water lick at her buttocks. She waited a moment or two and then lowered herself the rest of the way, sighing at the soothing, comforting heat.

The hot water drove Kelly into a dreamy, comfortable state. She sighed from behind her gag as her whole body relaxed. Adele tied her wrists off to a towel rack above her head. She let her hands hang there listlessly. It didn't matter.

Nothing mattered except the pleasant, warm feelings shooting through her body. Even the gag in her mouth didn't matter. Her dream man had somehow lowered its intensity so it was now no more than a comforting reminder of his presence in her body.

"I'm gonna let you soak for a while," Adele told her softly. "Then I'm going to wash you and let you soak some more."

True to her word, and unlike her essential nature, Adele waited silently, kneeling by the tub for about ten minutes while Kelly lay absorbing the soothing sensations of the water. She then waked her from her reverie and, untying her wrists from the towel rack, had her stand. There was a rubber hose with a spray attachment and Adele connected it to the faucet. She then let the hot water pour all over her friend's beautiful body. "You're just gorgeous, honey," she told her. She had soaped up a big, soft sponge and was softly rubbing foam all over Kelly's body. "You were just made for fucking, girl," she said, sweetly. "I've been telling you that all along. I don't think that you have to worry about that any more. You're going to get plenty of it from now on."

"No," Kelly thought lazily as she enjoyed the ministrations of her friend. "That's one thing I don't have to worry about. I'll get plenty of fucking." Her teeth and tongue massaged the simulated penis in her mouth. Each time she pressed on it, it sent a mild message of pleasure to her brain. "And sucking, too," she added. That was okay with her. Everything was okay with her. What was that she had thought earlier? "Everything will work out." That was it. Lost in her reverie, Kelly believed it. She would leave everything to the dream man. She had never lived as intently or as joyfully as she had these past two days. He knew what she needed. She didn't have to think about it any more, and if he thought she needed to be tied up and gagged or whatever else, then that's what would happen.

The young, blond woman's hands were working Kelly's flesh gently and diligently, cleaning every crevice and hole.

Kelly sighed and closed her eyes when the woman leaned over and took one of her teats in her mouth, sucking on it softly. "And he has brought me Adele," Kelly thought mistily. When Adele shifted her loving attention to her other breast, Kelly felt an overwhelming desire to return the favor. She felt Adele's hand cupping her pussy and she remembered her shock at feeling the woman manipulating her to pleasure this morning while she had her dream lover's cock in her mouth. Her reaction seemed so silly now. She didn't think there could be anything more natural than her growing affection and desire for the deliciously formed girl. Her pussy began to tingle and she was disappointed when the soft hand left her to resume its tasks.

Adele rinsed the thick layer of sweet smelling lather off of Kelly's body with the hose and then had her kneel down back in the tub. She had her raise her torso so she could do her long, reddish brown hair. Kelly loved the feel of her friend's hands massaging her scalp.

When she had finished washing the cream rinse from her hair, Adele had Kelly stand up again and pulled the plug on the water. "Stay right here," she told the nude woman as she dashed out of the bathroom, shutting the door behind her. Kelly's body shivered slightly as she waited. The thought occurred to her that it was decidedly anomalous to be standing in the tub of her own bathroom, her hands tied in front of her, while waiting for her apparently psychotic handmaiden to return. She saw herself in the mirror over the sink. The reflection showed her just from the neck to the tops of her knees. Her wet breasts glistened. Her bound hands stood out starkly as did her small, trimmed bush against her pale, shiny skin. She raised her hands over her head so just her lower belly and breasts were in the frame. "Everything any man would need," she thought to herself. She had forgotten about her ass. He used that too. She turned around, looking over her shoulder so she could see it. She felt a twinge of lust go through her as she remembered him piercing the dainty hole hidden by her small, round, rear cheeks. It shamed her how much she had enjoyed it. That's what he must want, she thought. It made his power over her seem so complete. She had proffered herself and loosened her muscles to prepare for him even though the very thought of being used there humiliated her. And she would do it again for him, tonight, if he wanted, or any other time.

Adele rushed in just as the remains of the dirty water were circling around the drain. She stoppered it again and turned on the faucet. Kelly felt the hot liquid gathering around her feet. She stood there as it rose. Adele was kneeling next to the tub expectantly, smiling, looking up at Kelly's beauteous form as if lost in thought. She then recollected herself and revealed a small bottle of expensive bathing oil, opened it and poured a generous dollop in. Kelly could smell the enchanting odor right away. When the water was high enough, she lowered herself down and then lay against the back of the tub. Adele raised her bound hands and reaffixed them to the towel rack. When the water was above her friend's breasts, she turned it off.

"Just lay back and enjoy it," Adele said kindly. She then realized her unintentional joke and started to laugh. Kelly, too, saw the humor in the oblique reference to her relationship with the dream man. She started to laugh as well. The two women, best friends, laughed hard and long, as they had done many times before. They were in this together. Neither of them would change a thing.

When Adele's raucous guffaws and Kelly's muffled amusement died, Adele leaned over and kissed her friend on the forehead. She stifled another giggle. "I'll be right back, honey," she said.

When Adele returned several minutes later, Kelly was in seventh heaven. She could feel the bath oil seeping into her pores. The room was misty from the steam coming off of the bath. The heat of the water made her whole body melt. Her hands hung limp above her. The blond woman had brewed Kelly a cup of chamomile tea in her favorite mug. She put it on the floor and loosened Kelly's gag and removed it. "You have to be quiet now," she said. "Ramón'll get mad if you say anything, okay?"

Kelly nodded her head in agreement. Adele brought the hot cup to her lips and let her take a sip. The tea was hot and tangy. There was a little slice of lemon in it. Kelly smiled her thanks to her friend. The familiar taste brought back to her the many nights she had sat on her veranda, enjoying her tea, peacefully appreciating the declining light and the beautiful world around her. Although she had just done it a few days ago, it seemed like a lifetime. Her eyes started to tear as she recalled how much had happened to her in the last forty eight hours or so. It was beyond her wildest imaginings. If only she hadn't dreamed of her fantasy lover. If only she hadn't reached her hand into the mist, if she had resisted the urge to pull the man through it to her side. Or was it somehow inevitable? Was this the fate that had always been awaiting her all those years she had toiled in school, proven herself in her internships, worked at her research project until she was almost too weary to make the drive home? How long would the man keep her as his plaything? What would happen tomorrow? Would they go to the lab? Would he come as well? How would she react in front of the pretty, young girls who worked for her? Would he want them too?

Adele saw her friend's distress. She leaned over the tub and caressed her face lovingly. "Don't worry, Kelly," she said earnestly. "It'll all work out. You'll see. He really cares for you. I know it."

Kelly knew she should not accept at face value what her mind controlled friend was saying. The man could make her believe anything he wanted. Yet, she decided to accept the reassuring words. Her face calmed and she smiled tenderly at the young, blond woman. She thought of the man and her need for him and her body shivered. She crossed her legs and bit her lip.

When Kelly had finished the tea, Adele let the water drain and then untied Kelly's hands from the towel rack. She helped her out of the tub. She took one of Kelly's large, fluffy, white towels and dried her body. She then wrapped it around her for warmth and had her kneel in front of the toilet, her back to her, as she dried and brushed out her hair and then fastened it into the ponytail Kelly liked to wear at night. She even had her stand in front of the sink while she brushed her teeth. When she was finished, she restored the woman's gag and had her exchange places on the toilet, this time raising the lid. She made Kelly spread her legs and douched her well used pussy and rear. As she did, Kelly remembered her statement to her earlier in the day that "Men really don't know anything, do they?"

She was not done. The happily content, naked, young blond woman found Kelly's shaving cream and razor and stroked her legs and armpits clean of stubble using the hot water from the sink to clean the razor as it jammed up with hair. She then had her lay down on the rug and spread her legs, her knees bent and raised. She put a folded towel under her behind, raising her hips.

"I'm gonna make you real clean down there," she told her friend. "I think Ramón will really like it."

Kelly had never wanted her pussy hair trimmed in the first place. Adele's insistence she buy and wear a bikini for their trip to Cancun had made it mandatory. Kelly had been careful to remove only what was absolutely necessary and she was letting it grow back. She didn't want it shaved clean now. The image of her bare pussy lips disturbed her. She tried to close her legs in protest. Adele gave her a stern, warning look. "Listen, honey," she said, annoyed, "if you don't do what I say, Ramón is going to get mad. And you don't want that to happen, do you?"

Kelly immediately recalled the man's power to make her suffer. At the same time, she was reminded her friend's first priority was pleasing Ramón. She was the one who had gotten the gag. She had gotten him clothes, she had placed the little rug in front of Ramón earlier after dinner so Kelly could service him. All she had done for Kelly, the soothing bath, the comforting tea, the reassuring words and the warm, tender caresses, had been so she would be a compliant whore for her master. Adele may have been feeling authentic affection and love for her, but she served Ramón. She was his accomplice, his co-conspirator. And she would help Ramón make her his slave.

Kelly opened her legs obediently and put her bound hands over her face. She cried while Ramón's pretty, blond minion carefully scraped away the remnants of her pubic hair. Each scrape of the sharp razor along her tender, private skin, bought another wave of unhappiness to her. They could do anything they wanted to her, Kelly thought. They could shave her head and put a ring through her nose. They could make her walk around on all fours and bark like a dog. They could tattoo and brand her, pierce her and whip her, do anything.

Adele finished her task quickly. There had not been much to shave anyway. She retrieved a hand mirror from the bathroom vanity. She placed it between Kelly's outstretched thighs and then lifted her back so she could observe the reflection of her hairless pudenda. "See how pretty it looks, honey," the pleased blond woman said. "It's real smooth and you can see your slit really well. It'll look like you're just waiting to get fucked."

Kelly had to agree. That's what it looked like. She would appear open and available all the time. A wave of despair passed through her. She was already open and available all the time to the man. So what difference did it make? The difference it made was that it made her feel humiliated and vulnerable. That was something the man wanted too. Something Adele clearly understood.

Adele let Kelly back down and went to the vanity and returned with a body lotion. She knelt between Kelly's legs and began applying it to the areas she had shaved. She rubbed it in softly and slowly. Kelly had closed her eyes and covered her face again with her hands. Adele's soft hands continued to stroke her clean, bare labial lips and then roamed to the insides of her thighs and over her belly. Kelly surrendered to the caresses. She began to feel her bare cleft moistening and a faint, familiar vibration in her pussy. She had been trying to ignore the low, simmering excitement caused by the penis shaped gag in her mouth. Adele's attentions had brought it back to the fore.

"You're so pretty, Kelly," Adele said to her softly. "Don't worry. Everything's going to be all right. I'm going to take good care of you. I'm going to make you feel good and you'll be happy."

Adele had begun to re-concentrate her attentions to Kelly's hairless gash. Warmth spread from her loins outwards to her belly and thighs, up her torso to her breasts, around her neck and into her brain. She felt Adele's thumb rubbing her pleasure bud softly, spreading her moisture over it, rolling it gently, teasing it. She felt the younger woman's shoulders brush against her upraised thighs and then, a second later, her tongue ascend lightly the length of her nether lips, dipping slightly into her crevasse. The delicate tongue sent a wave of pleasure through her. The gesture was repeated, this time a little harder and a little deeper. Kelly gasped with passion. She lowered her hands from her face and placed them on the blond head between her thighs. She didn't know whether to push the head away or clutch it to her. Her indecision left them laying softly on the short, straw colored hair of her tormentor.

Adele's thumb was still worrying Kelly's stiffened clitoris and Kelly moaned deeply as she felt her lust rising within her. She sucked on the leather presence in her mouth almost unconsciously, running her tongue along it, pleasuring it. The blond woman's tongue was probing deeper and deeper into her hot canal and the agile, gentle thumb was teasing her hard nubbin faster and faster. Kelly's thighs started to shudder and shake. She arched her back. She closed her thighs around the shoulders of the blond woman and wrapped her legs around her back. "Mmmmmmmmmm! Mmmmmmmmmm!" she exclaimed, as her pussy began to throb and pulse with her orgasm. Adele was pleasuring her cunt feverishly now, driving her lust higher and higher. "Mmmmmmmm! Mmmmmmm!" Kelly called out from behind her gag. Her moans echoed through the tiled room.

When Kelly had achieved quietus from her orgasm, Adele raised her head and pulled the well pleasured woman's legs from around her. Kelly's hands languorously stroked her belly and sought out her burning pussy, which was still echoing the hard contractions of her climax. Adele caught her bound hands in hers and warned her sternly. "That's not allowed, Kelly. You're not allowed to touch yourself."

"Not allowed to touch myself?" Kelly thought with shocked panic. "What does she mean?" She raised her hands away from her loins as if stung by a bee. They came to rest atop her breasts.

Adele, who had not lost hold of her wrists, gently urged her hands higher. "Not your titties, either, honey. I'm sorry, that's the way Ramón wants it."

Kelly's mind reeled with the import of the dream man's newly revealed regulations. The thought she could not touch her own body made her frantic. She felt like they were stealing it away from her a bit at a time. Suddenly, her breasts and her sex loomed in importance for her. As anyone else, Kelly spent most of her day oblivious to the existence of her sex organs. They were just a part of her, parts that obtained significance at certain moments and at certain times. Now she had been deprived of the rights of ownership of them, their existence loomed large in her mind. She wanted desperately to touch herself. Her breasts seemed to be yearning for her, her now hairless vulva craving her warm, comforting touch. Only the dream man and Adele would have access to them now. They would be free to use them, touch them, feel them, and she would not. She realized now that one of the reasons her hands had been tied, aside from the obvious ones, was so she would not make contact with her sexual parts. She recalled Friday night when she had stroked herself to pleasure, fondling her labia lovingly, cupping and squeezing her breasts. That pleasure and freedom was to be denied her. How could she bear it?

"Come on, Kelly," Adele said, a note of petulance in her voice. "Be a good girl and cooperate. I need to fasten your hands behind your back again. Ramón's waiting."

The reminder of the man's presence in her living room waiting to fuck her again, worsened Kelly's agony. She could feel her body begin to lust for him the moment he was mentioned. She knew she could not oppose him and hated herself for it. Why couldn't he make her happy and carefree like Adele? Why did he want to torment her, humiliate her? How could Adele be so caring and so callous at the same time?

Kelly looked up at her friend. There was no spite or meanness in her face, no sign of her enjoying Kelly's distress. The young blond woman placed her warm hand on Kelly's naked belly and rubbed it comfortingly. "Come on, sweetie, we're not going to hurt you. Ramón cares a lot about you and so do I," she said. "There's a reason for all this. It's very important. Ramón needs you and you need to help him. You can't hold back anything. You have to belong to him totally. Fighting him will just make you unhappy. I'm going to take good care of you. And don't worry," she added, smiling, raising her free hand and smoothing it gently over Kelly's plump breasts, "you'll get plenty of attention."

The feel of her friend's hand on her breasts, breasts that were forbidden to her, made Kelly moan. From now on, she would have to depend on someone else to stroke them. They would not feel the sensation of human touch unless it was at someone else's desire. And neither would her private place below. She had a vision of herself kneeling, gagged, begging for her lord to deign to caress her aching mounds, pleading for him to place his hand on her sex, to relieve her lusts. She would not be able to speak her supplications. She would have to plead with her forlorn eyes, jut her needy orbs out at him, unable to do more than whine or moan her desperate desire.

Adele's words were having a magical effect. Ramón needed her. It made her wet just to think it. She needed him too, more than anything she had ever needed before. The thought of shoving her friend aside and making a mad dash out the bathroom window had flashed across her mind in reaction to Adele's announcement that she had lost the right to touch herself, but immediately, the idea of separation from her lover made her ache with loneliness. She would submit. The thought of being governed like some strange prisoner, having fewer liberties than a child, made her cringe with unhappiness. She would do it, nonetheless, all for Ramón, so he would continue to need and use her. If she made him unhappy, opposed his will, he might abandon her, cast her aside for someone who would not. She couldn't imagine what the dream man's purpose was. Kelly didn't care. As long as he continued to let her near him, to feel his warm, comforting touch, the power of his mind as it stoked her lust and the hot radiance of his pleasure bringing cock, she would submit, maybe not happily, but she would submit.

Kelly nodded her bleak acceptance of her lord's will as expressed by his pretty, female disciple. Adele pulled Kelly's hands to her belly and untied them. "Now roll over on your tummy, sweetie, so I can tie you up."

The idea of losing the limited use of her hands, at having them again taken from her view, distressed Kelly, but, when her hands were made free, she dutifully rolled to her stomach and placed them behind her. She expected Adele to immediately begin to refasten them. There was a moment's delay and she heard the rustling of a plastic bag. She realized Adele must have brought it in when she brought the tea. Kelly had been too lost in her reverie to have noticed.

"I told you I had some more surprises for you," Adele said sweetly. "You don't want those nasty ropes around your wrists, do you? I've got something much better."

Kelly couldn't see behind her. She felt Adele wrapping something around her left wrist and buckling it closed. She tried to move her hand up to where she could see it. Adele grabbed it and kept in place. "No peekie," she said teasingly. The younger woman then placed a similar object on Kelly's right wrist. She pulled them towards each other and clipped them together.

"Now that's much better," she said proudly. Kelly realized her friend had placed some kind of slave bracelets on her wrists. She had seen them for sale once online. "Mmmmmmmm!" she protested. She didn't want to be bound up like one of those women on those web sites. She tried to pull her wrists apart. These were even worse than the rope had been. At least with the rope, her wrists were crossed and they could hang loosely behind her. With these, her wrists were confined facing each other and her shoulders were pulled back tautly. She protested again, "Mmmmmmmm!"

"Oh, stop carrying on," Adele said. "These are much better. There's a soft lining so your wrists won't get all marked up and they won't cut off your circulation. And they're real easy to hook together. I don't think I can tie a good knot to save my life. Now I won't have to." Kelly tried to pull the confining bracelets apart; they were locked fast together. "The guy at the store said that they're just about impossible to slide off since they fit so snugly under the hands. And your hands look so pretty pressed together like that," Adele said by way of justification. She placed her hands on Kelly's locked ones. "Oh, and tomorrow, I'm going to do your nails. That'll make them look even prettier."

The last time Kelly had done her nails was in high school. It was a level of vanity she had never really aspired to. It was yet another detail of her loss of the right to control her own body.

Adele went back to the bag and Kelly felt something going around her left ankle and then the right one. "And these are for your legs," Adele continued. "It's so you won't move around without permission. No more dirty ropes for that either. Although, I think Ramón really likes the feel of tying you off, so he might want to use them on you sometimes any way. That's up to him. Until then, these'll be real comfy."

Adele rose to her feet. She stood back and admired the accouterments she had placed on her friend's unwilling, supine body. "These look really good on you, Kelly," she said. "They kind of match your hair." Kelly's long, auburn ponytail was lying across her back. "They come in black too," the style conscious, young woman continued, "but I think I like the brown better." She paused for a moment, weighing the benefits of black and brown in her mind. "Maybe we'll get the black ones too. Your skin is real light and they might go really good together. We'll have to see. Come on now, you've got to get up."

Kelly, despondent at being so cruelly bound, recalled her vow to submit herself to whatever it took to make her keeper happy. She knew that rising from the soft, blue bathroom rug on which she lay was prefatory to being delivered to his presence. What difference did it make really how she was bound before him? It was just that the ropes had seemed temporary, makeshift, and these bindings bespoke more than that. It was as if her bondage had been institutionalized. An investment had been made, albeit at her expense, to acquire the formal tools of submission. The fact that Adele had gone to the trouble to get them implied some permanency to her condition. How long would they keep her like this, Kelly wondered unhappily as she rose to her knees. How long?

Adele helped Kelly rise to her feet from the kneeling position. She urged Kelly to turn around so she was facing the door. "Oh, I've got some more. I almost forgot," she said, chastising herself. Adele leaned down to the plain, white shopping bag and pulled out another object. It was a brown leather collar about two inches wide. Kelly's heart sank when she saw what it was. She submitted meekly as the taller, bigger breasted woman fastened it around her neck. Adele had also taken a three foot long leash out of the bag. She clipped its end to a ring in the front of the collar. "Now we won't have to lead you around by your arm," she told the sad, bound woman. "It makes you look like you're a prisoner at police headquarters. This is much prettier." She took hold of the leash and jiggled it so the chain swung between Kelly's breasts. Kelly felt like she was about to break down into uncontrollable, heartfelt sobs. She was leashed like a dog, her master's pet. Adele knelt down and she felt something being attached to her ankle bracelets. It was an 18" long chain. Kelly's felt like her heart would break from misery. How could this be happening to her? And her best friend too! Her world had been turned upside down.

Adele stood up. 'There!" she announced happily. "You're all dressed up! And you look so pretty. Wait till Ramón sees you! Having your hands behind you like that makes your tits stick out really nice. He'll want to fuck you all night long!"

At the mention of Ramón's intentions towards her, Kelly felt a surge of lust in her loins. He was out there, beyond the bathroom door. What would he think of her? How could he think of her as a human being if she was all trussed up like this? Adele placed her hands on Kelly's proffered breasts and massaged them gently. "Oooooouu!" she said, in her pleasant drawl. "He's so lucky. And you're lucky too!" As she said this last, she ran her finger slowly along the length of Kelly's hairless love lips, from the bottom up. The lack of hair and the fact they had been recently shaved made them much more sensitive. Kelly felt a surge of passion. It was a stark reminder of her newfound nudity there.

Adele opened the bathroom door and, giving Kelly's leash a little tug, began to lead her into the living room.

Ramón had gone through about forty technical journals while the women were in the bathroom. He was absorbing rapidly the information he would need to get started. He didn't need to make notes as his memory was photographic and his mind was so facile that he could retrieve any fact he learned accurately and at will. As an otherworlder, he was totally unfamiliar with earthly compounds and there was much to learn. His probing of the pretty scientist's brain had been of much help there. He could see where her project had been leading and he believed he could be of some help to her. She had made some mistakes in her assumptions. These were easily corrected. But her project was secondary to his needs.

He was also studying quantum physics, which meant he needed to learn calculus and trigonometry. And then there was molecular biology, metallurgy, computer technology and a number of other fields. He would bring his store of skills and information back with him to his world and add to the Whole's vast fund of knowledge. And he would be able to process materials he needed in his quest. He needed a weapon, for he knew without saying that his enemy would not submit to him willingly. Although the renegade had crossed a short while before Raijamoon did in his native world's measure of time, it had been more than five years ago here. His adversary would be very strong. And he would be wary.

He would know that someone would come for him. He probably even knew who it would be.

And he needed formulas to develop substances which would help sustain his familiar and his servants, to make them more useful to him and protect them from harm. It would be many weeks, maybe longer, before he was ready to move against the renegade, assuming he could find him.

Ramón had heard the laughter in the bathroom. Although the principal of human humor escaped him, he recognized it as a good thing. The women needed to be close. When he heard his familiar moaning her pleasure through the door, he was approving of his servant's actions. She would have to pleasure the other woman often.

He sensed Kelly's profound disturbance, even before she left the bathroom. When he turned to see her as she emerged, towed behind the younger, blond woman, her eyes downcast and wet, taking tiny, humiliating steps, he understood why. At first, he thought his servant had gone overboard. Then he realized she had read his needs and desires precisely. Nothing could have emphasized his familiar's need for subservience more than her present accoutrements. He would need to bond her to them, make her yearn for them. He noticed her bare loins with pleasure. She was more naked to him than she was before. And her availability for coital union could not have been more readily displayed. His male human nature stirred at the sight of the imprisoned woman. Her helplessness advertised his freedom to use her as he pleased.

As he watched Kelly shuffle miserably behind the younger woman, he was glad to see he had been right to use her former subordinate and friend as a tool for her further subjugation. The futility of opposition was made blatantly obvious when those closest to you were determined to facilitate it. The blond girl, acting merely on his telegraphed, unspecific desire, had on her own initiative found appropriate bindings for his auburn haired familiar. A night spent in chains would make her easier to deal with tomorrow when they had to emerge into the outside world.

Kelly was led to the middle of the room to a spot just opposite where her lord was sitting. As she drew closer and closer, Kelly's need for him grew stronger and stronger. She had been afraid he would see her habiliments as grotesque. When she finally found the courage to look up at him, she was relieved to see his approval in his powerful, deep, brown eyes. He sent her a wave of pleasing energy, a reward for her submissiveness. Kelly swooned as it passed through her. He got up from his seat and approached.

Adele was holding the end of Kelly's leash out as an offering to her master. She was beaming with delight at his satisfaction. She had read in his mind, after he had subdued her and she had learned of her life's purpose to serve him, his need for control over her friend. She also knew he could not 'reveal' his benevolent goodness and the holiness of his cause to the woman he had selected as his familiar in the same way he had to her. To serve the master properly, she had to be carefully led to total submission, convinced in her own mind that she had no choice. And Adele knew adorning her with objective signs of her helplessness would help do that. Binding her so securely and obscenely, stripping her of the shroud of hair that obscured her lord's view of her sex, would both be important steps in helping Kelly to abandon any thoughts of an individual identity. She was the master's vessel, his link to power. And she could only serve him well if she lost her sense of self, gave control over every aspect of her being to their common master.

She had meant it when she told Kelly she would care for her. She loved Kelly. The master had shown her that. She would calm her and pleasure her, and guide her to her destination.

Although she remembered the moment of her rebirth with great joy, Adele envied her friend's singular role as the focus of her master's lust and need. She could not conceive of a greater fate than to serve the master fully and absolutely, to give over your very being to him. When her friend Kelly learned to forget her happiness, she would be happy. When she learned to give up her all of her freedom, she would be free. She would live a life of absolute pleasure. Adele would help her do that.

Ramón took hold of the handle to Kelly's leash and pulled her towards him. The woman looked at him expectantly. He could see the lust in her eyes. He wanted her to learn that at each stage of her road to complete submission, her rewards of pleasure would grow greater. When the trussed woman was a foot away from him, he took hold of her breasts and passed a strong signal of sexual excitement to her. Her knees buckled and she swooned in response. When he ran his hand over her hairless lower lips, he sent another. She leaned forward, her body falling into him, overcome by the pleasure running through her.

The dream man led the woman over to a nearby easy chair and sat her down in it. Wrapping his large, strong hands around her bound throat, he felt her shame at being collared like a domesticated animal, her humiliation. He left that in place and tied her need for him to it so she would yearn for her demeaning collar, feel her lusts begin to burn whenever she wore it, feel lost whenever she did not. He bent her head down and placed his hands on her bound wrists, transmitting feelings of desire mixed with comfort and warmth through them. He leaned her back and took hold of her ankles by where the bracelets were mounted and did the same. Now, whenever she was accoutered in her bindings, she would re-experience the feelings he had sent her. She would crave, when free, to return to them.

His cock had grown to excitement as he had handled the impassioned woman. Adele had taken a position kneeling on the floor next to him, set so she could watch her lord enjoy the clean, sweet smelling and enticingly attired female she had returned to him. Ramón bent down and unbuckled the gag from behind the auburn haired head of his familiar. He eased it from her mouth. The woman's eyes peered up at him and then down at his rampant manhood. She needed no instruction. She pushed her head forward and wrapped her eager lips around his rigid rod.

The dream man took hold of Kelly's long, silky, reddish brown ponytail and guided her mouth along his long, thick shaft. Her tongue worked it hungrily. The warmth of her mouth sent a wave of exquisite pleasure to his male, human body. It was late and they all needed their rest. It was his last chance of the day to fill his connector to his dimension with the seed that would facilitate her emotional voyage there to gather the fuel that he would need. While he had been studying, and while the women had been occupied in the bathroom, he had let his body build up his reserves of fluids. He would fill all three of her orifices before he sent the female to her rest.

The bound and collared woman moaned as she received Ramón's radiating energy through the hard, meaty pole in her mouth. She felt it suffuse through her and her body became heated like a blazing fire. She was lost and she knew it. She would do anything to insure she could enjoy this wondrous experience again and again. When she felt the heavy, fleshy manhood begin to throb and pulse on her tongue, her pussy clenched with pleasure and sent her intense, repeated, almost unendurable spasms of ecstasy.

Kelly was breathless when the man slowly removed his still engorged cock from her mouth. Her mind protested at the loss. Adele, her beautiful, blond handler, rose to her feet and restored the comforting gag between her lips. She felt a pull on the chain that connected her braceleted ankles. The man was raising them, holding the chain with one hand and bringing her fettered legs up towards her head.

Ramón lifted Kelly's legs by the chain that connected them. He pressed it back until it touched the chair above her. The back sides of her long, pale flanks were exposed to him and both of her lower places of pleasure beckoned. Her hairless pudenda was squeezed tight by her thighs and he lowered her legs until her knees bowed out, and the naked slit spread before his eyes. It was glistening with the female's arousal. Without its furry beard, it looked clean and soft. The aroma of her skin was pleasing to him and accentuated his arousal. He took his free hand and stroked the soft skin around the enticing opening. The beauteous female moaned as he touched her. He felt her discomfort with the reality of her denuded sex. His mind played with it. He decided he would strengthen it, while at the same time he sent her a stronger, more compelling need to display it to him, to proffer it to him. She would struggle with her inner shame each time she did so.

Ramón stroked the female's sex until it was wide with invitation, her juices overflowing its banks. He poised his ready manhood at her gates and pushed himself inside. She gave a deep, impassioned moan from behind her gag as he filled her steamy canal with his hot cock. He could see her face between her bowed knees. It looked trance-like, as if her whole being was subsumed by the lusts he was driving higher and higher within her. He sawed himself within her cleft while, with his free hand, he stroked her hard button of pleasure. When he felt her fevered pussy clamp down on his prick, saw the woman's body convulse with pleasure, he released his sperm deep into her womb, sharp charges of ecstasy from his ejaculations piercing his frame. He felt his own knees bend and he closed his eyes, leaning his neck back. His alien soul rejoiced at the pleasure his human form was delivering to it.

His lust was on full burn. It radiated through the room like a furnace. Adele, kneeling by his side, was overcome with deep, sexual need, watching with adoring pride as her master pleasured the vessel she had prepared for him. She had lowered her hand to her loins and was stroking her pleasure lips fervently, her other hand wrapped around the end of a breast, pulling and tugging at her rigid nipple. Her eyes were glazed, her plump lips parted, her breath heavy. When she saw her master's moisture covered prick emerge from her offering's discharge laden cleft and descend into the small, dainty star of her rear, her climax overwhelmed her. She cried out her pleasure, a loud, staccato celebration of her master's virile power.

From within her mad delirium of lust, Kelly felt the thick prick part the small, now pliant entry to her bowels. Her mind cursed herself for the pleasure it brought her. The feel of the thick member dragging across the delicate membranes of her small anal ring made her raised thighs shudder and quake as she came for the third time and then the fourth as she felt the man's welcome flood of essence spread inside her.

Ramón, his body exhausted from his expenditure of lust, let himself lean over the moaning female, while his cock, still implanted in the women's murky depths, continued to glow with pleasure. His chest heaved from his exertions. At the same time, he absorbed the dwindling lustful psychic emissions of the two women, building his connection to them, strengthening his connection to this world. His powers were growing. He would need them tomorrow. And he would need the energies that would be transmitted to his familiar tonight in her dreams. Her psyche and her body needed rest. His sperm would meld with her cells, feeding her connections to him and the other realm.

The visitor, Kelly's dream man, rose from the body of his thrall and eased his manhood from her. He lowered her upraised legs to the floor gently. She was in a stupor, her mind dizzy with the aftermath of their impassioned coitus. Adele was recovering from her self administered bliss. He had no need to bar her from the pleasures of her own body. His control of her was different. He would need her alert and anticipatory of his needs. And she served his needs when she pleasured herself while bathing in the radiance of his lustful emissions, strengthening her devotion to him, reinforcing her satisfaction at the successful completion of his.

He needed to clean himself and the female needed to be placed at rest. He caressed the auburn air of his familiar, sending her a wave of rewarding warmth for her surrender to her lusts. He did not need to send a message to his lovely, blond, acolyte. She would know what to do.

As Ramón made his way to the shower, Adele rose to her feet and eased Kelly to hers. The bound woman's body sagged and leaned into her. She waited, happy at her friend's blissful state, as Kelly slowly recovered her senses.

"Come on honey," she whispered to her in a sweet, comforting voice. "I've go to get you to bed. You've had a long day and you have a big day tomorrow."

When she saw that the pale skinned, young woman was capable of walking, she took hold of the lead which dangled between her soft, round breasts and gently urged her to the bedroom. Kelly followed, contentedly, shuffling her chained feet. When they reached the bed, Adele assisted her in sitting down on it and, after removing the chain from her collar, rolled her over to her stomach on the mattress. The sheets were cool on her still burning skin. A radiating ember of fulfillment effused her flesh. Dreamily, she felt Adele unfasten her tightly bound wrists and then fasten them again, this time with a six inch long chain. Her shoulders relaxed at the increased distance between her hands.

"This will make you more comfortable," her happy, blond attendant told her. The svelte, younger beauty unfastened the chain between her ankles and linked the bracelets there directly together. Then, bending Kelly's legs backwards, connected the fastening between her wrists to her ankles with the 18" long chain. She then pulled the mesmerized body of her friend to its side so she was facing the place where her dream lover would bed down beside her. She stretched her long, naked body next to her, marrying her thighs, belly and breasts to those of the other woman. She could feel the remnants of her master's lusts emanating through the auburn haired woman's skin and it brought a wave of pleasure to her. She stroked the other woman's head, smiling her love and affection for her.

"Oh, Kelly," she whispered softly. "I'm so proud of you. You were perfect." She reached behind Kelly's head and released the straps holding her gag in place. Withdrawing it gently, she placed her lips on the object of her affection's and explored her mouth with her tongue. Kelly received her friend's attentions with joy. Her body shuddered with pleasure, both at her friend's ministrations and at her kind, welcome words. She had pleased the man of her dreams. For her, right now, there was no greater ideal.

Adele parted her lips from her friend's and restored the gag to her pliant, receptive mouth. She ran her hands over Kelly's plump breasts, caressing her nipples and then let her hands draw slowly over her taut belly until they had captured her pleasant, smooth labial lips. "Sweet dreams, sweetheart," she told her. "Tomorrow morning, before we go to work, I'll make you come again with my mouth."

Adele pulled the covers up over her friend and lowered the lights in the room before she left her. Kelly closed her eyes and let herself melt into the glow of her well pleasured body. Her lover would be here soon. He would lay himself down beside her and they would sleep for a long time together. Lazily, she tested the bonds that held her ankles and wrists joined. She had hated it when the leather bands had been applied on her limbs and around her neck. She now felt pleased her friend had adorned her with them. They seemed to glow on her body, sending her reassurances of her dream man's bond to her.

While the man finished his shower, Adele went to the back room and made up the simple, single bed with sheets and blankets she had found in Kelly's linen closet. There was a plump, soft pillow there and she laid it down. She had brought with her all the things she would need in the morning. She would help prepare Kelly for what would be a very taxing day.

The svelte blond had brought two plain, white bags in with her when she had gone shopping and she retrieved the second one now. From it, she pulled another set of leather confinements. These were for her. It was important her master sleep soundly, with no concern for her. And she wanted to be prepared for any use of her body he would desire. Her leather bracelets and collar would proclaim her devotion to him.

Sitting on the soft bed, Adele buckled the leather confinements around her ankles and wrists. After she had connected the collar around her neck, she rose to her feet and walked out to the small hallway that was the meeting place of the three other rooms of the house. She lowered herself to her knees outside the bathroom door.

Ramón was toweling himself dry. The pleasures of the shower, even though he was alone, were as satisfying as they had been the night before. What a world this was! He reveled in the sensual capabilities of his human body. These creatures' capacity for absorbing the delightful pleasures of their habitat amazed him. He would need to rest now, let his human flesh recuperate. He placed the towel in the rack and opened the bathroom door.

There, as he expected she would be, was his servant and acolyte, waiting submissively for him. She looked up at him expectantly. Her braceleted hands were on her thighs, rubbing them softly in anticipation of his presence. He stroked her tufts of straw blond hair and sent her a message of gratitude for her service to him. She moaned as she accepted it, parting her plump, red lips, running her tongue over them.

His cock stirred at the sight of the beautiful, graceful woman on her knees before him. He took it in his hand and proffered it to the anxiously awaiting woman's lips. They encircled him gently, lovingly, and the woman's tongue washed its bulbous head. She placed her hands on his thick, muscular thighs and inched closer to him, letting the hardening wand of flesh probe deeper into her mouth. He heard her moan with pleasure as she drew her lips down its length, until her face was buried in his loins. She then slowly withdrew, sucking gently, lovingly on his tool.

Adele was overjoyed to receive her master's meat. Her mouth and tongue craved his radiant energy that flowed from it. She stroked her fevered slit while luxuriating in her ministrations. She blessed the moment she had met the man and experienced his strength and goodness. When he came, spilling his precious seed into her, her pussy throbbed and pulsed with pleasure.

Ramón escorted the satisfied Adele back to her little room. She would fix it up over the next several days. Now, it was crowded with boxes and the effluvia of its owner's life. The blond woman turned her back to him to allow him to fasten her wrists together. She had left a small chain dangling from one wrist and it was simple to connect it to the other one. She lay down on the bed and rolled to her belly so her master could connect her ankles together and affix them to her wrists with the 18" long chain she had left out for him. He rolled her to her side so she was facing away from the wall and then took the last item from the white, plastic bag lying on the floor next to the bed. Adele held her mouth open willingly as he eased the long, thick leather prong of the gag into her mouth. He buckled it behind her head and then pulled the covers up over her body. He placed his hand on her golden head and passed a message of warmth and pleasure to her. She sighed softly, and when he gently massaged the appropriate part of her mind, she closed her eyes and went to sleep.

The man looked down at his peacefully resting servant. His seed would strengthen her commitment to him as it merged with her cells during the night. She would have a lot to do tomorrow. He would need her assistance in assuming control of the research lab and turning it to his needs. She would need to help guide her friend and, now, lover, through the day.

Ramón made a circuit around the small dwelling and turned off the lights. He made sure the front door was locked and then walked quietly to the bedroom. The female was already asleep, breathing deeply and contentedly. He eased himself down beside her. Before pulling up the covers, he softly caressed her fine, pleasing breasts and belly, sending, gentle, pleasurable messages to her. She stirred slightly in her sleep, sighing deeply. Her soft, round, enticing eyes fluttered. Her dreams had begun.

PART TWO: THE RISE OF A RENEGADE

CHAPTER EIGHT

If you travel west on US Route 10 from Los Cruses, New Mexico about 60 miles, you'll come across State Highway Route 146, a flat, straight, two lane highway that passes through the seemingly interminable, rough, semi arid country that surrounds it. Head south about 40 miles and take Route 9 west about another 40 and you'll come across the northernmost entry point for The Chiracahua Apache Reservation. There's a gate there with a small sentry hut run by the tribal police and you'll have to politely state your business or move on. If the usually alert guardians of the Reservation let you through, you'll have to drive another 40 or 50 miles, due south, before you come to the road that skirts the southeastern shore of Lake Palayas, a pristine, long, finger-like, aquifer fed lake redolent with trout, pike and other game fish.

About 10 miles south of the lake, there's a small road which leads east towards the southern portion of the long, rocky ridge known as Hachita Peak, which towers at its highest point about 6500 feet over the surrounding scrublands. At the end of that road, you'll approach a large gate, about 15 feet high topped with razor wire. It's electrified. There's a gatehouse there manned, not by the local constabulary, but by well built, rough looking but clean cut, Apache males dressed in tight, denim blue jeans and black t-shirts with high caliber automatic handguns strapped to their hips and dark sun glasses obscuring their eyes. They are employed as members of the large security force for the sprawling compound located another ten miles or so up the road. If you can confirm your business with the efficient, no nonsense guards, you'll be allowed to proceed, escorted, of course, to do your business with the compound's occupants. If not, you'll be politely turned back and given exactly one hour and twenty five minutes to leave the Reservation.

The expansive compound itself is nestled in the foothills of the mountain range. Before you get there, you will pass two more security checkpoints and a small airfield with a landing strip long enough to service even the largest of private jets. When you enter the compound, you will see a large, sprawling, hacienda and a number of smaller, but not inconsiderable out buildings including residences for senior staff, a barracks building for the security guards, a stable, a glass roofed building containing an indoor swimming pool and tennis courts, a garage to service the many motor vehicles used and useful in the conduct of the affairs of the residents of the compound and a long, two storied structure containing 24 motel like units and an elegant cafeteria for guests. There would be several other buildings, nondescript and surrounded by their own security fences whose purposes would not be readily apparent.

If you had arrived on the right day and at the right time, you would have seen a tall, broad shouldered man, about 37 or 38 years old with long, flowing blond hair and a clean shaven face standing on the large second story deck that faces west, proudly surveying the vast duchy which he controls. This would be Jonathan Blackthorne.

It was about 11:30 in the Shenandoah Valley when the enraptured scientist, her dream man and his servant found somnolence in their rural lodgment. In New Mexico, it was 9:30. On the second night of Dr. Kelly Jameson's captivity, Blackthorne was sitting in his large, brown, leather stuffed chair in his private study on the second floor of the hacienda. He had a small snifter of brandy sitting on the table next to him. The room was spacious and decorated in the style of the old Southwest, a large, woven, turquoise banded, cream colored Navajo rug partially obscuring the dark, polished oaken floor, heavy, dark, wooden furniture, even the pale, sun bleached, wind blown skull of a longhorn steer pegged on the wall. The lighting was dim, emanating from a series of small high hats in the low ceiling. On one wall was a large bookcase containing Blackthorne's collection of rare books and original editions. On the other was mounted an old, long barreled, muzzle loading rifle, said to have been once owned by Kit Carson himself.

In front of Blackthorne were two women. They had the light brown skin of Latin American *Meztitas*, shoulder length, strait, black hair, dark, thick overarching eyebrows and pleasant, young faces. The one on the left, Carmelita Rivera, was kneeling on the floor, her blue jeans, bright red t-shirt, modest, plain, white bra and panties and heavy *campeseno* work boots neatly arranged by her side. She had her hands behind her head, her fingers tightly intertwined and her pleasantly formed, heavy breasts were presented delightfully. Her back was erect and her knees were spread, and Blackthorne could see the thick, wiry, black bush that hid her love lips between her thighs. Her face had a mix of fear and wonderment on it, as if she couldn't quite figure out why she has stripped herself of her clothes and is kneeling in a submissive pose in this elegant, well appointed room before the blond *Norte Americano*.

Her sister, Guadalupe, younger, a little thinner and taller, was standing next to her. She was still clothed. She was shocked when Carmelita shed her body's coverings, but was more shocked that she could not seem to find the will to flee the presence of the handsome blond man. Her hands too were poised behind her head. She remembered the blond man vaguely from early the day before. She and her sister were part of a cargo of 25 or so immigrants who had paid a *coyote* to transport them to Tucson and had been hidden in a secret compartment in a large, twelve wheel, tractor trailer truck. The truck had stopped in a lonely part of the desert in the New Mexico panhandle. All of the hidden voyagers had been ordered out and forced to stand in the hot, early morning sun. Four dark haired, fierce looking Apaches carrying automatic weapons had waited there with them until a small helicopter had landed and the blond man emerged. He had walked up and down the line of illegals and then everybody, except the pretty Rivera sisters, had been ordered back in the truck which then continued on its journey. The blond man had flown away in his helicopter and the girls, inexplicably unconcerned at having been separated from their companions, had been loaded into the back of a large, black SUV. They had been held in a small, spartanly furnished but comfortable underground room. The men had not treated them badly, allowing them to eat and use the bathroom. An hour earlier, they had been given the opportunity to shower and had been brought here, to this room, a short while before. The man, who had been sitting in the large chair as he was now, had said nothing to them. For some reason Guadalupe did not understand, after several long moments of silence, during which the man had implacably maintained a steady gaze on their forms, she had placed her hands behind her head and her sister had started to strip.

Blackthorne had frozen the younger Rivera sister in place while he was rummaging around in the mind of her more voluptuous sister. Carmelita had not been a good girl back in her small, mountain Nicaraguan town. She had had two boyfriends who she had let fuck her. Well, he thought, she would get lots of fucking now. He turned his attention to Guadalupe. She had managed to reach the ripe old age of 18 with her innocence intact. She, in spite of her less developed breasts and thin frame, would be of more interest to him.

Jonathan Blackthorne, who had once carried the reference which could be best phonetisized as Jnthrn, had, about five years ago, jumped to this dimension and emerged from the lustful dreams of a 25 year old professor of biology at the University of Chicago. The shapely and handsomely attractive Professor Diane Lanier had earned her PhD. about a year before and was new on the University faculty. He had subdued her easily. Luckily for him, her pretty, 19 year old sister Nadine had been visiting from their Midwestern home. She had appeared, dressed in her baby blue, sheer, baby doll nightgown at the doorway to her sister's bedroom after having been awoken by her sister's frantic cries of passion. When the shocked Nadine took in a deep inhalation of breath prefatory to a scream, Jnthrn had simply turned and paralyzed her mind. Once he had driven her older sister to exhaustion with her third body shaking orgasm, he had made the pretty, dazed, younger girl strip, fall to her knees, place her forehead to the floor and accept the intrusion of his thick cock into her already moistened, tight canal while he rearranged her thinking to suit him. When he sent a large flow of his essence into her, causing her to moan and shudder in pleasure, she was claimed.

Nadine had been useful in effectuating his control over the beautiful, blond professor, engaging enthusiastically in their sexual trysts. Nadine had cute, coffee cup sized breasts, long, strait chestnut hair she kept in a ponytail and stood only about 5'4" tall. The soon to be former professor of biology was taller and more delectably filled out. To Professor Lanier's dismay, Nadine took readily to pleasuring her bound and gagged sister while Jnthrn recovered his forces for another bout of intercourse with her. She also made the professor's excuses to the University administration, explaining that Diane had come down with a severe case of the flu and wouldn't be able to make classes for a few days. With Nadine's assistance, Jnthrn, the sound of which had emerged in Nadine's mind as Jonathan, was able to solidify his control over her older sister, filling her with an almost continuous flow of his seed until her need for him had built up and become like an addictive drug. At the end of the third day, she had been fully enraptured.

This was Jnthrn's third jump. After his second, he had made up his mind he would not return from his next, assuming the dimension in which he found himself was as accommodating as his last one. He had not been disappointed. In fact, he could have not been more pleased. The sensual capabilities of these beings far exceeded that of the life forms he had previously encountered. He had made up his mind at once he would never go back to assimilation with the Whole.

Renegades were not unknown to the Whole, but it was rare. Jnthrn had studied the efforts of other aspects of the Whole who had 'gone native' so to speak. Their cases were carefully examined by those selected for the hazardous 'profession' of movement across dimensional barriers as warnings of the dangers of interdimensional travel. Jnthrn had learned from their mistakes. They had all been retrieved by another jumper armed with the moral authority of the Whole who had 'convinced' them of the errors of their ways and facilitated their return. Jnthrn was determined this would not happen to him.

His first goal was to lose himself. He compelled Diane to convert all of her holdings into cash and, with Nadine, they had fled the City of Chicago and headed south. Jnthrn had assimilated much of Diane and Nadine's stores of knowledge about the alien culture in which he found himself. The traveler had immersed himself in learning what he would have to know to meld in with the aboriginal population of the planet, principally by watching TV during breaks between his bouts of sexual relations with the two lust driven women. It was easy to build himself a native identity with Professor

Lanier's computer, which had been tied into the University's and, through it, to various governmental entities. There had been a social security card and a driver's license waiting for him at a commercial mail box facility when they arrived in St. Louis.

He spent the next week or so exploring the city and conditioning himself to his new environment. While he was out, Nadine stood guard over the bound and enthralled professor, seeing to her bodily needs and ensuring she was maintained in a steady, maddening state of sexual heat. Jnthrn practiced his command of spoken language and toyed with the minds of the people on the street. He had learned much about the sentient beings of this culture in the space of two weeks, perceiving as useful to his ends their tendency to easy corruption and their callous abuse of each other. He spent most of the time driving the female he had converted into his familiar further and deeper into an obsessive, mind wrenching need for his sexual attentions and his very presence, strengthening their bond and reshaping her as a more efficient conduit for the energies he needed to be drawn across the void between dimensions.

Professor Lanier's assets had been somewhat limited and the cash had run out fast. He could have easily transferred millions of dollars to himself by invading online banking records in spite of their ridiculously simplistic security precautions. That would have created a trail he did not want, and, perhaps, complications, as the financial institutions would undoubtedly recruit specialized governmental agencies to trace the stolen money. And, it would make it that much easier for the jumper sent to track him down to find him. So, when the cash was almost exhausted, he sold the pretty, cooperative, pert breasted Nadine to a pimp in East St. Louis for $25,000. The fast talking black man had been somewhat reluctant to make the deal, but when he saw how enthusiastically and joyfully Nadine serviced himself and his friends, and how pleased she was at the prospect of becoming his property, he jumped at it.

Afterwards, Jonathan, as he learned to think of himself (having decided to abandon his prior 'name' as a symbol of his determination never to return), desirous of making his trail harder to follow, moved his center of operations west, to Denver, Colorado. There, he converted several other, young, attractive disciples who would be more useful than the sometimes, bubble headed, younger sister of his familiar. He actually found it more efficient to have the enthralled Diane serviced and handled for his benefit by females strange to her, eliminating all ties to her former existence.

Another thing Jonathan had abandoned was the strict ethical code of the Whole. It had been easy for him. He had learned to despise the limitations on his 'personality' inherent in life as an aspect of the Whole. He realized that had he not hidden his yearnings for a more personal, individualized existence, he would have been considered what we would call mentally ill. Although lust was the fuel that connected him to the other universe, for he still needed to maintain that connection, he had found fear greatly enhanced its potency. To instill fear meant to inflict pain. He personally found physical violence abhorrent. Psychic pain was another thing. He often made the lovely, blond Diane writhe in acute distress as a reminder of her duties to him. He had felt a great wave of it when he let the former biology professor know of her baby sister's fate.

The conversion of Nadine to a whore had been so easy and so profitable, he had quickly enthralled and sold four more delectable, young women. Cruising the streets and parks of the city for appropriate candidates, he would, by the simple expedient of touching their arms or their hands, entrance them and have them accompany him back to the small apartment he had rented. He enjoyed breaking the pretty girls in before selling them. They cried and whined when he forced them to undress themselves in his naked presence and that of his other servants. He fed off of their fear and terror, as well as the passion he had stoked in them. One, a black haired, petit beauty who was in Denver just to visit some friends, begged and pleaded to be spared when he informed her of her impending fate. Unlike Nadine, whose memories of her prior existence he wiped out, he left these unhappy young women's memories intact, yet made them unable to disobey the commands of their new 'employers' or to resist the demands of the intense lust he instilled in them.

The money had been useful in setting up the computer equipment he needed and securing quarters where he could more easily keep his familiar in bondage. His education in this universe's laws and the basics of its technology and science increased exponentially. Meanwhile he built his powers through the lust and fear of his familiar and the servants he recruited. He knew the Whole could not terminate his bond to it. It was bound by its own morals and could not do anything to violate its taboo against taking any form of life. Cutting him from its flow of essence between the dimensions would mean the termination of his existence. And once he had access, the only limit on the amount of energy he could "pull through" was the capabilities of his familiar.

Every morning, he would drain the female of the energy she had obtained through her dreams. During the day, he would repeatedly drive her into frenzies of lust. She could not resist him even though he could not use his direct forms of mind control on her. He was her dream man, the epitome of her desires. He had been imbued with the physical form of her ideal. His servants, three appealing, young, now insatiably passionate women, all had regular employments and, after their conversions, had severed all other social relationships and moved in with him. They contributed their salaries to his needs but for the small allowances he permitted them, made sure the isolated house he had rented in a rural suburb was properly supplied with the necessitates of life and, in spite of the deep seated fear he had inculcated in them, adoringly and energetically complied with any and all of his sexual demands.

It was in his third month that he had his stroke of luck. He had just left the law office of a bright, up and coming, business attorney one of his servants had located for him and was in the elevator on his way out of the building when Dolores Marjoram, the 33 year old former trophy wife and now widow of prominent industrialist, Philip Marjoram, stepped in. Jonathan had recruited the handsome and well connected, young, female attorney because he had designed some improvements on existing technology and needed to establish a commercial entity to exploit them. This was in accordance with his second goal: wealth. Naturally, he wanted to enjoy and partake in the most refined and pleasurable experiences his new world offered. These things, he realized, cost money. More importantly, he needed access and use of the finest, most advanced laboratories and technology to build tools that would help him avoid the fate of prior rebels from conformity to the Whole. That would take great amounts of money. And quickly too.

The improvement of the primitive local technology had been simple. The hard part was to develop refinements subtle enough that they did not raise eyebrows as being sudden, miraculous breakthroughs. He did not want to draw untoward attention to himself. And he could not just walk into a company and plop an invention on their desk and receive cash in exchange. He would need to found a corporation, set up bank accounts, pay taxes.

Jonathan had left the pretty, street smart attorney disheveled and exhausted in her office after fucking her three times on her desk during their hour long interview. He had sat in her office chair while she suckled his cock fervently, kneeling between his legs, his hands on her head, redirecting her life's goals to serving him.

Mrs. Marjoram was an attractive 37 years old. She had taken advantage of all of the resources available to her through the wealth of her older husband to maintain her youth and vigor. Her thick, blond hair was stylishly cut to just below her shoulders. Her breasts were round and firm, filling the bodice of her Givinchy "little black dress" enticingly. Her long, well toned legs were shown off provocatively up to just above mid thigh. She was wearing killer black pumps and dark, sheer stockings. Dolores had been a moderately successful, aging, fashion model when she infatuated the much older, just widowed Philip at a party. She had been just 27 when they had married and he had been a spry 76. She hadn't expected him to last more than a few years. He had, to her dismay, lasted ten. Now, she wore her well tailored, stylish and revealing widow's weeds with aplomb, ecstatic at her new freedom and planning a long vacation in Acapulco. She had been visiting her attorneys, the ones whose firm name was too long to fit on a single line on an envelope and whose 75 associates and junior partners occupied the top three floors of the building, to discuss details of her husband's estate and how best for her to assume control of it. She and his 22 year old daughter by a prior marriage, a girl whom she detested virulently, were Mr. Marjoram's sole heirs with Mrs. Marjoram left a controlling 62%. The estate was worth over 300 million dollars.

Jonathan had developed the habit of probing the minds of women he came across while out in the world and had immediately sensed her usefulness. By the time the elevator had reached the bottom floor, Dolores had invited him to lunch. When lunch was over, they went to one of the first class hotels in the business district and rented a room. When she left at 9 o'clock that evening, she was his.

Jonathan realized his conquest of the heart of the beautiful widow would have to seem appropriately gradual and respectful to her dead husband's memory in order to avoid unacceptable public remonstrance. Consistent with his desire to live a low key existence, he didn't want their marriage to become grist for the scandal sheets. And so over the next six months, while he developed his cachet as a moderately successful entrepreneur from back east, his public courtship of the beautiful widow progressed gradually. Privately, he took every opportunity to cement her to his will. The day after their tryst in the elegant, downtown hotel, he took her, on the pretense of a trip to a mountain spa, to his rural homestead, where he taught her the meaning of fear and uncontrollable lust for four days.

They were married in Aspen, a huge affair that was the social hit of the season. Jonathan had realized he would not be able to squelch the publicity surrounding their union. However, the splash was just temporary and when they settled down to married life on the 2500 acre Marjoram estate fifty miles northeast of Denver, the public's interest in them quickly faded. Jonathan had the guest house converted to his private domain where he installed his familiar and his three randy acolytes. Dolores spent most of her days energetically serving him or them, popping out on the social scene under his strict psychic control from time to time, just enough to stifle any rumors.

Cathy Marjoram, Dolores's stepdaughter, who had boycotted the nuptials, had been convinced to pay them a visit when he had met her at a stockholders meeting for Marjoram Industries about a month after the wedding. Jonathan had voted all of Dolores' shares by proxy, and placed himself on the Board. He didn't need to elect himself Chairman. It was too soon for that anyway. From his vantage point as a Board member and representative of the majority shareholder he would be able to quickly assert authority over the direction of investments.

Cathy was a sweet, thin wisp of a girl with big brown eyes. She was shapely, but not voluptuous. She had looked lost in her prim business suit. Her hair was a light brown, long, almost to her waist. She had delicate hands that he remarked upon when they were introduced. Her handshake was soft, almost tender. She had earnestly expressed her hope she and her "father's former wife," as she put it, could live in relative peace. She had no real interest in the money. She merely wanted to be assured an adequate income so she could pursue aspirations as a concert pianist. She was slated to begin study in Paris in a few weeks. When Jonathan invited her to visit at the estate, holding her hand gently in his, the girl seemed dazed for a moment and then agreed. Two weeks later, she cancelled the Paris trip, signed an irrevocable power of attorney in favor of Jonathan and came to live with him and his dutiful wife permanently.

Jonathan had taken care of the servants right away. He had let go the butler who had served the Marjoram family for fifteen years and brought in and converted a 40ish, attractive and efficient, former hospitality manager from one of the downtown hotels. She had weeded out 'unacceptable' staff immediately, and the Blackthornes were now served by pretty, compliant, mostly illegal, Latina girls. The renegade had adapted them to his use one by one. They had been recruited from a business agent who operated out of San Antonio and had been brought directly there. No one would ever miss them, no one who counted that is.

In fact, he had developed a very helpful tool for his future endeavors when one of the nervous maids had been escorted into his presence in the large, well appointed library on the main floor for her 'interview'. Jonathan had begun learning Spanish a few days before and was not yet well versed, but he understood the girl's horrified, whispered ejaculation when she first felt the tendrils of his control wending through her mind. She had fallen to her knees, crossed herself and said, "Mi Dios, el Diablo!" in a soft, desperate voice before crawling naked between his thighs and receiving the essence that would bind her to his will. When he realized how useful the concept would be, Jonathan had immediately adopted it.

All the Hispanic girls who worked for them now believed they had been captured by a demonic power. And, for all practical purposes, they had. Jonathan had had a special design based on a pentagram made for him. He had mounted it on the wall of the library and a larger one in the servant's dorm. All of the servants now carried a tattoo of the pentagram on their bellies, just above their now hairless sexes, marking them, in their horrified minds, as the property of the devil. All of the other women now wore it too. It was to be the signifier of his control over them and all his future female servants.

The alien rebel had now achieved his second goal: comfort and luxury. He now needed economic power. He needed access to world class laboratories and high tech manufacturing facilities where he could conduct research and make prototypes with no questions asked. It had taken the equivalent of seven years of Earth time for the technicians of the Whole to isolate the emotional emanations of his familiar over the dimensional barrier. It was not like fishing where you just put your hook in and hope for the best. The emotional emissions of billions of people crash against the barrier daily and tens of millions of them break through. He calculated that, even under emergency conditions, it would take the technicians of the Whole at least three earth years to isolate the lusty needs of another female sufficiently bright and passionate to cast her emotions across the divide strongly enough to facilitate a pursuer.

Three years was a blink of an eye when you considered that he needed to make what would be revolutionary discoveries in the sciences of this dimension in order to fully accomplish his ultimate goal: to either free himself of the restrictions of dependence on the Whole or to find new ways of access to it that would liberate him from the necessity of maintaining his familiar. She would be a stone around his neck as long as his existence was dependant on her. And she would eventually wither and die. With his abilities to manage and rejuvenate his own flesh, he had estimated he could live 300 years or more before his physical powers diminished in any appreciable way. He could, conceivably, live in this dimension until he was 500 years old. By then, he might be able to find a way to develop and occupy a new male, human body. If he did, he could theoretically live forever.

So, he would need to replace his familiar many times. Although she was in the prime of health, his devoted female acolytes took good care of her in that respect, and he had planned to add a highly skilled, female physician to his coterie of servants as soon as he could, Diane's body would eventually burn out from its state of continuous stress, especially with the intensity of his use of her. It might take two years, three, five or ten, but her usefulness as a conduit to the other side would diminish, slowly at first, and then rapidly until she finally lost the ability to draw energies from the Whole. At that point, he would be finished. And if it happened, it happened. The years he would enjoy as a virtual god on this planet, wallowing in its sensual delights, would be well worth it. If there was a chance he could live many hundreds of years, he would go for it.

So, Jonathan needed to be able to do more than just influence policy. He needed to be able to run Marjoram Industries as a virtual fiefdom, allocating millions of dollars to research, first on how to detect the dimensional barrier with the primitive skills and technologies of this world and then how to exploit it. He was familiar, of course, with the principals that had led to the discovery and overcoming of the dimensional barrier on his side. You could not compare earthly science with the manner that the Whole absorbed and stored knowledge. Everything was different; the laws of science did not translate between universes. On this side he was dealing with whole new concepts. If you made a watch in

London and brought it to the deepest darkest forests of Africa, it would still be a watch. It would tell time. If you brought that watch over the dimensional divide, it would, if you were lucky, be no more than a lumpish, unrecognizable object, assuming it didn't just break down into its constituents and vaporize into dust in your hands, if you had hands.

Jonathan patiently built up his influence in the corporate structure of Marjoram Industries. It was a challenge because most of the decision makers in the company were men and he although could influence them with his mind, he could not control them. Not like he could with females.

A few weeks after his assumption of his duties as a Board member, he invited Charles Conway, who had taken over from Philip Marjoram as CEO a year before his death. Conway, a 43 year old, athletically built, up and comer, had believed he could easily deal with Mrs. Marjoram after Philip's death and saw himself with a bright future managing a Fortune 500 corporation. Now that Jonathan was on the scene, he saw the handwriting on the wall. He was on his way out. Jonathan was already on the Board and Conway expected that by the time next year's stockholders meeting rolled around, Blackthorne would be ready to take the helm. He had the strange man with a seemingly mesmerizing hold over Dolores Marjoram investigated. His people came up blank. And it was really a blank. They could find out nothing about him. It was if he had appeared out of thin air. If Conway had been able to get dirt on the suave, good looking interloper, he might have been able to push him off of the Board, even get Mrs. Marjoram, who was now known as Mrs. Blackthorne, to dump him and take back his control of her shares. Having failed in his efforts, Conway already had feelers out for a new position elsewhere.

Blackthorne had invited Conway and his lovely wife, Anna, to Sunday lunch at the vast Marjoram Estate. They had eaten on the southern veranda, at a table covered with a large, multicolored umbrella to keep off the worst of the sun's heat and served by the fawning and obsequious *Latina* servants dressed in pleasing, little, short skirted servant's uniforms. It was a pleasant, early summer day, slightly warmer than seasonal. Anna Conway, a sociable, well educated woman, about 32, looked appealing in her light, flowery sun dress. She had jet black hair down to just above her shoulders, a thin, long nose, and a narrow face. She was just short of what you would call beautiful, but her face was alert, and her intelligence and attentiveness to Dolores and her cheery disposition, conveyed an attractiveness all its own.

After lunch, Dolores and Anna adjourned to the garden and "Chuck', as Conway insisted Jonathan call him, went into the east rec room to watch the baseball game and finish their beers. The Dodgers were in town and it was potentially a good game. The Rockies were two games back and the Dodgers had lost three in a row. Jonathan had learned to appreciate the sometimes absurd game and he often used the company box at Coors Field. The game was a timeless, almost sensual experience in itself. And being in large, anonymous crowds was always of interest to Jonathan, who would scan the minds of the attractive women he found there, recording information he found, name, address, profession, passion, he could retrieve later.

They had watched the game for about twenty minutes, the Dodgers were ahead 3-1 in the second inning, when Jonathan brought up the subject that lay like a dead elephant on the floor between them.

"So, Chuck, are you going to stay on with us or what?"

Conway had been waiting for Blackthorne to raise the topic. "I'm not sure, Jon," he said. "It depends a lot on you."

"How's that?" Blackthorne inquired.

"Well," Chuck answered, his speech already outlined in his mind. The last thing he wanted Blackthorn to do was to fire him on the spot or to poison the well with other corporate boards by spreading word of his alleged incompetence or other supposed negative characteristics. "I can see Mrs. Blackthorne has a lot of faith in you," he told his rival. "Now that you're on the Board, I just kind of figured in a year or so you'd want to take over, run the place yourself. Not that there's anything wrong with that, but I'm young and at the peak of my abilities. I don't very much relish the role of a caretaker and so I've been looking around, as you probably know." It was good strategy to assume that almost anything you did would be known to your adversaries, especially ones who controlled fabulous wealth as did the Blackthornes.

"Suppose I asked you to stay on, Chuck?" Jonathan retorted. "Suppose I told you that if you did, you would become wealthy beyond your imagination, that you could live the life of ancient Roman Senator, able to exercise unlimited control over all who surrounded you, free to use them as you wished, anytime that you liked? If I could do that for you, would you stay?"

Chuck laughed. "I guess so, Jon. But nobody lives like a Roman Senator these days. And as for wealth, I know the company's doing well, but I really don't see that in the pipeline the way it's currently configured."

"Neither do I Chuck," Jonathan agreed. "Let's just supposed I could make it happen. What would you say then?"

Conway took a long sip of his beer. Blackthorne had always seemed strange to him. Now he knew the man was nuts. He felt like he was walking into a trap. He really didn't want to piss the man off. He just wanted to move on, that's all. He gave a conservative, reasoned response.

"I would have to say, Jon, that I'd need to be shown first, shown that you could do it, given an idea of how. And then I'd need to feel I still had the authority to pull the company in the proper direction. I don't mean any disrespect to you, Jon, or to Mrs. Blackthorne. I don't want to become known as anybody's 'boy'. I guess I mean that I want to make a name for myself, feel that I've accomplished something. I just wasn't made up to be second fiddle."

"But," Jonathan replied, "if I could prove I have the power of an Augustus or Tiberius or one of those other emperors who ruled absolutely for a long, long time, and that I could give you virtually anything you wanted, if I could prove that to you, then you'd do it, right?"

Chuck wanted to leave this uncomfortable subject. "Okay, okay," he said, laughing in an attempt to diffuse the situation. "So, bring on the dancing girls, we'll roast some Christians and turn lead into gold!"

"Well, I can't turn lead into gold. Not yet anyway. The dancing girls would be no problem. And if you want to burn Christians, that's not my bag, but I can arrange it. Okay?"

Chuck laughed again. "Okay," he said nervously. He really wanted to get out of there.

"Suppose we start with something more practical, Chuck?" the alien asked him. "You've been having some problems at home, haven't you?"

The CEO of Marjoram Industries bristled at Jonathan's inquiry. "I don't see that's any of your business, Jon," he replied.

"Ordinarily, I'd agree, Chuck, but bear with me please. Now, I know Anna's unhappy because she caught you cheating on her a few weeks ago. That's true, isn't it?"

Chuck was startled. Nobody knew about that but him, Anna, and the cute little barmaid down at Gibson's Tavern where he stopped in every Friday night for a few.

"Never mind how I know, Chuck," Jonathan continued. "She told you yesterday she wants a divorce because this isn't the first time, right?"

Aghast at the depth of Blackthorne's knowledge, Chuck just sat there. No one knew that either. In fact, he and Anna hadn't even talked about it. She had written him a note and he hadn't had the courage to speak to her since. No one else had read it, he was sure of it. She had always been supportive of his career, but probably came today just to get a good look at the fabled Marjoram estate for the first and last time.

"Let's say I can make that go away, Chuck. Anna would forgive you and never bother you about any of your affairs ever again. She would become a sweet little wife, suck you off whenever you wanted it, fuck your friends if you asked her, let you tie her up and whip her ass until it's red. Would that be proof enough for you?"

Chuck didn't know what to say. He didn't want a divorce. They had no children, that wasn't the problem. They had only been married for four years so there wasn't too much accumulated property to dispose of. It would still cost a lot, but that was just money. There were two, maybe three things that really bothered him. First, he loved Anna, or at least he loved fucking her. She was passionate and responsive, although Jonathan had hit it on the head. She didn't like to give blow jobs. Second, he was, hopefully, an up and coming executive. How would it look to the companies he might apply to to run them if he couldn't manage his own life? It was bound to get around he was being divorced because he couldn't keep his dick in his pants. That's not the way to make friends and influence people in the higher levels of corporate power. Not so much that he did it, but that he got caught.

And thirdly, and maybe this was the most important of all, no one said goodbye to him. He was the one who would decide when and if their relationship was over. His feelings when he first read his wife's note ran through him now. "You fucking cunt," he thought when her read her declaration of intent to leave him. "You don't say goodbye to me! You're mine! I won't let it happen!" He was so mad that if she had been there when he read the note he would have punched her in the face.

"M-maybe," was all he was able to get out in response to Blackthorne's question.

"I tell you what," Jonathan said to him, smiling, knowing his fish was hooked. "When she comes in here, I'm going to order her to suck me off. First she'll strip, then get on her knees and then she'll suck my cock until I come in her mouth. Then, after she swallows my spunk, she's going to turn to you, ask your forgiveness and suck you off too. Okay?"

Conway didn't know whether to run out of the room screaming for his wife to come and get out of there with him or to say yes. Suddenly, he began to get the feeling that the eerie, strange man from nowhere could pull it off. As to fucking his friends, maybe he'd make her do it as a punishment for writing him that letter. She could chew on it while they fucked her up the ass.

There wasn't sufficient time for Chuck to respond. As if on cue, Dolores and Anna came into the room. The rec room was set up with a large, digital TV in a corner with two long, light brown couches in front of it set off against each other to form a corner. You could sit on one and watch the TV and see the face of someone on the other couch at the same time. Anna and Dolores were laughing at some joke.

Anna, looking pleasant and happy, asked, "How's the game?"

"We don't know," Blackthorne answered her. "We've been talking."

"Nothing serious, I hope," she replied lightly. She sat on the couch next to Conway, about six or seven inches away from him, leaned back and crossed her long, delectable legs. Dolores, having received a signal to stay on her feet, stood at the end of the couch. If Anna had been alert, she would have seen a dark cloud cross her face, just for an instant, before she resumed a polite, gracious smile.

"In fact," Jonathan continued, "we've been talking about you."

"Me?" Anna asked, surprise and annoyance on her face. "And what have you been saying?"

"Well," Jonathan said, "I've told Chuck he doesn't have to worry about anything any more. That you're not going to leave him. In fact, you're going to be a better wife to him than you ever have before."

"Oh, is that so?" Anna replied, throwing a steely look at her erstwhile mate. She turned back to Blackthorne.

"I don't think I like...." was all she got out. A wave of confusion ran over her face, once and then again. Her lips moved as if she was going to speak, but nothing came out.

"I want you to do what I tell you, Anna," Jonathan said to her, his voice low and commanding. He didn't really need to say anything to her. He had already made most of the alterations in her brain he needed to. The show was for Chuck's benefit, so he could believe that it was really happening.

A tear formed in Anna's right eye. "Y-yes, Mr. Blackthorne," she said nervously. She could feel lust emanating from the handsome, blond man's body and resounding in her loins. She couldn't explain it. It frightened her.

"I want you to get up and stand in front of the TV. When you get there, I want you to take all of your clothes off. Leave those pretty sandals on. Then, when you're done, I want you to kneel down on the floor, spread your legs and put your hands behind your back. OK? And then, when I think you're ready, you can come over here and suck my prick."

Anna, her face a mask of fear and unhappiness, nodded dolefully. Why was she agreeing with him, she thought fearfully. Was she really going to do what he said? She felt she had to, that she had no choice. She looked over at Dolores. Her face had gone blank as if she had washed her hands of the whole thing. She could get no help there. Then she looked at her husband. He was staring at her, shocked and amazed she hadn't gotten up, slapped Blackthorne across the face and stomped out. There was also a gleam in his eye that told her he was in total agreement with the compelling blond man's commands. She looked back at Blackthorne as if for a reprieve. Maybe he was kidding?

"I'm waiting, Anna," he said.

Slowly, dismally, the attractive, 32 year old Anna Conway raised her body from the couch. She walked gingerly over to the TV and turned to face the others in the room. She winced when she saw that one of the pretty, short skirted, serving girls who had waited on them at lunch was standing in the back of the room, her hands placed behind her back, her legs parted, watching intently. Blackthorne had muted the TV, but the game was still going on behind her.

Jonathan increased his message of lust to the forlorn woman along with a surge of the need to obey. He also stoked her feelings of fear so that her hands were shaking when she reached them behind her neck to loosen the tied strands which held up her yellow and orange, flowered bodice. Her face was wrenched with confusion and horror as she untied the straps of her dress and pulled them forwards to the tops of her breasts. She hesitated there, perhaps hoping for someone to say it had all been a bad joke. When no reassurance was forthcoming, she gave a sob and lowered them past her pale, round, braless mounds.

Ana's breasts were plump, but not large. Their ends came to points and curved upwards slightly. Good for a 32 year old. Her nipples were small and flat, but had hardened with her fear and developing sexual passion. She couldn't figure out where it was coming from. She had never had the urge to do anything like this before, never fantasized about it. Why was it making her so hot? And she knew the further she went, the more obedient she was to the hard, blond man's commands, the hotter she would get.

"You know, Chuck," Jonathan said to his CEO, who was staring, unbelieving at the woman who he thought he had known for four years. "Anna has nice tits, but they'd be nicer if they were a little bigger. I have a guy you can call. He does a real nice job. I had him do Cathy's. You've met Cathy, haven't you, Dolores's stepdaughter? She's busy down at the guest house right now. I'll send her by the office some day next week and you can get a look at them."

Chuck looked at Jonathan, his eyes glazed, and nodded. He looked back at his trembling wife.

Jonathan too had resumed his gaze on the unhappy woman and when she saw the look in his eyes, the look of command, promising retribution for disobedience, she quickly shuffled the dress over her hips and let it fall to the floor. She was wearing a thin, white thong that barely covered her fluffy mass of black pubic hair. She crossed her arms across her taut belly and placed her hands over her private place, but only momentarily. Remembering her duty to obey, she took the sides of the thong in her thumbs and pulled it slowly down her thighs. She bent forward, causing her breasts to shift out from her body and drew the thong over her knees and down her shins. She pulled it free from her one foot at a time, carefully making sure it did not catch on her high heeled sandals and, at the same time, stepping out of the circle her discarded dress had formed around her. Punctilious about her clothes even in moments of stress, she picked them up and looked for somewhere to put them. Dolores, feeling an encouraging nudge from her husband and master, stepped forward and took them from her. Anna gave her a little smile in thanks and stepped back to her position in front of the TV.

Anna wondered frantically what was happening to her. Slowly, in obedience to Jonathan's command, she sank to her knees, spreading her long, slim thighs as she did so. When she felt the thick carpet on her kneecaps, a rush of pleasure soared through her. She sighed deeply and closed her eyes to let it pass. When she opened them, she placed her hands behind her back and looked at the two men anxiously. She felt her pussy burning with need. She couldn't understand how this was happening, but she understood that the strange, mysterious Mr. Blackthorne had something to do with it. He was smiling at her in appreciation of her obedience and when she saw he was pleased, another surge of passion coursed through her. She felt drawn to him, to whatever he was going to do to her. He said she was going to suck his prick. Her mouth and lips tingled at the prospect of having his cock. She wanted to do it now.

Anna felt her lusts building as she felt the eyes of the men and the women in the room on her naked flesh, her bare, proffered breasts, her available sex. She closed her eyes to block it out, but couldn't dissipate the vision of the muscular, broad shouldered, blond man's cold, hard gaze.

"Anna?" Blackthorne asked the clearly impassioned woman after about thirty seconds of heavy, pregnant silence had passed. "Are you wet yet?" His voice was pleasant, as if asking her if she needed some more tea or whether, perhaps, she would like a piece of cake. She looked at him uncertainly.

"I-I'm not sure," she said unhappily.

"Why don't you put your fingers in your pussy and see?" Blackthorn suggested.

Anna welcomed the suggestion to touch her burning slit. She drew a hand from behind her back and, after first running it over her soft, flat belly, let it fall to her loins. Her teeth bit her lower lip as she gently pried her engorged labia apart and touched her inner self. She was wet and her fingers slid inside her easily. She closed her eyes and let the feeling of her self penetration send her welcome messages of pleasure. She let her hand drift north and she rubbed her hardened pleasure bud softly. She moaned with desire.

"What's the answer, Anna?" Jonathan asked, interrupting her reverie.

"Y-yes," she answered dreamily.

"Then it's time to come here and take my cock in your mouth," Jonathan ordered. He had unzipped his cream colored, soft, loose linen pants and now revealed his thick, angry looking cock. Anna, who had opened her eyes at his voice of command, stared at it hungrily.

"Y-yes, Mr. Blackthorne," she said softly. Every cell in her body wanted her mouth to purse around the man's swollen member. She leaned over to her hands and crawled to him. She knelt between his legs and, taking hold of the huge instrument in her hand, directed it towards where she knew it belonged. She moaned as she let her lips tighten around it and pressed her head forward, engulfing it slowly into her. Blackthorne also moaned with pleasure. He would never get tired of the feeling of a hot mouth around his dick. Nor for the burning heat of a lustful cunt, or, for that matter, the steamy warmth of a woman's bowels, her tight, rear ring gripping his shaft firmly. He could come twenty five to thirty times a day, more if he really pushed himself. He never got tired of fucking or of sampling newly enraptured women. He had good food, near to the best the world could provide, lived in beautiful surroundings, had power, money. If he had to give it all up and keep just one thing, it would be the fucking. And of all the sexual acts he could force a woman to perform, kneeling between his thighs and sucking his cock was on the top of the list.

Blackthorne placed his hands on Anna's head while she slowly, lustfully serviced his hard prick. "Put your arms behind your back, Anna," Jonathan told her. "Grab your elbows ands spread your legs. Let your husband see your wet pussy."

Obediently, Anna released her hand from Blackthorn's shaft and put her arms straight across her back until she had grasp of her opposite elbows. She arched her back and spread her legs, proud to let her mate see the evidence of her excitement. Her lusts built higher and higher as she ran her lips down the length of the hard pole. She felt the man place his hands on her head and his will pour into her. She sensed that when she received his viscous discharge it would bind her to him irrevocably. She would obey him in all things as long as she lived. Some part of her persona rebelled at the thought. She was a graduate of Wesleyan University, had a masters in French literature, had friends, parents, people with whom she had bonds who she would lose forever.

She felt the man's body stiffen in preparation for his discharge. In a moment she would be lost, she needed to act now! All she had to do was get up from her knees, but the pleasure of having her mouth filled with the man's meat was too strong. She felt the first throb of his cock, tasted the sweet precum that oozed out of its end. It was too late. Anna, the elegant, sophisticated, educated, handsomely beautiful, liberated woman disappeared the moment Blackthorne's cum spurted on her fervent tongue. Mindlessly, she drew every drop of his essence from him. She moaned with pleasure as she felt her pussy clench and spasm in return.

Blackthorne reveled in his orgasm. His lust spilled throughout the room. Dolores and the maid swooned as his psyche pierced them and filled them with desire. He sent fierce messages of pleasure through his hands to the body of the now enthralled woman.

When his discharge was finished, Jonathan eased the lovely woman's head off his loins. He didn't need to tell her her duties. He had implanted them deeply inside of her. She would serve her husband joyfully. She would also report to him, Jonathan, anything her husband did that might not be in Jonathan's interests. All that had already been accomplished with a simple twist of her mind. He needed to complete the show for Conway's sake.

Conway's mouth was hung open in stupefaction. He had just watched his wife, who spurned oral sex, reach climax just from sucking off Blackthorne's cock. And she had done it willingly, enthusiastically. She had stripped in front of all of them without a word of protest. Could this be real?

Jonathan addressed the dizzy, satiated women. "Anna, listen to me," he said. The woman's eyes sprung open. "You aren't finished yet," he reminded her.

The woman's face lit up as if she had remembered she had left the gas burner on at home. Keeping her hands folded behind her back, she shifted on her knees and faced her husband, her new lord. Tears began to flow to her eyes. Her face cringed in misery. "I'm sorry, Charles," she said, earnestly. "I'll never do it again, I promise. Please, please forgive me. I'll do anything for you, I promise, please." She was staring into his face, searching for a sign of redemption. Her cheeks were wet and her chest heaved. "I'm so sorry," she whined in a long, mournful voice.

Conway looked at her. The man had done it. He had really done it. Anna, comely and enticing in her naked submission, her expression grim and remorseful, was his again and he could do anything he wanted with her. He hurriedly released his already stiffened cock from his pants.

"Come here and suck my cock, Anna. If you do a good job, I'll forgive you."

Anna sobbed in relief. She walked on her knees over to him and laid her head in his lap. Her rejoicing mouth engulfed his cock and she began to suck it lovingly. It took Chuck only a few minutes to come. His eyes rolled back and he groaned as he shot his sperm into her mouth. Anna drank it readily, joyously. When Chuck was done, he patted her on the head. "That was great, Anna," he said.

"So," Jonathan asked the sated CEO, "do we have a deal?"

CHAPTER NINE

Of course they had a deal. Jonathan knew it all along. He had pilfered Anna's mind at lunch and saw immediately Conway would play ball. He had just a few more words for Anna before she left with her new lord and master.

"Anna," he told her, "I want you to look at something." He pulled from his pocket a silver dollar sized, metal replica of the pentagram he had mounted in his library and in the servant's dorm and soon would have mounted in every room of the huge mansion, even the bathrooms. "I want you to take a good look at this, Anna," he said. She had turned when he spoke to her and she shifted towards him on her knees, a dollop of her husband's cum on her lower lip, her arms still dutifully pinioned behind her back as if held there by iron chains. Her vision shifted from Jonathan's face to his hand. As she gazed at the wide, dull, copper colored, round object, he created a wellspring of lust and fear inside the young woman.

"It's the symbol of your submission, Anna," the blond man told her. He was standing before her, the disk held at the level of her eyes. "It is the talisman of my will. Whenever you see it, you will remember what you have become: my servant, and the servant of my followers. It will strengthen your need for obedience and you will obey anyone who shows it to you. It will drive your lusts, cause your pussy to burn with need. Tomorrow, after your master goes to work, you will return here and a copy of this symbol will be marked on your body as a permanent reminder of who you now are."

Anna stared at the symbol with horror. She could not tear her gaze from it. The thought of carrying such a powerful and dreadful reminder of her enslavement on her flesh was terrifying and she felt a deep ache of fear inside her. Jonathan stroked that fear until it became a well of pain.

"As you feel now is how you will feel when even the thought of disobedience crosses your mind. Kiss the talisman and let its power fill you."

The frightened, anguished woman cringed at the thought of contact with the evil sign, but she was compelled to obey. She bent her head foreword, her straight, jet black hair framing her face like a curtain. Just as her lips touched it, Blackthorne sent another, fierce message of fear and lust through her. She moaned and sobbed and her naked body trembled, unable to tear her lips from the offensive object.

"All right, Anna," Jonathan finally told her. He released her mind and she collapsed to the floor.

The symbol, of course had no power. Jonathan was not a magician or a wizard. He couldn't put spells on things. But if a frightened, enthralled mind thought the device had power, then it did. Anna would cringe with fear and lust whenever she saw it. And more conveniently, if he ever had the need to take Anna way from Chuck, she would be useful to any of his followers who possessed one of the precious talismans.

Anna, at Jonathan's urging, rose from the floor and sought out her clothes. Chuck also rose to his feet. He watched his altered wife as she dolefully redonned her bright, happy dress and wondered if he had just sold his soul to the devil. He looked at Blackthorne. Maybe he had. But it was going to be a swell ride.

After that, gaining full control of the workings of Marjoram Industries was easy. He didn't grant his favors to all of the Board members, just the ones he and Conway agreed were essential. Anna was very useful in convincing the men's wives or lovers to come visit the mansion, where she cooperated enthusiastically in their enthrallments. The talismans were made in extremely limited editions and he granted access to them sparingly. He had had them constructed in a way that only the originals, made under his strict license from a dye he kept locked in a special safe he had designed in his bedroom, would be recognized by the women as authentic, thereby eliminating the risk of counterfeits.

And so over the next few months, Jonathan began to look for an appropriate location for what was his next need. He needed, in essence, a fortress which would provide him unlimited privacy, a place to conduct some of his experiments and a barrier that would make the task of his pursuer, when he came, more difficult. It would need to be remote, but not so inaccessible as to restrict his need to move about the country.

When he learned about the relative sovereignty of American Indian reservations, and came to appreciate the still powerful pull of old customs and beliefs among them, especially among certain Indian tribes of the American Southwest, a plan began to formulate itself. He made a study of various reservations and tribes and came to believe the Apache Chiracahua Reservation near the New Mexico panhandle was perfect for his needs. It was extremely remote. The citizens of the reservations were poor and the land barely supported them. Their beliefs in their heritage was strong. And the Apache warriors had been among the most fierce and feared in the American West.

He made a long, exhaustive study of Apache religion, history and culture. He even hired an Apache to teach him the language, something, to his instructor's amazement, he was able to master in a few short weeks. Having prepared himself, he flew down to Los Cruces and drove in a large motor home, along with his familiar and her three handlers, to the reservation. He had paved his way by sending a message via his instructor to one of the more prestigious shamans. Word was returned he would see him.

He met the old, haggard priest outside of a broken down trailer deep inside the reservation. Jonathan had learned as much as he could about the man before he came. He spent most of his days meditating and praying. He survived by giving blessings and performing ceremonies for fellow tribe members, receiving food and other offerings in return. No one was sure how old he was. His grandfather had fought with Geronimo in the last, great Indian uprising in the West. Sometimes, he would disappear for months at a time, only to be found one day back at his perch in front of the teepee, meditating in the scorching New Mexico desert sun, waiting for a customer.

Jonathan, his familiar and her handlers accompanying him, had to travel twenty miles along a washed out, dirt roadway to get to him. The small, dirty and rusty, aluminum trailer rested on its axles and sat about 100 yards or so off of the road. He was able to negotiate the motor home to within about 50 yards of it. It had no heat, hot water or electricity. The blazing desert sun glinted off of it almost painfully. He left the women in the van and slowly approached the ancient man who was sitting cross legged outside of a small, torn and tattered teepee. He had long, thin, sparse, grey hair that was being cast about by the strong, hot wind. He was wearing a faded, cotton, brown and white checkered, long sleeved shirt buttoned to his neck, an old and torn pair of bleached out jeans and worn, yellowish work boots with a hole in one of the soles. His eyes were dark and piercing, his face wrinkled, with deep gullies in his cheeks. "*Ta hey*," Jonathan told the man and sat down across from him. The man repeated the greeting and resumed his silence.

The two men, the otherworlder and the priest, sat in the desert sun for two hours wordlessly. The old man kept his eyes closed for most of the time, opening them now and again to take in the form of the blond haired white man and then closing them again. Jonathan could feel the old man probing him with his mind. He let him and examined him in return. He was a man wise in the ways of spirituality and a strong believer in the powers of emotions and dreams. Jonathan let his own powers flow through the man, letting him feel them, understand them. He could not control the old man or any males for that matter. He could read their emotions and, to some extent their minds, when thoughts and emotions were coupled strongly together. The old Indian, however, was a ruler of emotions and thoughts, and his musings were impenetrable.

At the end of the second hour, the old man suddenly got up and went into the shabby tent. He returned with a bottle of whiskey and two battered tin cups. He poured some liquor in both and offered one to Blackthorne. He raised his cup and said, "*Ta hey.*" Jonathan repeated the toast and drank the harsh, strong liquid down.

The man finally spoke in Apache. "*Many years ago, I had a vision about a man like you. He arose from the mist in the dreams of a white woman. He had powers like yours. The man came to me with an eagle's feather in one hand and in the upraised palm of his other hand he had the sun. He was a very powerful spirit. Everywhere he stepped the land turned green and fruitful. He gave the men strength and made the women fecund. He spilled his seed onto the ground and a great fire erupted, driving all of our years of suffering away. The people turned back to the old ways and the land, farther than an eagle can fly in a day, was ours again.*"

The man paused and took a breath. He was not finished and Jonathan knew better than to interrupt him. After several minutes, he resumed.

"*I do not know if you are that man or not. You have the powers the vision spoke of. The woman is here. I would see her.*"

Jonathan sent a strong message to his familiar in the motor home. Diane spent most of her days under the spell of lust and need he had imposed on her. She did have times of clarity, times, usually when she would bemoan her fate and yearn for freedom, but she was too strongly bound to the dream man to ever think of trying to leave him. Not that she would have had any opportunities to do so. She was carefully guarded at all times by the three young women her dream man had recruited. And each time she dared to conceive of her separation from him, her soul would ache and she would break into tears.

The naked, blond woman came tip toeing out of the motor home. She was unused to being unescorted and was usually fettered or bound. The bright, early afternoon sunlight blinded her at first. She put her hand over her eyes and saw the old man sitting in the dust and her lord sitting opposite him. She was frightened. He had sold his beautiful sister Nadine to those men many months ago. Was he going to sell her to the old man? Had she served her usefulness to her mysterious and powerful captor?

She began to cry as she approached the men slowly and fearfully, walking carefully over the rocky, pitted ground in her bare feet, her large breasts swaying and jostling, her hands up and out from her body for balance. Her thick blond hair had grown longer since she had been enthralled and, caught in the strong wind, it cascaded behind her like a flowing mane. Jonathan's servants kept her pale, voluptuous body clean and soft. Her outward appearance showed none of the ravages her psyche had borne. She was a beautiful, almost angelic sight. On her belly, above her hairless mons, she bore the tattoo of Jonathan's pentagram.

When she finally reached where the men were sitting, Jonathan compelled her with his mind to kneel next to the old man, her back erect, her knees spread, her hands crossed behind her. He could have wiped her fear away with a thought. He did not care to. He wanted the old man to feel the strength of his power in her.

When Diane was settled next to the old man, he spoke again. "*I want to feel her soul,*" he said. "*Do not interfere.*"

The old man got up from his cross legged position and knelt in front of the trembling, unhappy Diane. The man had spoken a strange language. There was something going on between the two men and she couldn't tell what it was. The man raised his head level to hers, placed his hands on either side of her face and peered into her eyes. He held her there, her vision locked to his, for a long time. His black, almost dead eyes were transfixing to her and she quickly lost herself in them. Suddenly, she felt like he was inside her. There was a bright light in her head and she could feel the inquiring probes of his consciousness piercing her brain. Her mind screamed in terror. She tried to move away from the old man with his gnarly, old hands, wrinkled face and steely black eyes. She was paralyzed. When her mind reached out for her master, seeking his essence, she could not find him. Her whole body cringed with anguish.

Finally, the man had seen enough and he withdrew his gaze from her. Diane felt she had been released from the torments of hell. Her chest heaved for breath and her body was shivering. The man knelt in front of her for a few moments, considering her naked body. He then came closer to her again, reached out his strong, hot, wrinkled hands and proceeded to examine every inch of her flesh.

Diane cringed as she felt his scratchy hands flow over her shoulders and arms. He examined both of her hands carefully before returning them to behind her back. He lifted her heavy breasts, weighing them, teasing the fat nipples to hardness and then pushing them against her chest as if testing their resilience. He then leaned over and took her teats in his mouth, one after the other, suckling at her long and hard until she moaned. She whined when he pushed her callously over into the dust and took his time feeling the muscles of her legs from the very tops of her thighs all the way to her ankles. Rolling her over, he ran his hands along her back and over her rump. He was silent as he worked; his only sounds an occasional grunt or wheeze.

The dazed and terrified familiar obeyed the man without questioning his right to manhandle her. Her arms stayed pressed behind her back obediently and she remained deathly silent except for little moans or cries when the man probed a muscle or moved her body this way or that. She didn't know whether she should pray the man find her body satisfactory for whatever purpose he had or reject her. In the first case, the dream man might leave her here with him so he could work some cruel, inhumane purpose on her. On the other hand, if she were found unsuitable, her unhappy ruler would certainly inflict prolonged, intense punishment.

When he had rolled Diane again onto her back, he placed his hands under her pale thighs and raised them, pushing them back until her knees touched her breasts. He then dipped his gray haired head and placed his lips on her hairless, exposed sex. Diane jumped with passion and fear when she felt his hot lips and tongue press against the tender flesh of her vulva. A fierce warmth spread from his mouth over her loins, up her torso and into her brain. Her body shivered as she felt him run his rough tongue along her crevasse up and down and back again until it softened and yielded and he could thrust it inside her.

Diane could see the man's scraggly, gray head between her thighs, feel his iron grip on her legs. Her back arched painfully over her folded arms behind her. She looked desperately for a view of her lord. She saw him, sitting calmly, looking dispassionately at her. She was frantic that her worries about being sold to the old man were coming true. She wanted to cry out to him, to beg he not send her away, but she knew too well the punishment for speech. She had started to cry again. Neither the old man nor the being who had enthralled her paid it any mind. The man's tongue had begun to excite her beyond tolerance and the confused and terrified woman gave out a low, unhappy moan of passion. The man's long, hot tongue was pressed deeply into her velvet passage. It was like he was trying to taste her, to gain the flavor of her soul. She could feel it washing along the sides of her lush canal.

The old man, satisfied at last, finally released her and pulled her back to her knees. She was covered with sweat and dirty and dusty from rolling on the ground. Her face was wet with her tears and her beautiful, long, blond hair was tangled and knotted.

Diane thought he was done with his exploration of her. She was wrong. The old man paused for a few moments as if digesting the knowledge he had gained from his callous exploration of her body. He then, without warning, reached up his hands and pushed her shoulders back, forcing her torso down. He relented only when her shoulders were touching the ground. Her knees were still under her and her thighs and back ached. Her belly and breasts were pointed to the harsh sun above. The rough, worn hands caressed her belly and, to the supine, blond woman's dismay, moved up and seized her breasts once again.

This time, he was not weighing them, assessing them. Having gained knowledge of her flesh, he now sought to explore her desires, her passions, her lusts. He began a slow, gentle massage of her generous mounds, teasing and squeezing them, worrying her stiffened nipples. His hands were hot and filled with a strange energy. She could not prevent the enflaming of her desire. Diane closed her eyes and let her mind become absorbed in the pleasures of the skillful, knowledgeable hands. Slowly, methodically, he stroked her, almost like he was drawing something out of her, milking her soul.

Diane was panting and squirming with need when the hands left her breasts. They ran back down her belly and she felt them stop at the site of her master's mark. She hated its presence on her body. Her master sometimes radiated his power to it, causing it to burn, filling her with fear and despair through it. Every time she saw it, on herself in the mirror, or on the other women who he used to torment and pleasure her, she cringed and felt the man's evil powers running through her.

Now, she felt the old man infusing the symbol with his own powers. The detested mark seemed to glow on her belly and the man's psyche flowed into her through it. She felt like her body had been filled with a fierce fire. She screamed and moaned in agony. Her body was frozen in place and she was unable to make any move to escape him. It went on and on. She felt like her insides were being scorched, burned away. Finally, after what seemed an eternity, he withdrew his hand and the fire subsided, leaving the pale skinned, blond woman panting and moaning.

As the agonizing burning diminished, Diane body became infused with a terrible energy. She started to shudder and shake as if some being had sprung to life inside her. Her pussy burned with need, her breasts ached. Her mind screamed for release. Then, eschewing all other physical contact with her, the old man placed one long, boney finger between her naked, exposed labial lips and began to stroke her needful slit. To Diane, nothing in the world existed except the small point of contact between the flesh of the man's gnarled finger and her sex. Her pussy became lush with her discharge and grew hot and fevered. Slowly, delicately, the finger teased her, driving her lust higher and higher.

The frantic woman's mind begged him to grant her completion, but he kept her passion burning on and on. When her orgasm came, it came on her all at once, her pussy exploding into hard, excruciatingly pleasurable contractions. Diane called out, "Ohhhhhhhhhhhhh! Ohhhhhhhhhhhhh! Ohhhhhhhhhhhhh!" as her spasms rocked her. When they subsided, and her mind was able to express her gratitude for relief, she found the cruel finger was still inside her, stroking her slowly and steadily until her lusts began to arise again.

When the old man had made the familiar come for the third time, he finally sat down back in his original place. He left the woman where she was, dazed, sweaty and panting, her back lodged in the dry, clingy dust, her legs bent and underneath her, her thighs spread wide. He poured himself and the stranger another whiskey and waited another fifteen minutes before he spoke.

"She will serve you better now, better than before. I can see you draw your power from your ghost world through her. It will be better now, stronger and more pure. She is your power and your weakness. You have need to protect her from the one who will come later."

Jonathan confirmed the man's prescience with a nod. The ancient, gray haired man continued.

"I have a task for you and then I will tell you whether I will serve you. A young woman will be here shortly, sent to me by her family to be cured, although she does not know that. She has taken up with the white man's filthy ways. She sells herself for their money and takes their white powders. Her soul is blackened with her sins. When she comes here, you must purify her and bind her to serve me. If you do that, I will serve you."

The men sat together, silently meditating. Diane remained lying where the old man had left her. After a short while, he went into the tent and returned with a dark brown hood which looked like it was made of unfinished deer hide, and a gourd filled with liquid. He lifted Diane's head and pushed the gourd against her lips, tilting it back until a milky, white liquid poured out, some of it spilling over her chin and down around her neck. The woman gulped it down gratefully. Then, placing the gourd aside, the man drew the hood over Diane's head and pulled it tightly around her neck. He let her head down to the ground gently and resumed his position.

There was no further movement or action until, about forty minutes later, a car's engine was heard in the distance. Jonathan turned and looked and saw a dusty, battered, old Chevy barreling down the dry dirt road, raising a huge cloud behind it. As it approached he could hear loud, tinny rock music blaring from its speakers. The car skidded to a stop, the music died and the car door swung open. A young woman emerged.

She was clearly a native, about 20 or 21 years old, and pretty in a saucy, insolent sort of way, with dark, black stringy hair and deep reddish brown colored features. She was wearing a short, tight, black spandex skirt which stretched over her enticing hips and a bright, tie dyed, multicolored t-shirt about two sizes too small. Her legs were covered by thick, dark tights that were torn in two or three places and she wore tall, black leather boots with pointy tips and high heels. Her large, loose breasts pushed firmly against the thin cotton cloth. Jonathan could see about three inches of her taut, brown belly. Her hair was held fast to her head by a black headband.

The girl stuck her head back into the car, pushing the front seat forward. As she leaned over, her skirt rode high on her thighs, exposing the gentle curve of her buttocks. After a second, she reemerged from the grubby vehicle slammed the door shut with a loud 'clang!' and began to march towards the two attentive men.

When she got a few yards away from them, she spoke, not in Apache, but in English. "Here, old man, I got your whiskey for you," she announced.

The old man turned to Jonathan and whispered in Apache concernedly, *"Don't let her drop the bottle."*

Jonathan, smiling, nodded his understanding. The woman stopped a few feet from the old man and held the bottle out to him. "My aunt told me to bring this to you and that you'd be able to give me some peyote buds," she stated matter of factly.

Jonathan screened her mind. Her aunt had paid her twenty dollars and gave her two bottles of whiskey for the old man. The other one was still in the back seat of her jalopy. She had said nothing about peyote buds.

The woman's Apache name was Faun that Leaps. She called herself Betty Leaps. Her stage name at the strip club she worked at near the air force base in Billingsly, about 200 miles west of where they stood, just over the Arizona border, was Faun. The place doubled as a whorehouse and Betty lived there for weeks at a time and then came back to the reservation to rest at her aunt's for several days. The girls lived in trailers at the back of the club which is where they did their entertaining. Betty spent most of her money on drugs for her and her Anglo boyfriend, a 37 year old biker named Billy. Billy was an ex-con who had done a stretch for armed robbery and drug distribution.

All this, Jonathan learned in a few seconds of searching Betty's mind. He also learned she had shot up a speedball about an hour and a half ago and was as high as a kite, which apparently interfered with her ability to see the naked white woman lying in the dirt. A moan from the hooded, obscenely displayed woman made Betty turn her head and look.

Betty's eyes only lingered on the form of the naked woman for a few seconds. From Diane's appearance, the implications of a nonconsensual arrangement that could be drawn from the hood tightly bound around her neck and her submissive, unusual posture, a reasonable person would have at least suspected there was something going on not necessarily in the supine, white lady's interests. Betty paid it no heed. Jonathan noted that her mind, while registering the other woman's probable distress, did not flinch or deviate a single iota from her goal. Betty looked at the two men quickly. "Having a party?" she asked jokingly. And then she looked back at the old man and said, "How about them Peyote buds?"

Diane had heard the car pull up, had heard the woman approach and had heard her speak. But Diane was not in receptive to communication or particularly concerned about what was going on around her at that moment. She had been happy to receive the drink the old man gave her, although it was hot and seemed bitter. She had been startled when he covered her head in the course, brown bag. Her face quickly became hot and sweaty and it was difficult to breathe. She dared not remove it or complain. Her lord would punish her severely, something she wanted to avoid with all her soul.

While the men had sat quietly, her mind had been concentrated on the echoes of her ordeal at the hands of the old man. Slowly, her body started to feel strange, as if it was beginning to float off of the ground. Her mind began to spin and she found it hard to focus. The sounds around her became loud and sharp. The arrival of the car had been like a roar in her ears, and the woman's voice was strange, almost unearthly. She recognized the words as English, but could not fathom any meaning from them. She started to realize the old man had given her something in the drink that was making her mind go wild. She had heard that American Indians of the Southwest were heavily into psychedelics, peyote, psilocybin. She was certain she had been dosed by the old man. Her concern quickly faded as her mind drifted away into a meditation on nothing. Her moan had been unconscious, an involuntary reaction to the mesmerizing images floating in her head.

Jonathan decided it was time to act. "Please hand me the whiskey," he told the young Apache girl in a soft voice. It was the first time he had spoken for hours. He was not thirsty or tired. He could regulate his body's needs easily and could sit there for many more hours without distress. He sent a strong message of obedience to the girl's mind. The girl looked at him quizzically and then handed him the bottle. He put it down next to him.

There was no need for Jonathan to speak his commands to the girl, the old man knew exactly what he was doing. But the effect of hearing the verbal commands on the subject of enslavement was to heighten her fear and confusion, as if the words themselves held the power that compelled her to obey.

"I'd like you to kneel, Betty, and take off your shirt. I want to see your tits," Jonathan ordered the girl in a soft, gentle voice. The girl looked at him as if he was off of his rocker, yet her knees slowly lowered until they were on the ground. She tried to say something, looking at the old man, and then her hands went to her waist and she lifted her shirt free, over her swaying breasts, over her head and then tossed it aside. Betty's breasts were large for her frame, but, despite her profession, completely natural. Her skin was dark and reddish and her areolas were even darker. Her nipples were long and fat. Betty went to place her hands on them, to cover them, then seemed to remember the white man had wanted to see them. She turned her body towards him so he could get a better view. Her eyes were frantic with misunderstanding as to why she was on her knees showing this strange man her tits. Her mouth moved several times. Nothing came out.

"Betty," Jonathan, said to the confused, upset girl, "please move a little closer to me so I can caress you." Betty complied immediately, even raising her chest so her lovely, heavy mounds could find a home in the man's hands. Jonathan reached out and took hold of them, sending waves of lust and fear into the dark skinned woman. She whined as it flowed through her. He then sent her a strong message of obedience, forcing his will over hers. It only took a few seconds. He altered her mind surgically, leaving her memories and personality in place, but depriving her of independence, rebelliousness, self interest. He terminated her brain's ability to receive stimulation from the drugs that were in her system and replaced it with an intense sensitivity to stimulation of her loins, her lips and the tips of her breasts. He drew new lines of pleasure from the tight ring of her rear entry to her brain.

The young woman moaned as Jonathan's hands continued to stimulate her. He passed to her a need to obey him so strong and deep into her psyche that her body shuddered when it received it.

Jonathan did not need to explain to the old man what he was doing. And he had not been concerned about the ability to meet the old man's challenge. He wanted to impress the strength and intensity of his powers on the priest so he would tell the others, bring others to him, until the tribe was willing to let him build his sanctuary here.

Jonathan removed his hands from the girl's breasts. She was panting with lust and consternation. She knew the man had done something to her, changed her. She knew she shouldn't have such a strong desire to be possessed by him, to serve him, but it was there, as undeniable as the need to breathe. She wanted to offer herself to him, be with him, go with him when he left. Nothing else mattered.

Jonathan sent the girl a silent message and she quickly turned and began to pull off her boots. When they had been shed, she leapt to her feet and loosened, removed and stepped out of her skirt. She then pulled her tights down over her thighs and then off of her feet, a thin, black thong with it. She resumed her kneeling posture in front of the compelling white man. Jonathan sent her a wave of pleasure for her obedience and she moaned.

"Face the priest, Betty," the powerful, dimension traveler told her. "Show him your pretty breasts."

The girl turned her body so she was facing the old man and lifted her breasts to him. The old man looked at them appreciatively.

"*She has nice tits,*" the old man said to Jonathan.

Jonathan did not reply. Instead, he moved on to conclude his demonstration of power. The hot sun beat down upon the girl. Her dark body was sweating and her knees were covered with dust. Her breathing was heavy, raising her chest up and down making her breasts flutter. She was cupping them in her hands, proffering them to the strange, old man. Blackthorne eased his control over her until her mind began to race with frantic worry about how the man had compelled her to strip and pose lasciviously before the old one. Although the girl had spoken English when she had arrived, she had learned Apache as a child and had buried it deeply within her. Blackthorne reached into her subconscious and opened it to let her ability to understand the harsh, guttural sounds bloom forth.

"*Fawn Who Leaps*," he addressed her, "*you have made your body into a pit of sin. You have shown your body to strange men, let them touch it and use it for the white man's money. You have used the white man's poison to dull your brain and to excite your body. You have abandoned the old ways, shown your disdain for your elders. Even today, you have stolen from this priest, keeping what was meant for him, lying to him, seeking to profane the medicines of your religion and sell them to the white man*"

The Indian girl shivered in fear. She could not move a muscle of her body, although every ounce of her will wanted to get up and run away. The man had some strange power over her, she realized it. Suddenly, she panicked. "The white man is a witch!" she screamed inside. Her mother, now dead from alcoholism and drugs, her father, who disappeared several years ago and had not been seen since, her aunts and uncles who had tried to keep her from her self destructive ways, all had told her the old tales about spirits who could take human form and steal your soul. Back at the pueblo, the other young people had told stories about the old man, saying that he dealt with devils. The older ones, when they heard that talk, quieted them and refused to speak of him.

She should have realized something was up when her aunt, her face serious and concerned, gave her the twenty dollars and told her to bring the liquor to him. She needed the money for gas to get back to Billingsly. She should have known better. And now, here she was, in the power of a demon. She started to cry and made an attempt to beg for release. She couldn't get any sounds past her lips and her fear deepened. She looked at the old man. He looked cruel and decrepit, evil. What were they going to do to her? Would they turn her into a snake or a rat, or imprison her in a stone? Would they burn her body as a sacrifice, her and the white woman who they held prisoner?

Jonathan let the lovely, desirable, dark skinned woman's fears rage inside her. He reached into her mind and fueled them, filling her with despair. He then drove her body to lust, causing her pussy to ache with need.

"I have come here to punish you for your sins, Fawn Who Leaps. I am going to take possession of your body and steal your soul. You will serve my priest, obey him in all things without question, without hesitation. Your body will burn with desire for the touch of men, and you will please those that my priest, your master, shall direct, offering yourself to them, yearning to be filled by them."

Jonathan stood and quickly removed his clothes. He was tall and muscular. His skin was pale, as pale as the bleached stones in the desert. His shoulder length blond hair blew in the hot wind. Before kneeling down behind the shaking, quivering girl, he removed one of his talismans from his pants pocket. When he was on his knees behind the girl, he placed it on the ground before her and then reached around her, seizing her full, soft breasts. He sent a strong message of pleasure and need through his hands to the terrified girl. Her hands were still under her breasts, cupping them. Blackthorne let his right hand descend across the shapely woman's taut belly and over her thick thatch of pubic hair until he felt her mound beneath. He traced a line down between her lower lips, parting them, letting the impassioned girl's moisture run free. She sighed deeply when his finger entered her and then began to tease the nub of pleasure at the top.

"When I enter you with my cock, Fawn who Leaps," he whispered in her ear, *"you will feel your soul begin to empty from your body and flow into my manhood. When I fill you with my seed, your lust will overflow and your will will be gone and you will be my servant forever. Bend over and spread your legs and offer yourself to me."*

Fawn-who-Leaps gave a mighty sob and leaned forward until she was on her hands and knees. Crying, she spread her legs obediently. When Jonathan poised the head of his cock outside her plush gates, rubbing the tip along her swollen lips, the lovely Apache girl's body shook with fear. Jonathan was feeding off of her terrified emissions. His cock radiated with intense energy and as he pushed it forward, parting the Apache girl's outer sex lips, submerging it into her hot, soft interior, the girl gave out a loud wail of grief.

The pretty, young whore who had called herself Betty felt her identity and will being drawn into the man's thick, hot cock as it filled her. At the same time, her body began to burn with intense, unquenchable desire. She moaned and rocked her hips against those of the demon who was filling her, stealing her, taking everything from her. She felt her lusts growing higher and higher, frantic that she was nearing the moment of her doom, unable to prevent herself from expediting its approach.

Blackthorne directed the panting, lustful girl's eyes to the amulet on the ground in front of her. *"Look upon my sign, Fawn Who Leaps,"* he told her. *"This is the sign you will serve and whose possessor you will obey. When you look on it, you will feel fear and lust. You will think of me and my power over you. You will feel loneliness and despair that only service to your master can dispel."*

Jonathan sent the girl a wave of unhappiness and misery as she stared at the metal disk. She moaned in anguish as she felt its power over her. And then the black hearted, white skinned demon pushed a strong wave of lust through the girl. He came at the same time, flooding her delicate chamber with his spunk. The girl's passion overwhelmed her and her pussy pulsed and spasmed in return. "Ohhhhhhhhh!" she yelled as the intense pleasure mixed with her knowledge that she was lost. "Noooooooooo! Nooooooooo! Ooooooooooh!"

The broad shouldered, blond man groaned with satisfaction. His mind drank in the girl's despair as the hot sun baked his body. He could feel the sweat running off of him as he relished the throbbing of his meat inside the girl's pulsing sex. "Ohhhhhhhhhh!" she moaned again. "Ohhhhhhhh!"

Fawn Who Leaps felt the man's hot juices spread into her womb, damning her. Her eyes were fixed on the evil symbol of his power on the ground in front of her. She felt the loss of her will and her soul even as her body radiated with satisfaction at her powerful climax.

Jonathan let his manhood slide from the sobbing woman's channel. He leaned over and retrieved the talisman and handed it to the old man. "*She is yours,*" he told him.

The two men sat and drank some more whiskey. The sobs of the lost Apache girl subsided slowly until she silently, in despair, placed her head on the ground in the dust in front of her.

"*You have strong power,*" the old man finally said. "*The word will spread quickly about what you have done to this girl and the men will come to see and to use her body. Come back in thirty days and I will assemble many members of our tribe. They will want to see your power for themselves. You will have what you want. My grandfather fought the white man, and his father and his, the Americanos and the Spaniards. My people are poor and weak. You will make them strong and give them hope. Our women will no longer serve as sluts in their bars and the men will not take the welfare and the money of the Indian Agency. The spirits of our fathers and mothers will sing as the people return to the old ways."*

Jonathan, pleased, rose to leave. After he was dressed, the old man went back into the tent and retrieved the gourd that contained the hallucinogenic he had fed Jonathan's familiar. He spoke to him again. *"Give her this to drink, no more than once a day. Her dreams bring you power. When she drinks this, she will dream while she is awake and draw more energy for you from your ghost world. Keep the dream hood on her so all that she sees will be in her mind. And one more thing, leave me one of your white women so my people can see what you have done to her and how I can force her to serve them. The one with the fiery hair."*

Jonathan realized the old man had seen into his mind and learned of the other women in the camper. He also realized the old man would serve him well, but only so long as he, Jonathan, kept his promises to the Apaches. That was no problem. They were fierce and loyal and deserved to be strong and have power. Over the years to come, they would be very useful. He would reward them manyfold.

Blackthorne called for the redheaded Marie to come out of the trailer. He knew the three women had been peeking from its windows, watching. Marie, the 24 year old former kindergarten teacher from a small town just outside Denver, came trotting happily out, apparently in anticipation of his or the old man's use of her. She was naked and her breasts swayed pleasantly as she stepped hurriedly but cautiously over the rock strewn dirt the 20 yards or so over to the two men. Her hair was bright orange, loose and free down to below her shoulders. Her skin was almost pink, and she had round, soft hips and strong, heavy thighs. Her eyes were big and round and starry blue. She carried the tattoo of his talisman over her hairless mons. Jonathan hated to lose her. She was the first of the three acolytes he had recruited and she had served him energetically and well. He quickly overcame his momentary qualms. She, like all of them, was an inferior being. What difference did it make? He could get a hundred red heads who would serve him just as enthusiastically. Whatever fate the old man ultimately had in mind for her, it was no business of his.

When Marie stepped near to him, she saw the hardness in his eyes. She looked at him and the old man and a look of anxiety and uncertainty crossed her pretty face. Jonathan ordered the now unhappy Maria to kneel before the wrinkled, shabby, old Indian and compelled her into his service. The old man showed her the amulet and her body shuddered with fear.

The pleased traveler called the other two women and they came and retrieved the woozy and dazed Diane and brought her back to the trailer, her face still covered with the deerskin hood. The old man, whose name Jonathan still didn't know, had retrieved two long, leather thongs from his tent and was tying the hands of Marie and the Apache girl behind their backs. He had another gourd of psychedelics and poured long drinks into each of the girls' obedient mouths. He looked at Jonathan. "*I have my own ceremonies to perform,*" he said by way of explanation.

As Jonathan maneuvered the van around to begin his drive off of the reservation, he saw the old man leading the two bound and naked, compliant women into the tent.

CHAPTER TEN

And so Blackthorne had his fortress, or would have once the formal arrangements were made and he could start having it built. He contacted the company's chief of the engineering division, a man whose pretty, little wife he had converted some weeks before. He went over detailed topographic maps with him and started to plan what facilities his fortress would need. He had introduced some innovations to the company's products that had the marketplace abuzz. Already profits had started to climb. He had a couple of other ideas under development and, once he was able to arrange the acquisition of the appropriate smaller companies, he would introduce them.

A few weeks after his successful meeting with the old shaman, the Apache who had taught him showed up at his office unannounced and instructed him as to the time, date and place he should return. This time, unwilling to lose another of his acolytes, he recruited three red headed, college students up at the university in Boulder to take with him.

Jonathan didn't really know what to expect. His retinue was met at the gate to the reservation by three black SUV's and they were all driven for about two hours on little one lane, rocky roads to where the gathering would be. The drivers were taciturn, young, Apache males, well built, and dressed in jeans, cowboy boots and straw cowboy hats. When they arrived at the gathering place, a large, flat plain covered with mossy grass and near a large spring fed lake, he saw, not the teepees and Indian ponies he expected, but a wide array of pick ups, banged up cars, motorcycles and a number of trailers. He got out of the SUV and a tall, broad shouldered Apache with dark glasses and wearing a neat, cotton flannel shirt and jeans said, "*Ta hey*, Mr. Blackthorne. The welcome tent is over here."

The place looked like a Fourth of July picnic. There were huge braziers grilling thick steaks, big pots of beans with large slabs of bacon in them cooking over fires. Men and women congregated everywhere talking and laughing. A three guitar band was playing country and western songs on a small stage in front of which men and women were dancing two-steps. Children were running around kicking balls, chasing each other. Pretty Apache girls dressed up in flowing summer skirts and halter tops smiled at him as he passed. From his quick estimate, the must have been about 200 people there. And new vehicles were pulling in all the time.

Jonathan had brought Diane, his three acolytes, and the three red headed girls from Boulder with him. Replacing Marie had not been difficult. In fact, he took the opportunity to add some variety to his diet of female lusts and emotions and selected a tall, graceful, black skinned woman who had shown up at a business conference his company had sponsored. He discovered the thrill of her jet black skin and eager mouth in his hotel room that afternoon. The contrast between her pigment and that of his other two pale, white servants he had found appealing as they made love before him for his benefit on the soft, thick rug in the study at the Marjoram Estate guest house.

Jonathan had no need for any security for his servants since they were all converted and wouldn't have run off even if given the chance. He had left his control of the new women purposely light so they would be nervous and uncertain as to their fate. Although they had been marked with his sign, he had blocked their minds so they would remain ignorant of the tattooed pentagrams on their bodies until he presented them to the shaman.

The welcome tent was a huge, yellow and white striped canvas tent supported by about twenty 8' high poles around the circumference and taller poles in the middle. There was a long table filled with a large rack of grilled chicken, thick, red slices of London broil, and an assortment of other grilled meats. There were big platters of home fries, baked beans, potato salad and garden greens. Another table had an assortment of liquors and mixers and next to it was a big barrel filled with bottles of beer drowning in freezing cold water and ice.

"Getchya anything?" the good looking, young Apache who had greeted him asked. Blackthorne, with all the world to choose from in terms of refined elegant refreshments, had developed a taste for beer.

"How about a Heineken," he asked.

"And the girls?" the man inquired.

"Oh, just sit them down some place and get them some Cokes or something," Blackthorn answered. He had to admit he was taken aback by the normalcy of the surroundings. He looked around the tent and, from what he could see, he could have been at a Rotary picnic. Among the small, milling crowd under the tent, there were several middle aged men in white, short sleeved shirts and black rimmed glasses, a couple of older women dressed in long, off the rack summer dresses. If you looked closely though, you could see they all were of definite Apache heritage. Their skin was dark and their faces carried the strong, almost Asiatic features typical of their race. Jet black hair was universal and a couple of the women had long pig tails in braids with small colorful feathers attached at the ends.

Blackthorne's greeter returned with a bright green, open bottle covered with perspiration. He handed it to Blackthorne with a smile. The girls had all found chairs by the side of the tent and were drinking soda from cans, looking like virginal debutants waiting to be asked to dance. They looked at him nervously, not knowing what to expect from all of this. The only exception was Diane, whom he had specially entranced before they arrived. She was holding her unopened can of cola in her lap with both of her hands, her eyes glazed, her shoulders slumped. All his women were dressed in short, puffed out skirts and sleeveless tops with long 'v' necks that showed off the sides of their pretty breasts.

The man who had been assisting Blackthorne introduced himself. "My name's Bob Cloud," he said, holding out his hand. "I'm from the Water Clan. It's good to meet you."

Jonathan shook his hand and probed the man's mind. He found honesty and good will. So far so good. He realized he was incredibly vulnerable in the midst of these people. He could never do anything to control all of them at once, not even more than a few. He was here with his familiar, who the shaman knew was his biggest vulnerability. But he felt he could trust the old man. Anyway, the die was cast.

Bob introduced him to the Tribal Council President and a few of its other members. They all shook his hand heartily, grinning and expressed their gratitude for his coming. He got sidetracked by the Tribal Business Manager who peppered him with questions about investments, interest rates and long term economic forecasts. A broad beamed, middle aged woman came up to him, smiling. "My name is Barbara Feathers," she told him, "Juniper Clan. I'll be the high priestess for the ceremony." Her face was pudgy and jovial. She was wearing a long red, patterned dress that swept the ground. Her jet black hair was in a long, single braid behind her back. The bodice of her dress was cut in a low semi-circle, showing off the tops of her large, fluffy breasts. She had a firm handshake, like a woman used to physical labor. She looked over at the line of seated, confused looking, white woman. "Which one is Diane?" she asked.

Blackthorne led her over to the girls. He started from the other end. "This is Linda, Mary and Donna," he said. "They're gifts for the Shaman. The next three are Darla, Yolanda and Christine. They are my principal servants and they take care of Diane, who is right here." He pointed to the dazed, confused pretty, blond woman.

"Oh, she's so pretty," the matronly Apache woman exclaimed. She crouched in front of Blackthorne's familiar and ran her fat hand over the blond woman's dazed head. "How are you doing, sweetie?" she asked her in a pleasant, syrupy voice. She looked at Blackthorne. "Does she talk?"

"No," Blackthorne answered.

"Oh, that's ok, dearie," the woman responded directly to his familiar. She rose to her feet and walked down the line of seated women, touching each of them on the cheek. She especially remarked Yolanda's clear, smooth, coal black skin. When she reached the three red headed, college girls, she said, "Oh, I'm sure the shaman will like them. They're all so cute."

Linda, Mary and Donna looked back at the woman quizzically. They had heard the strange man who had taken them from the streets of Boulder say that they were presents and then heard the reference to the shaman. It really didn't compute. How could a person be a present?

It was Bob who saved him. "Mr. Blackthorne, I'm sure that you want to rest up for the ceremony. We have a special tent for you. Don't worry about the food, I'll have something sent over for you and the girls."

Barbara Feathers had one more thing to mention. "Mr. Blackthorne, we have roles in the ceremony for Diane and her caretakers, but we didn't figure on the other three. Maybe you can just present them at the appropriate point. Okay?"

Blackthorne was amused at the woman's concern for protocol. "Okay with me," he replied.

Bob led him to a spacious, white tent about thirty or forty yards from the welcome tent. It was set off by itself for privacy. Two mean looking Apaches stood by the doorway and nodded at him when he went in. The inside was well appointed with a thick, woven rug on the floor, several large throw pillows, a table and some chairs and a large, king sized mattress draped with a light brown, hand woven blanket. It was covered with colorful designs of geometric patterns and representations of various gods and spirits. At the four corners of the bed were wooden stands from which hung leather thongs with feathers, bones and snake rattles attached to them.

There was also a large manikin standing in the corner on which was hung a deerskin costume littered with colorful bead and feathers. It was pale white. Blackthorne looked at Bob. "That's for you to wear, Mr. Blackthorne. I hope you don't mind. The shaman gave us the sizes."

Blackthorne went over and examined the bright, colorful getup. "Why not?" he thought.

"There's a headdress that goes with it. It's considered very holy and so we'll keep it in the security tent until the last minute. Don't worry, you'll look great. I'll be in costume too," he added, smiling broadly. "I'm the snake god."

When Bob left, Blackthorn had the girls all kneel in a semi-circle around the bed. Except for Diane. He sent her an order her to strip and get on top of it. She mounted it obediently and crawled to its center. Blackthorne tossed off his own clothes and followed her. Someone had thoughtfully placed a thick, wooden stake in the ground at the head of the bed and set a long, leather thong next to it. Jonathan tied off the woman's wrists in front of her and then raised them and tied the other end to the post. He laid the pale skinned beauty's body out and ran his hands over her soft belly and breasts, sending strong, irresistible messages of lust to her.

Diane had been on a low burn all afternoon. The close proximity to her dream lover caused her to yearn for him intently. She was confused about all the people and where they were. When her captor put his hands on her skin, all of that went away.

Jonathan put his lips on hers and buried his tongue in her mouth. Diane moaned in response, hungrily greeting him. He placed his hands on her breasts and poured his energy into her. Her body melted under his as waves of pleasure seared her mind. Her thighs opened in invitation and Blackthorne positioned himself to penetrate her. His cock was hard with lust and he pressed it between her engorged love lips, sighing as her moist heat welcomed him.

The old man had been right. Since his handling of the woman, her body had been an unexcelled conduit for pleasure. It was if he had purified or sanctified her. Her psychic emissions of lust flew out of her. And after she had slept during the night, or after her daily session under the influence of the hallucinogen, he felt surges of pure essence of the Whole rushing from her body.

Now, as he stroked himself inside her, his mind reeled as it gathered up her emanations. He took his mouth from hers and suckled at her hardened teats, inhaling her passion as it flowed from where the old man had stroked her. Diane moaned and writhed beneath him. Her body clenched and shuddered as she orgasmed, her pussy gripping his fevered prick. Her hands struggled at their bonds above her head, yearning for the feel of him. He felt his forces rising and he let them go, groaning with delight as his fluids pumped from his pulsing rod.

Not yet satisfied, he remained within her, sawing his still hard cock along her pleasure bud. The frantic, passion overwhelmed woman came twice more before he spilled himself in her again.

Afterwards, Blackthorn rose from the bed and compelled his acolytes to disrobe and attend to their charge. They leapt to their task and, joining Diane on the bed, stroked and caressed her, keeping her lusts burning. The three red headed college girls stared in amazement, confused, uncomfortable looks on their faces. They too had felt the heat of

Blackthorne's lust and their eyes conveyed their yearnings. Jonathan left them simmering there, as his mind turned to food.

As if waiting for a signal from him, a voice outside the tent announced the arrival of his meal and he answered that the voice should come in. It was Bob again and he was followed by three, pretty, young Apache girls carrying trays of comestibles and two bottles of Heineken. Blackthorn was nude, his long, thick limp cock was still wet with the passionate discharges of his familiar. The girls just tittered, averting their eyes, sneaking furtive looks at his manhood. He could feel the lust burning in them. But, he had decided, the pretty Apache girls would be, for the most part, off base for him, unless proffered for his amusement.

They placed the trays on the tables and scurried out.

"It's just about six o'clock," Bob said. "The ceremony will begin as soon as it gets dark. I'll come get you around 7:30."

After he ate, and while his acolytes fed Diane and themselves, he compelled his three red headed offerings to suckle at his cock. He didn't come, but let the eager mouths of the three girls send him languorous sensations of pleasure while he drove their lusts and reinforced their compulsions to obedience. Their faces looked so pretty as he presented his manhood to their lips one by one. Their expressions migrated from shock and confusion as they realized their irresistible compulsion to open their lips and consume the thick hard rod, to ecstatic pleasure as they felt the radiation of his power through it, to being dazed and confused after he withdrew without climax, their minds befogged by lust.

Bob had gone over what was anticipated from Jonathan at the ceremony and, although he had plenty of lust to spare, Jonathan had decided he would preserve himself to ensure a good show. He was resting on the bed when Bob returned. There were three, strong men with him. Bob announced it was time to get ready and that the women would have to be brought to the women's tent to be prepared for the ceremony. Jonathan nodded his consent and the men stood the women up and proceeded to bind their hands behind them with leather thongs. One of the redheaded girls began to cry when she felt her wrists being bound off. Jonathan stood and sent all of them strong messages of fear, pain and obedience, drawing sustenance from their misery as he touched their bright fiery heads one by one. The men hooded the females and led them off, the three redheads still in their pretty, short, flowery skirts and his acolytes and Diane nude. He was apprehensive about the necessity for separation from the beautiful, blond familiar, but he let it go.

As soon as Bob and the men left with the females, a portly Apache woman entered followed by three young, bashful, Apache beauties. They were all dressed in long, white, deerskins sheaths, adorned with beads and feathers. Their long, black hair was tied back in braids behind them. Jonathan was still nude and his lust arose immediately as he felt the minds of the three young girls reach out to him. The older woman paid his erection no mind as she urged him over to the bed and had him sit on it.

"*I'm Cocheta,*" she said in Apache. "*We will only use our Apache names during the ceremony. This is Nascha, Prita and Lolotea. We are to get you dressed and stay with you until the ceremony begins. The girls will serve you afterwards. They are a gift from the shaman and our people.*"

The three young girls were nervous and edgy, but also pleased to have been selected for their honored roles. While Cocheta drew the native garb piece by piece from the manikin, the girls dressed him. The pants to the costume turned out to be leggings that were held tight to the tops of his thighs by leather thongs. He could feel the lust from the young women as they slid the smooth, supple, white leather up his legs. He stood while they fastened them at the crux between his thighs and his loins. Jonathan knew he could have all four women writhing on the floor passionately in an instant, but held his powers in check. Nonetheless, one of the girls took the opportunity while tying off his right legging to circle his cock with her small, smooth hand and caress its length. Her black eyes stared up at him and her tongue washed her lower lip.

"*Lolotea!*" the older woman said, "*Control yourself!*"

The rest of the dressing ritual proceeded without incident. The smooth, white shirt fit him perfectly. A thick, colorfully beaded belt went around his waist and a supple, soft, bright red breechcloth was wended through it, covering his otherwise exposed loins and rear. When the women had finished adorning him, they stepped back and curtsied and then fled wordlessly.

The man who had called himself Bob then came in. He had shed his white world clothes and was wearing only a long, colorfully beaded loincloth. His body and his face had been painted in slashes of bright, red, yellow, black and green. His stature seemed to have grown as he presented himself in his true identity. Blackthorne heard from outside the tent the heavy, rhythmic, rumbling of drums. Three strong, young men had come in with Blackthorne's greeter, all dressed and adorned like him. Bob spoke in Apache to the ceremonially attired white man.

"*I am Kajika, he who walks without noise. I greet you, Jitendra, Lord of Conquerors. I will lead you to the People.*"

Kajika turned and took from the men behind him a black, bearskin headdress with a long tail of eagle's feathers attached.

"*I give to you the symbol of your power.*" He intoned, holding it out to Blackthorne. Jonathan solemnly took it from him and placed it on his head. Kajika made a motion that he should follow and he exited the tent followed in turn by the other men of Kajika's escort.

It was a dark, moonless night and Jonathan could hear now the voices of what sounded like hundreds of people chanting to the beat of the drums. He was led along a pathway through the tents until he came across a field that was lit almost as bright as day by a series of large torches mounted on fifteen foot poles circling around. A large fire was burning in the middle and the crowd of Apaches surrounded it. They did not look like average middle Americans now, as they had all donned various forms of native costume. Many of the men had their faces painted in what Jonathan took to be war paint, and the women wore short, deerskin dresses and paint on their faces of various colors, yellow, red, white, black. Bright, luminous feathers abounded. The children had been apparently put away for the night.

Jonathan was led around the fire. At the north side, he saw a large, three foot high platform. In the middle, sat the old man. He didn't look like the wizened wino he had met a month ago. He was wearing a long, feathered headdress and had a heavy, bearskin robe over his shoulders. His face was painted half yellow and half green with a line of red down the middle. There was an empty chair beside him covered in soft, tanned deerskin. In front of the platform, at each corner, he saw the kneeling figures of Fawn Who Leaps and Marie. Their hands were bound behind them to stakes in the ground and their backs had been pressed against them. Their knees were pegged apart. A thong tightly bound their necks to the stake, forcing their heads up. Their faces, breasts and shaved loins had been painted a bright red. They looked delirious and Jonathan scanned them to confirm that they had been drugged.

Kajika indicated Jonathan should assume his seat and then disappeared. The old man nodded to him and then waved his wizened, gnarled hand. The throng of celebrants silenced themselves and the drums came to rest. The old man stood and walked to the end of the platform

"*Men and Women of the People,*" he shouted, "*tonight we celebrate the return of strength and honor to us.*" His voice was not now the scratchy growl Jonathan had heard a month ago. It was strong and powerful. *"Jitendra, Lord of Conquerors, has come among us as it has been prophesized. Tonight he will show you his powers and the People will rejoice."* He turned and waived at Jonathan, inviting him to step forward. Blackthorne rose from his seat and stood next to him, dwarfing him with his greater stature and bulk. He got the impression he was intended to speak.

"Great Chiricahua Nation," he called out. *"I have come from the ghost world to redeem the promises made to your fathers and bring life back to the People. The Chiricahua Nation will live again."* There was an outpouring of throaty yells and high pitched Indian style yelps from the surrounding crowd. Blackthorne saw the woman who had called herself Barbara Feathers standing to his right. She gave him a nod and, scanning her mind, he realized this was the time to present his gifts to the shaman. He nodded back to her and the three naked, frightened, young, red headed college students were led out by three colorfully dressed and bedecked Apache women. The girls' hands had been tied together behind their heads and connected to a thick leather thong that was wrapped several times around their necks and which terminated in a leash. Their nervous eyes flitted around the crowd as they were dragged towards the platform, their hands raised behind them and their breasts and bright orange, furry triangles presented for all to view.

When the distraught, young women were standing in front of him and the old man, Jonathan gave them a strong surge of his power, suffusing their bodies with intense, piercing, psychic pain. All three girls collapsed to their knees, their faces masks of misery. He removed from them the block he had put in place and revealed to them all that had happened since they met a pleasant looking stranger on the streets of Boulder. The girls' faces became frantic with fear. Suddenly, everything around them became sinister and threatening. With a wave of his hand, Jonathan sent them intense pulses of lust, and their eyes widened and their bodies began to writhe. The Apaches around him stared with wonder and respect as they witnessed his power to control them. He had secreted one of his medallions in the folds of his tunic and he removed it now, presenting it to each of the beautiful, naked and bound white women. He had instilled them with its power when they had been captured and the evil, enthralling nature of it came back to their minds, causing them to moan and cry. He spoke to them in Apache, conveying directly to their minds the meanings of his words.

"You bear on your loins the mark of the medallion and will serve any male who possesses it. It will drive you to lust and fear. You will obey without question fully and with all of your life forces any commands given to you. You will open your selves willingly, stoked with desire, to anyone who wishes to make use of you." The crowd was silent as it watched the submission of the three helpless white women. Jonathan turned to the old man, *"I give these females to you to serve you and your people as you see fit."*

The old man bowed slightly to Blackthorne to acknowledge the gift. He produced from under his robes the copy of the medallion Blackthorne had given him previously. Jonathan gave the women a command to crawl to him on their knees and to kiss it.

Miserable, crying, and their bodies shaking with fear, the three shapely and desirable, redheaded young women obediently shuffled towards the shaman on their knees. One by one, they kissed the powerful circle of copper colored metal. A pretty Apache girl ran up and gave the shaman a gourd and he poured the milky psychedelic mixture into their mouths, forcing them to swallow it and spilling it over their chests and breasts. The old man then placed his hands on them, caressing their naked breasts, stroking their heads. He waved his hand and the three native women who had led the girls in tugged on their leashes and led them to the side of the podium. Stakes had been pounded into the ground there and, after being forced to kneel again, their leashes were tied off to them.

The shaman waved his hand once more to signal the continuation of the ceremony and he and Blackthorne resumed their seats of honor.

The drums began a mesmerizing beat and a chorus of male voices cried out in song. The crowd began to sway back and forth to the beat. From the side, four fabulously bedecked men came out, feathered headdresses trailing, carrying rattles and drums. It was Kajika and his three escorts. They began an ecstatic, rhythmic dance around the fire, twisting and turning, raising their heads up and down, kicking their knees high in the air. A pretty Apache maiden offered Blackthorne a cup of an aroma laden, thick, syrupy mixture. He scanned her mind quickly and realized it was the Apache corn beer, tis-win, a potent brew. He accepted the glass, signaling his gratitude and gave the smiling young woman a surge of pleasure in response. He eyes widened in amazement and she scurried off the stage.

There were four dancers and they pranced around the fire in a clockwise direction. Four men ran out and each planted a 4' tall stake in the ground around and close to the fire, one for each direction, north, south, east and west. At some signal Blackthorne could not discern, the dancing men came together and stood before the platform on which Jonathan and the old shaman sat.

The drums and the crowd became quiet. Jonathan waited expectantly for the next development. Suddenly, four naked and bound, young white women were led into the circle from the left side of the crowd. They were gagged with thick, leather covered sticks lodged crossways over their mouths and tied off behind their heads, giving them obscene grimaces. Their arms had been folded up and tied crossed behind their backs with leather leads running from each wrist over their shoulders, in between and then under their naked breasts, around their torsos and tied off again behind their backs. They were presented to the two men on the dais, their painted faces filled with mind numbing fear, their beautiful, pale, nude bodies trembling, looking ghost like in the lights of the dancing torches.

* * * *

Paula Fowler and her three friends had been driving through the New Mexico desert about three days ago when they stopped at a small, run down, gas station just outside of Los Cruces. They had left their homes in Connecticut the week before. It was the trip of a lifetime for them, one that they had been planning all during senior year of high school. They had worked all summer to earn the money for the trip, waitressing, babysitting and the like. Los Angeles was their goal where they all hoped to get jobs as models or actresses. Penny had the name of an agent who was a friend of her father's and he had promised to get them photo shoots for a portfolio. They all knew it was a long shot, but what's the sense of being young if you don't gamble. Promising their parents that if they didn't make it in a year they would come home and go to college, the girls had decided to travel the scenic southern route across the country and to take their time and enjoy the sights.

The black haired, scraggly, service station attendant offered to check their oil when they pulled in for gas while they went into the small convenience store to stock up on sodas and, for Jane and Samantha, cigarettes. Samantha had wanted to use the credit card her dad had given her, but the place only took cash. Paula wondered if the man who was servicing her car was a real Indian. She had never seen one in real life. He had the dark skin and broad face she had come to associate with that race. He was standing by the side of the car when the pretty, 18 and 19 year old girls emerged from the store. He smiled as he took their gas money and told them that everything was "all set" under the hood.

They had driven about an hour along the flat, straight highway when the car engine began to whine and make strange sounds. Penny was driving and she pulled the car to the shoulder. It stalled and made a great hissing sound as steam poured out from under the hood. They all got out and commiserated about their bad luck. Jane went to get her cell phone out of her purse in the car to call Triple A. It was missing. Samantha looked for hers and it was gone too. So was Paula's and Penny's. They realized the attendant at the gas station had probably stolen them. It was odd though that he hadn't taken their wallets or anything else.

There was no one on the road. The flat, empty highway stretched for miles straight as an arrow over the forbidding, dry landscape. The late August sun beat down on them cruelly. They all turned when they heard a car engine coming towards them. It was a dirty, dull red van. Jane recognized it as having been at the gas station when they stopped there. The van slowed to a stop next to them. It was driven by a young woman with dark skin and pleasant features and long, strait black hair. She smiled. Another young woman, looking the same, sat in the passenger seat and she was the one to address them. "*Ta hey*," she said. "Having trouble?"

The girls explained their predicament. The girls in the van didn't have cell phones. They offered to drive the marooned white girls to their place about fifteen miles from there and let them use the phone. The black haired girls were friendly and none of the white girls wanted to stand around in the blistering sun if they didn't have to.

To Paula, the ride seemed longer than fifteen miles. It actually took about an hour. The van left the highway and drove for a long time along a single lane dirt road. It pulled up, finally, in the driveway of a tumbled down farmhouse.

There were several cars already parked there and when they went inside the house, there were four strong, mean looking men sitting on an old brown couch drinking beers and watching a fluttering, old, color TV.

It was then things got really hairy. Paula screamed when the biggest one grabbed her and threw her face down to the floor. She protested and flailed her arms and legs. The man circled her right wrist with a thong and then pulled it tight. He dragged it behind her back and, holding it with his one hand, gathered her left wrist and tied it to her right one. She was pulled to her feet and one of the girls from the van popped a mouth filling, spongy, rubber ball between her lips and then covered them with a wide band of clear packing tape. The man dragged her from the room.

When they went into the kitchen, there was a plump, older woman standing by an opened trap door in the floor. The man led the struggling and crying Paula down the stairs and, when they reached the bottom, dragged over to a heavy wooden door that opened into some kind of storeroom. He pushed the bound young girl onto the floor and pulled off her sneakers and socks. He then used another leather strap to bind her ankles together. He made her kneel and, pulling the lead from bound ankles between her thighs, pushed her head down and tied it around her neck, knotting it in the crux of her throat. He put a black hood over her head and drew it tightly under her chin.

The other girls had been brought to the room too, and Paula could hear their whines and cries near her. After a while, the door opened and one of the girls was taken from the room. A short while later, she was returned sobbing and wailing, and another girl was taken. Paula was the third to be selected. When her hood was removed, she saw she was in the middle of an underground, low ceilinged room. It was dark and the room was lit only by a small wattage single bulb that hung from the rafters. The young women who had removed her from the storeroom were the ones from the van and they proceeded wordlessly to undress her.

Paula had been wearing a short, black and white checkered skirt. She started to struggle when she felt the long haired, dark skinned, young woman tug at it in an effort to draw it down her hips. The woman gave her a vicious slap across the face. Her voice stilled by the ball in her mouth and the tape, Paula gave a muffled cry at the violent blow. Thereafter, she was cooperative, and she was soon led, crying, hooded and nude, back to her little prison.

Paula didn't know how long she was kept prisoner there. She had to kneel absolutely still since any effort to move caused the leather binding around her neck to tighten. Once every couple of hours, the two black haired girls would return and take the prisoners from the storeroom one by one to let them void in a bucket, eat some crackers and drink some water. It was hot and stifling in the little room. The hours dragged by agonizingly slowly. She could hear the people upstairs moving around, the toilet flushing, the television, the faint murmur of their voices through the floor. She knew when it had become night from the complete and deadly silence that permeated the house above her.

Her friends remained mostly silent, as did she, except for the occasional groan of pain from their confined limbs or sobs of grief and fear. It was the interminable darkness that was the worst. It was like she had been transported to a different world, one in which she was all alone. That, combined with the effect of being unable to say a word to anyone, to beg for release, to ask what the cruel people wanted from her, made the pretty blond girl sink into deep despair.

She did not know how long she had been a captive. It was after a long, long time when, after letting her use the bucket and have some water, the women rehooded her and led her back up the stairs. No one had even talked to her since she and her friends had been abducted. She heard words now, the deep voices of men and the lighter, more pleasant sound of women. The voices weren't speaking English. It was a language the young girl had never heard. The sounds were sharp and guttural. Her speculation that she had been kidnapped by Indians had seemed so absurd when she thought of it, but now seemed to be all too probable.

The girls helped her negotiate the steps down from the porch in the front of the house. Paula was ambivalent about the fact of having been brought outside. It was wonderful to be out of the dismal basement. The sun was hot on her naked body and felt good. But she knew that whatever horrible fate awaited her, she had taken a decisive step towards it.

To her dismay, when the feminine hands which had been escorting her released her arms, strong, masculine hands took their place. Rough hands caressed her breasts and ran over her naked buttocks making her squeal, until a woman's voice shouted a protest. Her wrists were untied from behind her back and retied in front. After they were bound in close to her waist with a rope that ran around her torso, Paula was forced to step up into the enclosed well of the bed of a pickup truck. There was a rough plywood sheet on the floor and the men made her lie down on it. The uneven wood scratched her naked back and rear. She felt straps go around her neck, her waist, her thighs and her ankles, connecting her tightly to fastenings that had been screwed into the board beneath her.

The frightened girl cried and pleaded in her mind for someone to save her. She realized she was going to be taken somewhere. All kinds of things raced through her mind from a Mexican whorehouse to the Texas Chainsaw Massacre. She felt and heard her friends being laid down beside her. She couldn't tell whose soft, naked, arm, hip and thigh rubbed against hers. Whoever it was, she was sobbing heavily. She heard another thick board being maneuvered into place above her. It settled cleanly with a dull thud into the ridge that had been made there for that purpose. Then there was the sound of lumber or something heavy being loaded on top of the board. When the noise of the loading stopped, there was about fifteen minutes of silence and then she heard and felt the engine to the truck come to life and felt the sensation of motion.

It seemed like hours later that the truck came to a stop. Her body was sweaty and dirty and her throat was parched. A little fan had been running somewhere over her head pulling fresh but still hot air into the small enclosure. During the hot, tortuously long drive, Paula's emotions had run the gamut between dismal, unhappy resignation to her fate, whatever it was, to rebellion, anger and fear. She felt her heart in her throat and a sinking in her stomach when the vehicle finally came to a halt and heard the sounds of its doors opening and then slamming shut.

The lumber, or whatever it was, was removed and the top to her prison opened. She was unstrapped and pulled from the truck.

There were people all around, Paula could hear them. She was appalled and ashamed to be hooded, naked and helpless in front of them. Voices were laughing and she could hear guitar music off in the distance. A rough hand grabbed her breast and squeezed it, followed by a deep, male laugh. When she was steady on her feet, she was led away and, when she was kneeling again, her arms and ankles were rebound behind her to some sort of stake in the ground and her hood was removed.

She was in a large tent. Penny was kneeling next to her. She watched as Jane and then Samantha were brought in, and knelt down next to her. A long pole was laid across the backs of the girls' necks and connected to tent poles on either side of them. Paula whined and protested through her stuffed mouth when one of the women came behind her and, holding a fistful of her long, blond hair, pulled her up fully erect and leaned her head back against the pole. Another black haired, dark skinned woman placed another pole in front against her neck. It pushed against the bottom of her chin and raised it until it was lifted high. The pressure of the pole forced her to maintain a strict posture, kneeling straight and tall, her torso extended. Her vision was directed upwards and so she could not see, but rather felt, strong women's hands drag her knees apart and tie them off to the knees of the girls on either side of her, forcing her legs open.

The cruelly bound girls were left there for quite a while. The posture was uncomfortable, making Paula's back and neck ache. The width between the poles just enough so that she had no problem breathing. The ball was still in her mouth and the tape still sealed her lips or she would have tearfully begged one of the dark haired women who kept coming in and out of the tent to release her or at least to tell her what was going on. They would stop and look at her and her friends admiringly, speaking that strange language to each other. Some, unable to resist the erotic display of the naked, helpless white girls, would take the time to caress one or more of their heads or stroke their breasts and lower bellies. Paula was embarrassed, but happy, when one of the women brought a bowl and held it between her legs so she could pee in it.

The nineteen year old, blond girl was more frightened than she had ever been in her life. There seemed to some kind of big party going on and she was sure her part in it was not going to be something she would like. She yearned for her father, her mother or someone to come and save her. After she had been kneeling there, helpless, for about two hours, a wide hipped, jovial, older woman, wearing a long red shift came in and examined each one of the girls carefully. Paula flinched when the woman grabbed her nipples between her thumbs and forefingers and pinched and tweaked them until they became hard. She caressed her naked hips and felt the soft, tender inside of her thighs. She placed her hand on Paula's sex and stroked her until she became moist and lubricated, her breath becoming heavy and her breasts beginning to ache. There had been two younger, middle aged women, dressed in work boots, t-shirts and jeans, sitting in the tent, chatting with each other amiably while watching over them, and the lady in the red dress said something to them. One of the women left the tent and returned with a tray with some food on it.

She had not eaten in a long time, and Paula happily let one of the women feed her little pieces of a thick, rich, deep yellow, corn bread. She had a can of Coca Cola and gave her several long, soothing sips. When the dark skinned woman thought the bound, naked, blond white girl had had enough, she forced the ball back into her mouth. She didn't bother putting the tape back on.

About a half hour after the red dressed woman left, eight pretty, young, black haired girls came into the tent. The older woman was with them. One by one, the unhappy white girls were untied from the stakes and brought out the rear of the tent. The area behind the tent was marked off from the rest of the tents by a 7' high set of canvas panels which whipped and clapped in the strong breeze. The two girls who handled Paula were dressed in jeans, t-shirts and sneakers and kept giggling and laughing to each other as they brought her to a large, tin washbasin that had been placed on the ground. There was one for each bound white girl. They made Paula step into it and commenced to wash her body with pailfulls of steaming hot water they ladled from another, larger tub. They had bars of soap and washcloths and they scrubbed her whole body. She was grateful to have the grime and sweat washed off of her, but her fear of what fate the young, happy, pretty girls were preparing her for was too heavy on her mind to enjoy it.

She could see her friends suffering the same awful anxiety as their bodies too were washed. Penny's eyes were filled with tears as the girls who were servicing her made her spread her legs so they could wash her furry sex. She had long, straight brown hair that fell midway down her back. Her hips were soft and graceful. Her youthful breasts were round and plump, but not too big for her slender frame.

Jane, the tallest of the group, had short cropped, blond hair that covered her head in tiny ringlets. Her breasts were small and pointed and she had slender hips, almost like a boy's. She had trimmed the patch between her legs and all Paula could see was a little tuft of blond hair above her long slit.

Samantha was the buxom one. Her breasts swayed and jumped as the girls who were washing her pushed them about playfully. She was a brunette, like Penny, but her hair was wavy and shoulder length. Her hips were wide and created a concave effect as her taut belly sloped to her mons.

All of the girls were crying and they looked at each other forlornly. It was surreal to be a bound prisoner under the bright blue, open sky and with so many seemingly ordinary people around. The pretty, black haired girls kept up a chatter in their strange tongue, making the experience seem other worldly. Other women, and an occasional cowboy hatted man, came wandering through the enclosed area. The women paused and watched for a while, exchanged witty or admiring comments to their companions and then left. The men would ogle them and, as soon as they were noticed by any of the women, shooed away. Two older women kept the flames under the main tub burning and, from time to time, one or the other of them would bring a pail of fresh, presumably cold, water to pour into it.

The hot water felt good as it poured down over Paula's head, matting her long, blond hair. One of the girls stood on a stool and worked sweet smelling soap into her scalp. She was standing in front of Paula and her breasts, loose under her thin, faded yellow t-shirt pressed against the distressed girl's face when she leaned over her. After the shampoo came a smooth, pleasant, cream rinse.

One of the girls ran off to get a towel and Paula had the momentary urge to hop out of the wash basin and make a run for it. Her heart pounded as she thought of it. She could make the opening in the enclosure in about ten strides. She had run track and she believed if she could get to open ground she might be able to outpace her pursuers.

But where would she go? She had no idea where she was. They had driven for a long, long time and the roads they had gone over for the last hour or so of their journey had been rough and bumpy. It was hot and they were somewhere in the desert, miles away from anything. Even if she got away and didn't tear her bare feet to shreds, she would probably die of thirst or exposure before being rescued. And what would they do to her if they caught her? Her hands were bound behind her and she would not be able to defend herself. The girls in the basement where she had been confined for who knew how long had slapped her hard across the face just for struggling when they were undressing her.

In spite of the risks, Paula had just about worked up enough nerve to make a dash for it when the other girl returned with a large, fluffy towel. Her fear and hesitation had quashed her hopes for escape. Her heart sank as she was assisted from the tub. The two girls took turns drying her. The hot desert sun plucked the moisture off of her body quickly. She was then led back into the tent and, once she had knelt and her hands and ankles had been reaffixed to the stake in the ground, her knees reconnected to her friends' on either side of her, the girls brushed her long hair until it was straight and free of tangles.

What kind of girls are these, Paula asked herself dolefully. How could they do this? They had to know that she and her friends had been kidnapped, that they were prisoners. They seemed sweet and kind, not cruel. If only she could talk to them. She tried to beg them with her eyes for help. The only response she got was a soft caress on the side of her face by one of the girls and a kiss on her forehead. When all the girls had had their hair brushed, to Paula's dismay, the poles were put back in place.

The imprisoned girls were given another snack after a little while, some rough bread with a slice of steak on it. Paula could not stop her eyes from tearing as she chewed the little meal as slowly as she could to forestall the reinsertion of the spongy ball she had carried in her mouth for what seemed days. Every time she swallowed, she could feel her neck press against the pole in the front of her throat. With her imprisoned, upturned head, she felt like an animal being fed on a feed lot. After she was given a long drink of what tasted like Sprite, the ball was reinserted.

After a short while, things seemed like they were starting to happen. Women kept on running nervously in and out of the tent. They had doffed their regular clothes and were wearing ceremonial Indian garb, long, white, clingy, doeskin dresses with colorful patterns sewn into it, moccasins, and bands of beads across their foreheads. Some of the women had painted their faces with strange, sinister designs or with broad bands of yellow or red.

Paula could tell from when the tent flap opened and closed that it was getting dark outside. People seemed to be walking past the tent all in one direction, garbling their strange language, laughing. From time to time, she caught a waft of English being spoken in terse, clipped tones. The tent seemed to be filling up, with more women staying once they had entered than leaving. She saw the young girls who had washed her, now bedecked in ceremonial garb, take a kneeling position in the back.

The older woman who had worn the red dress came sweeping in. She was wearing one of the long, white, leather dresses and she uttered some commands. Her dress was fancier and more colorful than the others. She took at look at the displayed, young white women, walking down the line of them, peering into their uplifted faces, feeling their breasts and their tummies. She knelt by Paula and, once again, placed her hard, calloused hand over her sex and stroked it, letting a thick finger drag between her lower lips. She peered deeply into Paula's eyes until the pretty, white girl's extended and grotesquely displayed body shivered with fear and her blood ran cold.

The tent had become crowded with the Indian women. Something was definitely going to happen soon, Paula just knew it. She whined and, straining her neck, looked over at her naked and bound friends who looked frantically back. A small, brass bowl was placed in front of each of the unhappy, naked and kneeling, young white women and the big woman clapped her hands. Paula could hear the sounds of drums outside the tent.

All of the women sank to their knees and went silent at the sound of the big woman's clapping hands. She knelt in front of them towards the girls in between Paula and Jane, who was on her left. Samantha and Penny were on the ends. The women all placed their hands together in front of them palms up and closed their eyes. A single torch now lit the enclosure and the flame leapt this way and that, sending sinister shadows all over the canvas.

Then the big woman began to chant. It was a nasal, repetitive, staccato chant, alien and strange. Every once in a while, the other women would join in. Paula struggled to free her bound limbs. The strange ritual was a dire portent to her. She was ashamed at her nudity and the brash display of her breasts and her sex in front of all these ceremonially attired women. The desperate girl tugged and yanked at her bindings, moaning and crying, twisting her imprisoned neck frantically. After about fifteen minutes or so, without missing a beat, the leader crawled to the little bowls in front of the girls and dropped something in them. She took out a long taper from the fold of her dress and lit its end from the torch. She then transferred the fire to the little bowls and a thin layer of white smoke arose.

The smell was pungent and strange and Paula tried to wave her head around so she wouldn't breathe it. "Oh god! Oh god! Oh god!" she thought. "They're going to burn us! They're going to sacrifice us!" She had read in history class how the Indians used to torture white people and had always remembered a colorful painting of a man being burned to death in the midst of a chanting, dancing crowd of Indians. The terrible image had stayed with her a long time and now she recalled it.

Paula had remained obediently silent but for her sobs and moans all during her captivity. Now she tried to call out to the women for mercy. "..leeee! ...leeeee!...leeeeee!" she tried to yell, her filled mouth unable to form the complete words. Her frantic voice was muffled by the stifling object they had put in it. She could hear the muted and strained voices of her friends as they made their own supplications. Their noises could barely be distinguished amidst the monotonous, rhythmic chanting. Paula pulled at her bound wrists in agonized fear.

The big woman waved her arms and the chanting sunk down to a low moan. The girls who had washed them ran up to the bound and frightened girls and, stepping behind them, took solid grips of their heads, immobilizing them. The big woman approached Penny, to Paula's right and two other women came with her holding wooden bowls in their hands. Out of the corner of her eye, Paula could see the woman daubing the contents of the bowls on Penny's pretty, uplifted face. She came to Paula next, and the girl felt the woman's strong fingers make lines and circles on her. As she moved to Paula's left, the girls released her. Paula looked over at Penny and moaned in despair when she saw the bright green, yellow and red markings covering her cheeks, chin and forehead.

When all the girls had been painted, the big woman stood. She had a rattle in her hand and she began to shake it and walk around the helpless, bound girls. Two of the women in front released the pole which had so cruelly pressed against Paula and her hapless friends' necks. Two others approached Paula and, when the big woman untied her hands and ankles from behind her, quickly forced her to the ground onto her breasts and belly. A woman sat on her flailing legs and she felt strong hands pull her arms up behind her back and cross them. Paula cried and screamed in pain as her shoulder muscles strained. She felt a leather thong tying them together tightly and then she was pulled back up to her knees and the ends of the thong were draped across her shoulders, between and under her bare breasts and than back around her where they were tied off together.

Her arms aching, oddly trussed, Paula felt the ball being pried from her mouth. She opened it to scream for help, mercy, anything, when a thick piece of wood covered thickly with leather jammed between her teeth. It had leather laces fixed at its ends and she felt them being tied behind her. When the primitive gag was secured, a coarse, leather bag was pulled over her head. Before it shut out her vision, she saw her friend Jane, her eyes widened with terror, her lips pulled back in a strange grimace, her painted face almost unrecognizable.

The girls were led by a leash around their necks. A strong hand held it close to Paula's chin and every time her knees gave out from frantic fear, it pulled her up and made her keep walking. The drums were loud now and she could hear what sounded like hundreds of people chanting and singing all around her. She sensed people on either side of her, jammed closely together. Her head was swimming with foreboding and her stomach churned. The drums stopped and there was silence.

Suddenly, her hood was lifted and she was dragged forward. Her eyes couldn't believe what she saw although her ears had given her sufficient premonition of it. There was a large, raging fire in the middle of a vast crowd. Its dancing light made macabre the crowd of people that encircled it. All of the people wore Indian costumes, and the dark, strange faces of most of them were painted.

She didn't have much time to look at them since she was hurried to a large dais. Two naked women were kneeling there, bound to stakes on either side of it. They looked like they were in some kind of trance. One was white, with pale skin and flaming red hair. The other was clearly an Indian girl, with dark skin and long, black hair. Their red painted faces were slack and their eyes rolled back strangely. Sitting in chairs on the platform were two men, one an old, wizened Indian man with a cruel expression and half covered by a heavy, fur robe and the other, a tall, broad shouldered white man dressed in a bright, white costume and a large, black, furry hat.

Paula felt like she was being presented to the men. She became conscious of her nakedness, her cruel bindings and her lurid, painted face. The tall, younger man's eyes caught hers and a wave of fear passed through her. She felt like the man had penetrated her mind. She was struck by a painful, inner loneliness, despair so deep she almost fainted. She was grateful when he shifted his steely, mesmerizing gaze to the other grotesquely bound women.

Paula had not noticed the painted and feathered men who had been standing near the platform when she was brought there. One of them came up next to her and took hold of her leash from the Indian woman. The man's appearance terrified her. He was painted all over with strange designs and had a sinister, macabre headdress on filled with feathers and shells and little pieces of bone. He was breathing heavily and was wearing only a loin cloth. His strong, muscular, dark skinned body was covered with sweat.

The old man stood and waved his hands at the crowd and the drums and chanting began again. Paula felt herself being dragged away from the dais toward the fire. "Oh, god!" she thought, "He's going to throw me in!" She fought against the man. He was strong and he dragged her by the leash, his hand under her chin, until they reached a place on the side of the fire. He pushed her to her knees harshly. Paula tried to crawl away. He grabbed her foot and dragged her back. He pulled her up by her hair and forced her back against a wooden stake. She felt him tying off her bound wrists behind her to it. When he was done, he wrapped a wide leather band around her neck and secured it there too.

Paula peered hopelessly out at the crowd of weirdly decorated, lustful faces. The fire behind her lit them grotesquely. She could see her shadow and the shadow of her captor flutter about, long and large, as the huge flames danced behind her, throwing out an intense heat. Through the crowd's rhythmic, tonal singing, she could hear the loud crackle and pops of the raging conflagration. The demon like man who had bound her to the stake placed looped thongs around her ankles and then raised them, tying them off cruelly to her thighs. Her knees were spread and tied off to stakes on either side. She was completely immobile, balanced on her knees, her bare body ready for whatever these mad, devilish people wanted to impose on her. Her heart cried out in frantic fear. "Uhhhh! Uhhhhhh! Uhhhhhhh!" she screamed through her enforced grimace. "Uhhhhhhhhhh!"

The demon man began to dance around her as the dread filled drums reverberated through her whole body. "This can't be happening!" she thought dismally. It was like a horror movie! It couldn't be real!

Blackthorne felt the lust arise from the crowd. The strangely painted faces of the bound and naked white girls had been pretty. Their eyes had been full of fear. He had probed each of their minds and filled them with sharp stabs of despair. He read their stories quickly, enjoying reliving their days of terrified seclusion, their mind numbing anxiety as they were prepped for the ceremony. This was his test. The Apaches had kidnapped these women, women he had never seen before, to see whether his manipulation of the other females was a trick of some kind. He could imagine them tearing him apart if he failed. But he would not fail. It would be easy. His powers were surging as a result of the lustful crowd and the abject fear of their sacrifices to him.

Slowly, Blackthorne rose from his chair and stepped from the platform. The ominous drums and the musical chants from the crowd seemed an appropriate backdrop to his prospective subjugation of the forlorn, desirable young girls. He decided to do the long haired, blond girl first. She was facing east, where the sun rose. He walked over to within a few feet in front of her. He drank up her frantic terror as her wild eyes met his. The Apache dancer stopped and pulled away to give him room. He sent the powers of his mind into the mind of the kneeling, helpless, spread-eagled girl. Her body shuddered and her eyes, already wide from her bone chilling fear, grew wider as she felt him alter her, twist her perceptions, bind her to him.

Paula felt like the fearsomely attired white man had reached his hand into her brain and clenched his fist over it. She immediately saw him for the god that he was, an evil, vengeful god who fed on pain and fear. She could not break from his gaze and her body shook in her bonds. Suddenly, a pain worse than she ever felt before surged through her. It was not a physical pain, but a pain in her soul. Her insides twisted in agony. All of her fear and despair over the last few days seemed to become magnified a hundred fold. She watched as he stripped his loincloth and flung it on the ground. His cock was hard and thick. And then she felt the man caress her brain with his mind, mingling an irresistible wave of intense, sexual desire with her agony. She began to hunger for him to possess her, lay his hands on her flesh. She tried to resist the dreadful urges he had forced upon her. What was left of her conscious mind rebelled while all other parts of her yearned for him. She had been right, in part, in her speculations about why the people had captured her, prepared her, said their heathen prayers over her. She was a sacrifice. This man was their god of lust and she was their offering to him. And she had been thrown into a fire, or rather, one had been built inside her, as every pore of her body burned with desire for the cruel god who was now her master.

Jonathan's rampant loins were offset by his pale, white leggings and tunic, and the enthralled young woman's gaze was drawn to it. He stepped closer to the wildly impassioned girl so he could lay his hands on her. He took her full, firm, proffered breasts in his hands and he let his psychic force flow through them. The naked woman's eyes rolled back and she gave a great moan of lust, fear and despair all in one. He could feel her emotions run wild inside her. He caressed the plump, soft mounds, enjoying their feel and weight, letting his own passions grow until his need swelled within him. Reaching behind her head, he untied the harsh gag that bisected her widestretched lips. He took his hot, thick cock in his hand and presented it to her yearning mouth, tantalizingly just out of her reach.

Paula had never felt a need so intense as the need to encompass the white demon's flesh between her lips. She strained her neck and pursed her lips to capture it. Her bound hands twisted behind her, straining to get free. Her feet pulled hard on the bindings on her ankles, yearning to bring her to him.

When Jonathan sensed the crowd had taken full measure of the storm of lust he had generated in the pretty, young, white girl, he pushed his outstretched rod towards her mouth. He could feel the surge of passion in her mind as he slid it over her hungry lips and entered her.

Paula had never felt such pleasure before as the thick meat filled her mouth and dragged along her tongue. She had sucked her boyfriend's cock. It was never like this. She pursed her lips around the man's member and drank at it feverishly. She could feel lust radiating from its every pore. It was magical, it was suffused with power. She could only move her head slightly and she was frustrated in her desire to stroke it, to bring it ecstasy. When she felt it begin to slowly slide in and out, she gripped it tightly with her lips, madly intent on granting it every measure of pleasure she could give.

Blackthorne, his hands still on the delirious girl's head, made the adjustments to her being that would make her a slave to the amulet. He showed it to her in her mind, sending her a terrifying fear of it and a terrible lust for its creator and his minions. He washed away all other desires except to serve her masters with every ounce of her being. He preserved a part of her though. She would remember her transformation, she would remember that she had been damned and that she had experienced mind numbing lust and pleasure when it happened.

Paula felt the man's passion rising and rising. She reviled herself for her shameful need for his essence. Although she knew the man had forced himself upon her, had altered her mind, she cursed herself for her sinful lust.

When the man's cock began to throb and spasm in her mouth, Paula's body began to shake convulsively. Her pussy had been burning and it now exploded, sending shockwaves of pleasure through her. She consumed the man's copious spunk greedily, feeding on his long, full flow of salty, viscous fluid. As it entered her body, she felt his semen meld with her, binding her to him and the evil symbol he had placed in her mind.

Blackthorne left the blond girl to wallow in despair and sorrow over the loss of her soul. He stepped before the next helplessly bound girl, who faced south. She was thin with long, brown hair. Her pretty brown eyes stared back at him frantically. Her weirdly painted face cringed when she felt the first powerful pulse of his psyche enter her mind. Before he plunged his manhood into her soon to be yearning mouth, he took a moment to reveal to her what she was about to become. He felt her mind rebel in frantic panic. She tried to plead with him to spare her, her words distorted by her grotesque gag. Her eyes begged him for mercy. Her torso yanked and tugged at the bindings behind her. And then he filled her with a desperate, gnawing need for him. A minute later, she closed her eyes dreamily as she drank at his throbbing tool.

He finished with the thin, boyish, short blond haired girl quickly. She was the prettiest of the kidnapped girls, her body long and elegant. While she sucked eagerly on his prick, her will bound irretrievably to his, he probed her innermost thoughts and fears. He sensed her hidden and suppressed disappointment for her pert, pointy breasts. He converted it to a deep, intense shame and, at the same time, made them almost unbearably sensitive to stimulation so they would be the seat of her desire, so she would yearn to have them suckled and caressed despite her humiliation at exposing them. Her slender hips and long torso were boyish. He drew a ring of need around her small, rear entrance so that if anyone wanted to use her there, she would groan and writhe with pleasure.

The last was the voluptuous brown haired one. After he filled her with fear and lust, he knelt before her and placed his lips on her teats, sucking on them long and hard until her body shook and shuddered with a frantic need for completion. He placed his hand between her widespread, bound thighs and took possession of her vulva, pouring his power through it, making the young woman jerk and spasm with pleasure. He made her come three agonizing times before he removed her gag and fed her his essence.

When he stepped back from the dazed and enslaved, brown haired girl, he signaled the male dancers to release all four of the enthralled, pretty white girls from their stakes and to loosen their legs. Painfully stupefied at their ordeal, the women rose slowly to their feet. He sent them a command and the beat of the drums entered their bodies. Their demon minders circled them, dancing wildly and then led them around the raging fire. Their hands still bound painfully behind them, the desirable, young women's bodies jerked spasmodically as they mindlessly followed the painted demons. Blackthorne signaled that the three redheaded college students should be released and they joined in the *danse macabre* around the fire.

Paula knew she was lost. She could not stop her body from responding to the drums, was compelled to circle the fire, dancing frantically, displaying her naked and bound body for all to see, proving the blond god's mastery over her.

From the left of the platform, Jonathan saw a procession of white robed, Apache women enter the circle. They were chanting and doing a shuffling dance as they entered, banging small leather covered drums and shaking rattles. The heavyset, Apache woman he had met in the welcome tent was leading them. Behind them came his three lovely and dutiful, naked acolytes. On their shoulders they carried a platform strewn with colorful desert flowers. In the middle, knelt his familiar.

She wore a grotesque mask of some demented demon. She was mounted on a frame, her head and neck caught in a yoke that raised them for the crowd. Her arms were bound, crossed and up behind her back. Her body had been painted all white but for her dangling breasts and her hairless pudenda which had been painted red. Yolanda, the black beauty, was in front, two rails over her shoulders holding her master's precious captive high. Darla and Christine proudly brought up the rear, all naked, their bodies decorated with painted designs. They set the platform down on the ground before the dais where the old man sat watching the proceedings approvingly.

The familiar was writhing in her bonds, overcome with lust. He could feel her energies pouring out of her. The Apache women, with the help of his acolytes, had been fueling her passions while the ceremony was going on. Jonathan felt a surge of lust in himself. He sent his three servants off to join in the dance around the fire and he stepped behind the moaning and panting, masked and painted woman. Her legs were spread and he could see between whitened thighs her reddened pussy, dilated and moist, ready for his penetration.

He stepped forward and circled his hands under her torso, seizing her loose, round, bright red painted breasts in his hands. As he let his passion enter the needy female's body through them, he pierced her burning, welcoming shaft with his steely pole. The female came at once, her inner flesh throbbing around his meat, her moans of pleasure escaping from behind her hellish mask. He felt himself coming and he poured his essence into her.

Jonathan Blackthorne's mind reeled with joy. The huge fire roared in front of him. The steady, monotonous, rhythmic chanting and the heavy, insistent drums seemed to enter his lustful, powerful body. His hot cock pulsed with a driving, forceful pleasure and his mind fed on the untrammeled lust of his familiar and all of those around him. He could see the figures of the women he had claimed dancing wildly about the conflagration, their long and eerie shadows echoing their spastic and frantic movements. This is where he belonged, he thought, madly. This is what it means to have your own destiny, not to serve, no matter how happily, the suffocating, numbing belonging to the Whole. Here, he ruled. And in the end, if his tenure in this dimension was short, if he was destroyed, it would have been worth it. He would never go back!

* * * *

The festival went on for three days. After he had finished his role in the ceremony, the three, young Apache girls had been presented to him formally as a gift of the Apache people. The maidens stripped themselves before the crowd and knelt in front of him, their crossed wrists proffered in a gesture of submission. They were to serve him for one year, until the next year's festival, when three more would be chosen from a selection of enthusiastic volunteers. He ceremonially bound their hands with leather thongs. He did not convert them until later. They serviced him joyously in his tent of their own volition all night and into the early morning hours. When he awoke in the morning, he had them kneel before him and passed his will into them, making them cringe and cry with fear when they realized their misapprehension about what being one of his bond women meant. In public, and after their year of indenture to him was over, they would seem happy and content to have been chosen to serve Jitendra, Lord of Conquerors, unable to relate to anyone the misery they had suffered at his hands.

The three redheads he had given to the shaman and the four kidnapped girls were set up in individual tents where they enthusiastically provided sexual services to the single men of the tribe, and a few married ones when their wives were not looking. Afterwards, the four kidnapped girls were given to the Snake God and his fellow performers. They graciously permitted Jonathan to have his turn with them.

The lovely Paula was his favorite of the four, although he took great pleasure in giving the lanky blond girl, Jane, her first ass fucking. She moaned and cried with shame and lust as he stroked himself in her small, energized anal ring. Later, when the work started on his mountain fortress, Bob set up a little bar and trailer park near the construction entrance and staffed it with them. With the old man's blessing, Maria and the other redheads joined them. The lovely Fawn Who Leaps was kept by him as a sort of temple whore since it was not appropriate for an Apache girl to serve as a prostitute to non-Apaches.

Jonathan didn't spend the entire three days fucking. He met with the tribal leaders several times as they worked together for an appropriate site for his complex. Blackthorne had Conway and a couple other executives fly down to conference about design details and they took a helicopter tour of the proposed situs. When Jonathan returned to corporate headquarters, work was already under way on drawings and cost estimates.

The research facility was the first building completed, even before the sumptuous hacienda. It was to serve as his dream lab. The old shaman had agreed to assist him in trying to find a reliable way to pierce the dimensional barrier through the dreams of strong willed, intelligent, emotionally vibrant, young female subjects. As part of his company's affirmative action program, much lauded in the media, Blackthorne would personally interview prospective employees at job fairs at universities and colleges across the country. After his visits, several of the more promising ones would, after terminating all of their social relationships and winding up all of their other affairs, drive their own way to the gates of his compound, not sure really why and who their other pretty companions were. They would be shown their way to the research lab where they would spend the next several months, or longer if they seemed promising, as subjects in the dream experiments.

Marjoram Industries prospered. The company had gone public about two years before Philip Marjoram's death in an effort to raise needed capital and about 10% of it was in the hands of outsiders. Ruling a publicly traded company was a pain in the ass, with all of the government scrutiny and SEC regulations, and one of the first things Jonathan did was have the company buy it back. One by one, he acquired smaller companies whose product lines could easily assimilate his subtle improvements to earth technology or supply goods or services necessary in his research.

Now, five years later, Blackthorne was the master of a huge empire. The Fortress, as the vast complex deep inside the Chiracahua Reservation was known, served as his nerve center and his keep. His research into breaching the dimensional wall continued. In secret laboratories all over the United States, he had scientists and theoreticians working on it. Their silence was, of course, amply rewarded. This required a constant flow of enthralled, compliant women and untraceable funds to provide them with lifestyles they could only have imagined.

These needs were satisfied with the alliances he had formed with organized crime syndicates throughout the country. These humans were frail and consumers of many vices. Pimps, whorehouses, strip clubs, porn sites, all were able to provide desirable young females who could disappear without too much question. In turn, Blackthorne was able to insure their other sex workers remained enthusiastic and obsessively loyal to their employers. Blackthorne had stocked his entire elegant 24 bedroom guest complex at one stroke one night when he converted all of the stunningly beautiful erotic dancers who had been specially invited to participate in a 'go-go-a-rama' at a Miami strip club. A special bus driven and attended by loyal Apaches had been waiting in the parking lot. After a spectacular show and when their night was over, the girls all obediently turned their earnings over to the club manager and marched onto the bus where, dazed and confused, they were given a cross country journey that terminated in southwestern New Mexico.

Runaways, girls who had decided to use their bodies to make an easy buck, drifters, illegal immigrants, black, brown, yellow and white, even drug addicts who had not managed to ravage their bodies yet, were all easy prey. A surge of his power was all it took to turn them from one addiction to another. And a judicious culling of model agencies, college towns and rural backwaters produced a steady stream of clean, wholesome, attractive, young girls.

The international interests of Marjoram Industries easily facilitated the flow of drugs and other contraband in and out of the country. And he had his tendrils deep into governmental operations to ensure attendance to his needs and influence the administration of justice. Those he was unable to corrupt, could be convinced to cooperate in other ways.

It had started in the early days. Marjoram Industries had purchased a tract of land on which it intended to build a new factory. It was one of Blackthorne's pet projects. The mayor of the small burg in which the land was located was against the development and his influence was enough to stymie the issuance of necessary permits. Jonathan learned he had two young, pretty daughters attending college at the state university. He made a little visit to them and had afterwards invited the mayor to a "man to man" discussion with him at the Marjoram Estate. The sight of the two naked beauties happily cavorting together in an impassioned embrace on the carpet in his study had convinced the mayor to see the error of his ways. Blackthorne released the girls on parole back to the mayor and the project went through. Three months later, the mayor had a fatal 'accident' and the girls were recalled to duty.

Some politicians made it easy. Senator Grant had been concerned his family situation would provide negative publicity during his reelection campaign. He, his irresponsible, alcoholic wife, his rebellious 20 year old daughter, Geraldine, and the growingly intractable senior campaign aide the Senator had been fucking were among the first guests invited to the fortress once the social amenities had been completed. They were no problem now and all lived together as one big, happy family. The Senator was recently touted by the press as being among a small circle of public figures who were viable candidates for the Oval Office in the next election.

Conway had proven a disappointment. In spite of the millions Blackthorne had lavished on him, and the three compliant mistresses he had provided, Conway had been discovered feathering his own nest. The news had come from the elegant Anna, who had overheard Chuck talking on the phone one night with someone about some funds he needed 'processed'. Chuck drowned on a fishing trip to Alaska. His mistresses were all reassigned by Bob. His widow, Anna, signed over all his assets to Jonathan. He let her spend some time with him before sending her to work down at the guest complex. She was still there and from time to time he had her brought up to the hacienda where, before using her, he relaxed his control long enough so she could beg and plead for her freedom.

Earlier today, he had said farewell to select senior executives of his latest acquired company. They and their wives and girlfriends had been invited down to the Fortress for the weekend to celebrate the new venture. On Friday evening, when his corporate jet delivered them, there had been a welcoming banquet. Saturday morning, the men all were scheduled for 'conferences' and the women were invited for a brunch with his gracious, still beautiful wife, Dolores. The highlight of the late morning repast was a personal introduction to their host. The seven unsuspecting females all stood in a little semi-circle smiling and wearing their fashionable best as he went around shaking their hands. Their happy smiles, one by one, turned into looks of surprise and apprehension.

He spent several hours both Saturday and Sunday enjoying their conversions in the basement of his hacienda.

They were waiting there in little cages when the men were ready to leave, after having spent their time appreciating the graces of the beautiful and engaging whores he kept around for just such purposes. After making proper obeisance to their new masters and wearing Blackthorne's mark on their bellies, the women were given last minute 'instructions' and were allowed to dress and go on their way.

The plane had left an hour ago and he was finishing his business of the day with the two pretty *Meztisas* his men had picked up on Saturday morning. His connections on the other side of the border, only fifty or so miles away from the Fortress, had alerted Bob, otherwise known as Kajika, He Who Walks Without Noise, to their presence on the truck and Bob had arranged for the truck to be halted. It had been a quick trip on the helicopter to meet them and convince them to go with Apaches in their SUV. The other *illegales* had been adjusted so they would forget the truck had ever stopped.

Bob had become Jonathan's right hand man. He recruited all the security staff, supervised the connections with the underworld and was constantly on the lookout for 'corporate opportunities' in the underground economy. The Latina girls had really been recruited for the entertainment of the hard working, Apache security guards. Either this very night, or within days if Jonathan decided to play with them awhile, they would be sent down to the security barracks to join their *hermanas* who eased he burdens of life for the ruthless, efficient, Apache warriors who worked for him. They particularly enjoyed the subjugated Latina girls as a revenge for ancient grudges. The Spaniards, and later the Mexicans and their hirelings, had decimated the thriving Chiricahua Nation, destroying their villages, murdering their families, enslaving their women. The survivors had been forced to move into the mountains. Later, it was the *Americanos* who took their land and slaughtered them when they protested.

The two young, brown skinned women trembled in fear

before him. The waves of terror that emanated from their bodies were sweet. But, Jonathan had something else on his mind right now. His pursuer would arrive any day, he just knew it, if he hadn't arrived already. For the last three years Jonathan had had his agents scouring the country for signs of him. He would go to Chicago first. While the Whole had no way of pinpointing Jonathan's location now, they would know where his jump terminated. It would not take long for the pursuer to realize that the beautiful, successful Professor Diane Lanier had disappeared without a trace soon after his arrival. From there, even though Blackthorne had covered his traces well, it was only a matter of time before the retributive agent of the Whole found him.

Well, he thought, maybe it was about time. His researches had been lagging and his familiar was showing signs of toll after five years of serving as the conduit for the massive energies he drained daily from the other dimension. She was physically well taken care of. He still maintained his original acolytes, save the poor Marie, who had been replaced with Yvonne, and they assiduously attended to their duties of keeping the former biology professor in a state of almost continuous arousal. Daily ingestions of psychedelics had not left much of her conscious mind. He had detected a slight waning of her ability to absorb the essences necessary for his survival. She would not last forever.

The pursuer would have a familiar as well. If Jonathan could locate her, make her his own, he might be able to transfer his bond to the Whole to her. That would give him at least five more years to solve the riddle of freeing himself of the burden and vulnerability of needing a familiar at all.

The corrupted dream man redirected his attentions to the pleasures at hand. At an urging from his mind, the distraught, virginal Guadalupe Rivera began to remove her clothes.

End Book One